Incidents Of The War
Humorous, Pathetic,
And Descriptive

by

Alfred Burnett

Double9
BOOKS

Incidents Of The War
Humorous, Pathetic, And Descriptive
by Alfred Burnett

ISBN: 978-93-67142-85-1

Published by

DOUBLE 9 BOOKS

2/13-B, Ansari Road
Daryaganj, New Delhi – 110002
info@double9books.com
www.double9books.com
Tel. 011-40042856

ABOUT THE AUTHOR

Alfred Burnett was an American author and journalist known for his writings during and after the Civil War. His work often blends humor with poignant observations, capturing the diverse experiences of soldiers and civilians during this tumultuous period in history. Burnett's ability to depict both the absurdities and the harsh realities of war offers readers a unique perspective on the complexities of human nature in times of conflict.

His writing remains valuable for its historical insight and its exploration of the emotional landscapes shaped by war. Alfred Burnett's works often reflect the tensions and contradictions of his time, highlighting themes of bravery, folly, and the human condition. Through his vivid anecdotes and sharp observations, he brings to life the camaraderie and struggles faced by soldiers and civilians alike. His unique blend of humor and pathos makes his writings both relatable and impactful, preserving the legacy of an era.

CONTENTS

SKETCH OF THE AUTHOR

BY ENOS B. REED

The author of the following sketches, letters, etc., has been known to us for lo, these many years. We have always found him "a fellow of infinite jest," and one who, "though troubles assailed," always looked upon the bright side of life, leaving its reverse to those who could not behold the silver lining to the darkling clouds of their moral horizon. We could fill a good-sized volume with anecdotes illustrating the humorous in Mr. Burnett's composition, and his keen appreciation of the grotesque and ludicrous— relating how he has, many a time and oft, "set the table in a roar," by his quaint sayings and the peculiar manner in which they were said; but we are "admonished to be brief," four pages only being allotted to "do up" the veritable "Don Alfredus," better known by the familiar appellation "Alf."

Mr. Burnett has been a resident of Cincinnati for the past twenty-seven years, his parents removing thereto from Utica, New York, in 1836. Alf, at the Utica Academy, in his earliest youth, was quite noted as a declaimer; his "youth but gave promise of the man," Mr. B., at the present time, standing without a peer in his peculiar line of declamation and oratory. In 1845, he traveled with Professor De Bonneville, giving his wonderful rendition of "The Maniac," so as to attract the attention of the *literati* throughout the country.

Perhaps one great reason for Mr. Burnett's adopting his present profession was a remark made by the celebrated tragedian, Edwin Forrest. Mr. B. had been invited to meet Mr. Forrest at the residence of S. S. Smith, Esq. Mr. Burnett gave several readings, which caused Mr. Forrest to make the remark, that "Mr. B. had but to step upon the stage to reach fortune and renown." "Upon this hint" Mr. B. acted, and at once entered upon the duties of his arduous profession. In his readings and recitations he soon discovered that it was imperative, to insure a pleasant entertainment, that humor should be largely mingled with pathos; hence, he introduced a series of droll and comical pieces, in the rendition of which he is acknowledged to have no equal. As a mimic and ventriloquist he stands preeminent, and his entertainment is so varied with pathos, wit, and humor, that an evening's amusement of wonderful versatility is afforded.

Mr. Burnett is a remarkably ready writer—too ready, to pay that care and attention to the "rules," which is considered, and justly so, to be indispensable to a correct writer. To illustrate the rapidity with which he composes, we have but to repeat a story, which a mutual friend relates. He met Alf, one afternoon, about five o'clock, he being announced to deliver an original poem in the evening, of something less than a hundred verses. In the midst of the conversation which ensued, Alf suddenly recollected that he had not written a line thereof, and, making his excuses, declared he must go home and write up the *"little affair."* In the evening a voluminous poem was forthcoming, Alf, in all probability, having "done it up" in half an hour "by Shrewsbury clock."

Mr. Burnett has contributed various poems to the literature of the country, which have stamped him as being possessed of a more than ordinary share of the divine afflatus. Among them is "The Sexton's Spade," which has gained a world-wide celebrity. The writer has been connected with Mr. Burnett in the publication of two or three papers, which, somehow or other, never won their way into popular favor: either the public had very bad taste, or the "combined forces" had not the ability to please, or the perseverance to continue until success crowned their labors.

In the commencement of the war, Mr. Burnett was on a tour of the State, in the full tide of prosperity. Immediately after Sumter fell, he summoned to him, by telegraph, his traveling agent, together with Mr. George Humphreys, who had, as an assistant, been with him for years. A consultation was held, which resulted in the determination of all three to enlist in the service of their country. The agent repaired to Chillicothe and joined the 27th Ohio; Humphreys joined the 5th Ohio, and Mr. Burnett enlisted as high private in the 6th Ohio, and served with his regiment in West Virginia, throughout that memorable campaign.

Mr. Burnett was subsequently engaged by the Cincinnati *Press*, *Times*, and *Commercial*, as war correspondent. His letters were read with great avidity, and were replete with wit, humor, and interesting anecdote. His extensive acquaintance enabled him to gather the earliest information, and his letters were always considered among the most reliable. A number of them will be found in the succeeding pages.

That "Incidents of the War" will be found instructive and entertaining, we can but believe, although Mr. Burnett's professional engagements precluded the possibility of his devoting that time and attention to its preparation which was almost imperative. It lays no particular claim to merit as a literary production—being a collection of letters and incidents, which Mr. B.'s publishers thought would be palatable to the public in their present form.

In the volume will be found several pieces for the superior rendition of which Mr. Burnett has been highly extolled. At the close will be found a famous debate, which, although not an incident of the war, is peculiarly spirited, and was delivered by Mr. Burnett before General Rosecrans.

For the graphic illustrations accompanying the volume, Mr. Burnett is indebted to Messrs. Jones & Hart, engravers, and Messrs. Ball & Thomas, photographic artists.

Mr. Burnett is still engaged in giving readings and recitations, in city and village, and, since the death of Winchell, stands almost alone in his profession. Upon a visit to England, some years since, he gained the praise of the English press and public, as a correct delineator of the passions, mimic, and humorist. He is never so well pleased as when before an audience, and receiving the applause of the judicious.

In conclusion, let us hope that "Incidents of the War" may be welcomed by that large number who have had relatives in the armies of the Union, and whose names may, perchance, be found in its pages, while we know the numerous friends of Mr. Burnett will hail its appearance with unfeigned delight.

CHAPTER I

In a two-years' connection with the army, a man with the most ordinary capacity for garnering up the humorous stories of camp may find his *repertoire* overflowing with the most versatile of incidents. A connection with the daily press is, however, of great service, especially as a letter-writer is expected to know all that occurs in camp—and *more too!*

The stories that I shall relate are no fictions, but veritable facts, to most of which I was myself an eye-witness.

The hardships of camp-life have been so often depicted by other pens that it will be unnecessary for me to bring them anew before the public. A few jolly spirits in a regiment frequently sway the crowd, and render the hours pleasant to the boys which otherwise would prove exceedingly wearisome; and many a surgeon has remarked, that it would amply remunerate Government to hire good, wholesome amusement for the benefit of the soldiers when not on active duty. Frequently, when visiting various hospitals, have I noticed the brightening eye of the patients as I have told them some laughable incident, or given an hour's amusement to the crowd of convalescents—a far preferable dose, they told me, to quinine. A word of praise to the suffering hero is of great value.

I remember, the day after the battle of Perryville, visiting the hospital of which Dr. Muscroft was surgeon. I had assisted all day in bringing in the wounded from the field-hospital, in the rear of the battle-ground. The boys of the 10th and 3d Ohio were crowded into a little church, each pew answering for a private apartment for a wounded man. One of the surgeons in attendance requested me to assist in holding a patient while his leg was being amputated. This was my first trial, but the sight of the crowd of wounded had rendered my otherwise sensitive nerves adamant, and as the knife was hastily plunged, the circle-scribe and the saw put to its use, the limb off, scarce a groan escaped the noble fellow's lips. Another boy of the 10th had his entire right cheek cut off by a piece of a shell, lacerating his tongue in the most horrible manner: this wound had to be dressed, and again my assistance was required, and I could but notice the exhilarating effect a few words of praise that I bestowed upon his powers of endurance had. This was invariably the case with all those whom it was my painful duty to assist. The effect of a few words of praise seemed quite magical.

Men frequently fight on, though severely wounded, so great is the excitement of battle, and I am cognizant of several instances of men fainting from loss of blood, who did not know they were wounded, until, several minutes afterward, they were brought to a realization of the fact through a peculiar dizzy, sickening feeling. Brigadier-General (then Colonel) Lytle, who commanded a brigade during that battle, it is said, by boys who were near him, after the severe wound he received, fought on several minutes. A field-officer, whose name I have forgotten, being shot from his horse, requested to be lifted back into the saddle, and died shortly afterward. Captain McDougal, of Newark, Ohio, commanding a company in the 3d Ohio, who, with sword upraised, and cheering on his noble boys, received a fatal shot, actually stepped some eight or ten paces before falling. Colonel Loomis, of the celebrated Loomis Battery, who did such service in that engagement, says he saw no dead about him; yet there they lay, within a few feet of his battery. Loomis at one time sighted one of his favorite pieces, taking what he called a "fair, square, deliberate aim," and, sure enough, he knocked over the rebel gun, throwing it some feet in the air; at the sight of which he was so elated that he fairly jumped with delight, and cheer after cheer rang out from the men of his command, and it was not until a whizzing shot from the remaining guns of the rebels' battery warned him that they were not yet conquered, that his boys were again put to work, and eventually quieted their noisy antagonists. At one time, during that fight, the rebels tried to charge up the hill from "Bottom's farm-house," but were repulsed. At that time the 10th and 3d Ohio, aided by the 15th Kentucky Regiment, were holding the eminence; the rebels were protected by a stone wall that skirted the entire meandering creek, giving them, at times, the advantage of an enfilading fire; our boys were partly covered by what was known as "Bottom's barn." Many of our wounded had crawled into this barn for protection, but a rebel shell exploding directly among the hay set the barn on fire, and several of our poor wounded boys perished in the flames.

Colonel Reed, of Delaware, Ohio, was in command at Perryville, some time after the battle, and it is a disgraceful fact that the rebels left their dead unburied. At one spot, in a ravine, they had piled up thirty bodies in one heap, and thrown a lot of cornstalks over them; and on the Springfield road, to the right, as you entered the town of Perryville, a regular line of skirmishers lay dead, each one about ten paces from the other; they had evidently been shot instantly dead, and had fallen in their tracks; and there they laid for four days. One, a fine-looking man, with large, black, bushy whiskers, was within a few yards of the toll-gate keeper's house, (himself and family residing there,) who, apparently, was too lazy to dig a grave for the reception of the rebel's body.

As a matter of course, the first duty is to the wounded, but these people seemed to pay no attention to either dead or wounded. And it was not until a peremptory order from Colonel Reed was issued, that the rebel-sympathizing citizens condescended to go out and bury their Confederate friends; and this was accomplished by digging a deep hole beside the corpse, and the diggers, taking a couple of fence-rails, would pry the body over and let it fall to the bottom: thus these poor, deluded wretches found a receptacle in mother Earth.

Accompanied by Mr. A. Seward, the special correspondent of the Philadelphia *Inquirer*, the day after the fight I visited an improvised hospital in the woods in the rear of the battle-ground. There we found some twenty Secesh, who had strayed from their command, and were playing sick and wounded to anybody who came along. They had guards out watching, and, as I suspected they were playing sharp, I bethought me of trying "diamond cut diamond;" so I dismounted, and having on a Kentucky-jeans coat, I ventured a "How-de, Boys?"

They eyed us pretty severely, and ventured the remark that they needed food, and would like some coffee or sugar for the wounded boys. I went inside the log-house, telling them I would send some down; that we were farming close by there; "Dry-fork" was the place; we would send them bread. After we had gained their confidence, they wanted to know how they could get out of the State without being captured; said they had not been taken yet, although several of the Yanks had been there; but the "d—d fools" thought they were already paroled.

We told them that as soon as they got well we would pilot them safely out. They said they had already been promised citizens' clothing by Mrs. Thompson and some other rebel ladies. They then openly confessed that there was only one of them wounded, and that they had used his bloody rags for arm-bandages and head-bandages only for the brief period when they were visited by *suspicious*-looking persons; but, as we were all right, they had no hesitancy in telling us they were part of Hardee's corps, and were left there by accident when the rebel forces marched.

By a strange *accident* they were all taken prisoners that afternoon by a dozen Federal prowlers, who kindly took them in out of the wet.

Skeered! That Aint No Name for It

About a mile and a half to the rear of the field of battle there stands, in a large, open field, a solitary log-house containing two rooms. The house is surrounded by a fence inclosing a small patch of ground. The chimney had been partly torn away by a cannon-ball. A shell had struck the roof of the building, ripping open quite a gutter in the rafters. A dead horse lay in the little yard directly in front of the house, actually blocking up the doorway, while shot and shell were scattered in every direction about the field in front and rear of this solitary homestead. I dismounted, determined to see who or what was in the house—

"Darkness there, and nothing more."

A board had been taken from the floor, exhibiting a large hole between two solid beams or logs. An empty bedstead, a wooden cupboard, and three chairs were all the furniture the house contained. Hurrying across the field, we caught up with a long, lank, lean woman. She had two children with her: a little boy about nine, and a girl about four years of age. The woman had a table upon her head. The table, turned upside down, contained a lot of bedding. She had a bucket full of crockery-ware in one hand, and was holding on to the table with the other. The children were loaded down with household furniture of great convenience. As it was growing dark, I inquired the nearest road to Perryville. The woman immediately unloaded her head, and pointing the direction, set one leg on the table, and yelled to the boy—

"Whoray up, Jeems; you are so slow!"

"How far is it, madam?"

"O, about a mile and a half. It aint more nor that, no how."

"Who lived in that house?" said I, pointing to the log-cabin I had just left.

"I did."

"Were you there during the fight?"

"Guess I was."

"Where was your husband?"

"He wor dead."

"Was he killed in the battle?"

"No; he died with the measles."

"Why didn't you leave when you found there was going to be a fight?"

"I did start for to go, but I seed the Yankees comin' thick, and I hurried back t'other way; and jest as I e'enamost got to the brush yonder, I seed the

'Confeds' jest a swarmin' out of the woods. So, seeing I was between two fires, I rund back to the house."

"Wasn't you afraid you'd be killed?"

"Guess I was."

"What did you do when they commenced firing?"

"I cut a hole in the floor with the ax, and hid between the jists."

"Did they fight long upon your ground?"

"It seemed to me like it wor TWO WEEKS."

"You must have been pretty well scared; were you not?"

"Humph! *skeered!* Lor bless you, *skeered! That aint no name for it!*"

SKEERED! THAT AIN'T NO NAME FOR IT.

Camp Fun in a Burlesque Letter to a Friend

The other morning I was standing by Billy Briggs, in our tent.

"Hand me them scabbards, Jimmy," said he.

"Scabbards!" said I, looking round.

"Yes; boots, I mean. I wonder if these boots were any relation to that beef we ate yesterday. If they will only prove as tough, they'll last me a long time. I say, Cradle!" he called out, "where are you?"

Cradle was our contraband, with a foot of extraordinary length, and heel to match.

"What do you call him Cradle for?" I inquired.

"What would *you* call him? If he aint a cradle, what's he got rockers on for?"

Cradle made his appearance, with a pair of perforated stockings.

"It's no use," said Billy, looking at them. "Them stockings will do to put on a sore throat, but won't do for feet. It is humiliating for a man like me to be without stockings. A man may be bald-headed, and it's genteel; but to be barefooted, it's ruination. The legs are good, too," he added, thoughtfully, "but the feet are gone. There is something about the heels of stockings and the elbows of stove-pipes, in this world, that is all wrong, Jimmy."

A supply of stockings had come that day, and were just being given out. A pair of very large ones fell to Billy's lot. Billy held them up before him.

"Jimmy," said he, "these are pretty bags to give a little fellow like me. Them stockings was knit for the President, or a young gorilla, certain!" and he was about to bestow them upon Cradle, when a soldier, in the opposite predicament, made an exchange. "Them stockings made me think of the prisoner I scared so the other day," said Billy.

"How's that?" said I.

"He saw a big pair of red leggings, with feet, hanging up before our tent. He never said a word, till he saw the leggings, and then he asked me what they were for. 'Them!' said I, 'them's General Banks's stockings.' He looked scared. 'He's a big man, is General Banks,' said I, 'but then he ought to be, the way he lives.' 'How?' said he. 'Why,' said I, 'his regular diet is bricks buttered with mortar.'"

The next day Billy got a present of a pair of stockings from a lady; a nice, soft pair, with his initials, in red silk, upon them. He was very happy. "Jimmy," said he, "just look at 'em," and he smoothed them down with his hand—"marked with my initials, too; 'B,' for my Christian name, and 'W' for my heathen name. How kind! They came just in the right time, too; I've got such a sore heel."

Orders came to "fall in." Billy was so overjoyed with his new stockings he didn't keep the line well.

"Steady, there!" growled the sergeant; "keep your place, and don't be moving round like the Boston post-office!"

We were soon put upon the double-quick. After a few minutes, Billy gave a groan.

"What is it, Billy?" said I.

"It's all up with 'em," said he.

I didn't know what he meant, but his face showed something bad had happened. When we broke ranks and got to the tent, he looked the picture of despair—shoes in hand, and his heels shining through his stockings like two crockery door-knobs.

"Them new stockings of yours is breech-loading, aint they, Billy?" said an unfeeling volunteer.

"Better get your name on both ends, so that you can keep 'em together," said another.

"Shoddy stockings," said a third.

Billy was silent. I saw his heart was breaking, and I said nothing. We held a council on them, and Billy, not feeling strong-hearted enough for the task, gave them to Cradle to sew up the small holes.

I saw him again before supper; he came to me looking worse than ever, the stockings in his hand.

"Jimmy," said he, "you know I gave them to Cradle, and told him to sew up the small holes; and what do you think he has done? He's gone and sewed up the heads."

"It's a hard case, Billy; in such cases, tears are almost justifiable."

CHAPTER II

A great many stories have been told about General Nelson, with whom the writer was upon the most intimate terms. That Nelson was a noble, warm-hearted, companionable man, those even most opposed to his rough manner, at times, will readily admit.

Nelson was strongly attached to the 6th Ohio. From his very first acquaintance he said he fell in love with it, and his feeling was reciprocated, for the 6th was as ardently devoted to him.

At Camp Wickliffe the General was very much annoyed by women coming into his camp, and he had given strict orders that none should be admitted on the following Sunday, as he intended reviewing the division that day. His chagrin and rage can only be imagined by those who knew him, when, upon this veritable occasion, he saw at least thirty women huddled together, on mares, mules, jacks, jennies, and horses. The General rode hastily to Lieutenant Southgate, exclaiming—

"Captain Southgate, I thought I ordered that no more of those d—d women should come into my camp. What are they doing here?"

"I promulgated your order, General," replied Captain Southgate.

"Well, by — —, what are they here for?" and riding up to the bevy of women in lathed and split bonnets, he inquired, in a ferocious manner, "What in — — are all you women doing here?"

Now, the party was pretty well frightened, but there was one with more daring than the rest, who sidled up to the General, and, with what was intended to be a smile, (but the General said he never saw a more "sardonic grin" in his life,) she answered for the party, and said:

"Sellin' pies, Gin'ral."

"Selling pies, eh! Selling pies, eh! Let me see 'em; let me see 'em, quick!"

The woman untied one end of a bolster-slip, and thrust her arm down the sack, and brought forth a specimen of the article, which Nelson seized, and vainly endeavored to break. It was like leather. The General gave it a sudden twist and broke it in two, when out dropped three or four pieces of dried apple.

"By — —, madam, you call them pies, do you? Pies, eh! Those things are just what are *giving all my boys the colic*! Get out of this camp every one of you! Clear yourselves!"

The camp was thus cleared of pie-venders, who escaped on the double-quick.

General Nelson was a strict disciplinarian, and frequently tested his pickets by a personal visit. Upon one occasion he rode through a drenching rain to the outposts; it was a dark night, and mud and water were knee-deep in some parts of the road. A portion of the 2d Kentucky was on guard, and as the General rode up he met the stern "Halt" of the sentinel, and the usual "Who comes there?"

"General Nelson," was the reply.

"Dismount, General Nelson, and give the countersign," was the sentinel's command.

"Do you know who you are talking to, sir? I tell you I am your General, and you have the impudence to order me to dismount, you scoundrel!"

"Dismount, and give the countersign, or I will fire upon you," was the stern rejoinder.

And Nelson did dismount, and gave the countersign, and at the same time inquired the sentinel's name, and to what regiment he belonged. The following day the man was sent for, to appear forthwith at head-quarters. The soldier went with great trepidation, anticipating severe treatment from the General for the previous night's conduct. Imagine his surprise when the General invited him in, complimented him highly, in the presence of his officers, and requested, if at any time he required any service from him, to just mention that he was the soldier of the 2d Kentucky who had made him dismount in mud and rain, and give the countersign.

On another occasion he was riding along the road, and was accosted by two waggish members of the 6th Ohio.

"Hallo! mister," said one of the boys, "won't you take a drink?"

"Where are you soldiers going to?" inquired the General.

"O, just over here a little bit."

"What regiment do you belong to?"

"Sixth Ohio."

"Well, get back to your camp, quick!"

The boys, although they knew him well, took advantage of the fact that the General displayed no insignia of his rank, and replied:

"They guessed they'd go down the road a bit, first."

"Come back! come back!" shouted the General. "How dare you disobey me? Do you know who I am, you scoundrels?"

"No, I don't," said one of the boys; and then, looking impudently and inquiringly into his face, said: "*Why! ain't you the wagon-master of the 17th Indiana?*"

Nelson thought activity the best cure for "*ennui*," and consequently kept his men busy. One day, calling his officers together, he ordered them to prepare immediately for a regular, old-fashioned day's work; "for," said he, "there has been so little work done here since the rain set in, that I fear *drilling* has fallen in the market; but if we succeed in keeping up that article, I am sure *cotton* must come down."

He was exceedingly bitter in his denunciations of the London *Times* and rebel British sympathizers, remarking to me, one evening, that he was exceedingly anxious this war should speedily end, "for," said he, "I would like nothing better than to see our people once more united as a nation; and then I want fifty thousand men at my command, so that I could march them to Canada, and go through those provinces like a dose of croton."

I was present at the Galt House, in Louisville, when General Nelson was shot by General Davis, and immediately telegraphed the sad news to the daily press of Cincinnati. The following was my dispatch:

General Nelson Shot by General Davis.

Louisville, September *29*.

Eds. Times: I just witnessed General Jeff C. Davis shoot General Nelson. It occurred in the Galt House, in the entry leading from the office. The wound is thought to be mortal.

Alf.

Later.—General Nelson Dead.

Louisville, September 29, 10 A.M.

General Nelson is dead. I will telegraph particulars as soon as possible.

Alf.

THIRD DISPATCH.

Particulars of the Affair.

Louisville, September 29, 11 A.M.

Eds. Times: Jefferson C. Davis, of Indiana, went into the Galt House, at half-past eight o'clock this morning. He met General Nelson, and referred to the treatment he had received at his hands in ordering him to Cincinnati. Nelson cursed him, and struck Davis in the face several times. Nelson then retired a few paces, Davis borrowing a pistol from a friend, who, handing it to him, remarked, "It is a Tranter trigger—be careful."

I had just that moment been in conversation with the General.

Alf.

The particulars were afterward given in a letter, which is here inserted:

Louisville, *September 29, 1862.*

The greatest excitement of the day has been in discussing the death of General Nelson, and the causes which led to the terrible *denouement.*

Sauntering out in search of an "item"—my custom always in the morning—I happened to be in the Galt House just as the altercation between General Nelson and General Jeff C. Davis was reaching its climax, and of which I telegraphed you within ten minutes after its occurrence. From what I learn, from parties who saw the commencement, it would seem that General Davis felt himself grossly insulted by Nelson's overbearing manner at their former meeting; and seeing him standing talking to Governor Morton, Davis advanced and demanded an explanation, upon which Nelson turned and cursed him, calling him an infamous puppy, and using other violent language unfit for publication. Upon pressing his demand for an explanation, Nelson, who was an immensely powerful and large man, took the back of his hand and deliberately slapped General Davis's face. Just at this juncture I entered the office. The people congregated there were giving Nelson a wide berth. Recognizing the General, I said "Good morning, General," (at this time I was not aware of what had passed). His reply to me was: "Did you hear that d——d insolent scoundrel insult me, sir? I suppose he don't know me, sir. I'll teach him a lesson, sir." During this time he was retiring slowly toward the door leading to the ladies' sitting-room. At this moment I heard General Davis ask for a weapon, first of a gentleman who was standing near him, and then meeting Captain Gibson, who was just about to enter the dining-room, he asked him if he had a pistol? Captain Gibson replied, "I always carry the article;" and handed one to him, remarking, as Davis walked toward Nelson, "It is a Tranter trigger."

Nelson, by this time, reached the hall, and was evidently getting out of the way, to avoid further difficulty.

Davis's face was livid, and such a look of mingled indignation, mortification, and determination I never before beheld. His hand was slowly raised; and, as Nelson advanced, Davis uttered the one word, "Halt!" and fired. Nelson, with the bullet in his breast, completed the journey up the entire stairs, and then fell. As he reached the top, John Allen Crittenden met him and said, "Are you hurt, General?" He replied, "Yes, I am, mortally." "Can I do any thing for you?" continued Crittenden. "Yes; send for a surgeon and a priest, quick."

A rush was made by the crowd toward the place as soon as he was shot. No effort, as far as I can learn, has been made to arrest General Davis.

A few minutes after the occurrence I was introduced to the Aid of Governor Morton, who told me he saw it all, from the very commencement, and that, had not Davis acted as he did, after the gross provocation he received, Davis would have deserved to have been shot himself.

It is a great pity so brave a man should have had so little control over his temper. Although very severe in his discipline and rough in his language, the boys of his division were devotedly attached to him, *because he was a fighting man*. The 6th Ohio, especially, were his ardent admirers. He was hated here, bitterly hated, by all *Secessionists*; this of itself should have endeared him to Union men.

The Louisville *Journal*, this afternoon, in speaking of the affair, says:

"General Nelson, from the first, thought the wound was a mortal one, and expressed a desire to have the Rev. Mr. Talbott, of Calvary Church, summoned. This gentleman resides about three miles below the city, but was unable to get home on Sunday after service, and passed the night at the Galt House. He immediately obeyed the summons, as he was well acquainted with the General. The reverend gentleman informs us that the dying man spoke no word concerning the difficulty, and made no allusion to his temporal affairs, but was exceedingly solicitous as to the salvation of his soul, and desired Mr. Talbott to perform the rite of baptism, and receive him into the bosom of the Church.

"After five minutes' conversation, to ascertain his state of preparedness, the clergyman assented to his wish, and the solemn ordinance was administered with unusual impressiveness, in the presence of Dr. Murray, the medical director, Major-General Crittenden, and a few other personal friends. When the service concluded, he was calm, and sank into his last sleep quietly, with no apparent physical pain, but with some mental suffering. The last audible words that he uttered were a prayer for the forgiveness of his sins. That appeal was made to Almighty God. Let, then, his fellow-mortals be proud of his many virtues, his lofty patriotism, and undaunted courage, while they judge leniently of those faults, which, had they been curbed, might have been trained into virtues. Let it not be said of our friend—

"'The evil that men do lives after them,
The good is oft interred with their bones.'"

The Funeral

The funeral of General Nelson took place yesterday afternoon. The corpse of the General was incased in a most elegant rosewood coffin, mounted with silver. The American flag, that he had so nobly fought under at Shiloh, was wrapped about it; his sword, drawn for the last time by that once brave hand, lay upon the flag. Bouquets were strewed upon the coffin.

Major-General Granger, Major-General McCook, and Major-General Crittenden, and Brigadier-General Jackson, assisted by other officers, conveyed the remains from the hearse to the church-door, and down the aisle. As they entered the building, Dr. Craig commenced reading the burial service for the dead. As soon as they reached the pulpit, and set down the corpse, the choir chanted a requiem in the most impressive manner. Rev. Dr. Craig then read the 15th chapter of the First Epistle of St. Paul to the Corinthians, 21st to the 29th verses:

"For since by man came death, by man came also the resurrection of the dead.

"For as in Adam all die, even so in Christ shall all be made alive."

After the reading of this, the Rev. Mr. Talbott, he whom General Nelson had sent for immediately upon being shot, and who had administered to his spiritual welfare, and received him into the Church, delivered one of the most beautiful and eulogistic discourses I ever heard.

He said that the General had been, in private life, one of the most congenial and warm-hearted of men; his hand ever open to the needy. He had known him well.

The last half-hour of his life was devoted entirely to the salvation of his soul; he did not refer to worldly matters. Mr. Talbott told him he must forgive all whom he thought had injured him. His reply was, "O! I do, I do forgive—I do forgive. Let me," said Nelson, "be baptized quick, for I feel I am fast going."

Mr. T. then administered to him the sacred rite, and in a few minutes, conscious to the last, smiling and serene, he passed to "that bourne from which no traveler returns."

"A more contrite heart and thorough Christian resignation," said the divine, "I never saw."

The discourse over, the body was conveyed again to the hearse.

Lieutenant-Colonel Anderson, of the 6th Ohio, had command of the escort, which consisted of two companies of the 2d Ohio, and two companies of the 6th, all being from his old and tried division. No relatives, I believe, were here, except Captain Davis, a foster-brother, belonging to the 2d Minnesota Regiment.

General Nelson's gray horse was led immediately behind the hearse, the General's boots reversed and fastened in the stirrups. An artillery company and cavalry squadron completed the *cortège*, which moved slowly down Second Street to the beat of the muffled drum.

He has gone to his long home! Though rash and impetuous at times, we must not forget our country has lost a noble defender, a man of true courage—one who was looked up to by his division.

To-day he *was* to join them; and as I went through the old Fourth Division, last Sunday, the boys were all in a jubilee, because Nelson was going to be with them, and they remarked, "If he is along, he'll take us where *we'll have fighting!*"

As I have before told you, everywhere Secessionists are rejoicing at his death, and Kentucky ones especially. The Union men of Kentucky have lost a noble defender.

Yesterday General Rousseau's division of ten thousand men was reviewed. They are a splendid body of men.

There will be no examination of Jeff C. Davis before the civil authorities, but the affair is to be investigated by a court-martial.

A singular incident is related of General Nelson. It is said that the Rev. Dr. Talbott, who resides a few miles from the city, wished to return home on Sunday night last. Nelson refused him the pass. On Monday morning it was this reverend gentleman who was sent for by Nelson, and received Nelson into the Church, and who performed the funeral services to-day.

Yours, Alf.

The gallant Colonel Nick Anderson, who so bravely led the 6th Ohio at Shiloh, and more recently at Murfreesboro, in speaking of Nelson, says:

"And what is said will be assented to by all who shared his familiar moments, that, outside of his military duties, he was a refined gentleman. Whatever may be said of his severe dealing with his subordinates, his violent manner when reprimanding them, every one who knew him will bear witness that it was only to exact that iron discipline which makes an army irresistible. His naval education, in which discipline is so mercilessly enforced, will explain clearly his intensity of manner when preparing his forces for the terrible trials of the march or the battle-field. However much he was disliked by subordinate and inefficient officers, he was beloved by his men, the private soldiers.

"How carefully he looked after all their wants, their clothing, their food—in short, whatever they needed to make them strong and brave! for it was a maxim with him, that, unless a man's back was kept warm and his stomach well supplied, he could not be relied upon as a soldier. All who know Buell's army will bear witness to the splendid condition of Nelson's division.

"General Nelson earned his rank as major-general by no mysterious influences at head-quarters, but by splendid achievements on the battle-field. It has been said that his division was the first to enter Nashville; so it was the first in Corinth; but these are the poorest of his titles to distinction. It was his success in Eastern Kentucky, in destroying the army of General Marshall; and, greatest of all, his arrival, by forced marches, at Pittsburg Landing, early enough on Sunday afternoon, the 9th of April, to stop the victorious progress of General Beauregard, that placed him among his country's benefactors and heroes, and which will 'gild his sepulcher, and embalm his name.'

"But for Nelson, Grant's army might have been destroyed. His forced march, wading deep streams, brought him to the field just in time. An hour later, and all might have been lost."

An officer of his division has recounted to me some thrilling incidents of that memorable conflict.

"It was nearly sunset when Nelson, at the head of his troops, landed on the west bank of the river, in the midst of the conflict. The landing and shore of the river, up and down, were covered by five thousand of our beaten and demoralized soldiers, whom no appeals or efforts could rally. Nelson, with difficulty, forced his way through the crowd, shaming them for their cowardice as he passed, and riding upon a knoll overlooking his disembarking men, cried out, in stentorian tones: 'Colonel A., have you your regiment formed?' 'In a moment, General,' was the reply. 'Be quick; time is precious; moments are golden.' 'I am ready now, General.' 'Forward— march!' was his command; and the gallant 6th Ohio was led quickly to the field.

"That night Nelson asked Captain Gwynne, of the 'Tyler,' to send him a bottle of wine and a box of cigars; 'for to-morrow I will show you a man-of-war fight.'

"During the night Buell came up and crossed the river, and by daylight next morning our forces attacked Beauregard, and then was fought the desperate battle of Shiloh. Up to twelve M. we had gained no decisive advantage; in fact, the desperate courage of the enemy had caused us to fall back. 'General Buell,' said my informant, 'now came to the front, and held a hasty consultation with his Generals. They decided to charge the rebels, and drive them back. Nelson rode rapidly to the head of his column, his gigantic figure conspicuous to the enemy in front, and in a voice that rang like a trumpet over the clangor of battle, he called for four of his finest regiments in succession—the 24th Ohio, 36th Indiana, 17th Kentucky, and 6th Ohio. 'Trail arms; forward; double-quick—march;' and away, with thundering cheers, went those gallant boys. The brave Captain (now Brigadier-General) Terrell, who alone was left untouched of all his battery, mounted his horse, and, with wild huzzas, rode, with Nelson, upon the foe.

"It was the decisive moment; it was like Wellington's 'Up, guards, and at them!' The enemy broke, and their retreat commenced. That was the happiest moment of my life when Nelson called my regiment to make that grand charge.

"Let the country mourn the sad fate of General Nelson. He was a loyal Kentuckian; fought gallantly the battles of his Government; earned all his distinction by gallant deeds. All his faults were those of a commander anxious to secure the highest efficiency of his troops by the most rigid discipline of his officers, and in this severe duty he has, at last, lost his life.

"His death, after all, was beautiful. He told Colonel Moody, in Nashville, that, though he swore much, yet he never went to bed without saying his prayers; and now, at last, we find him on his death-bed, not criminating or explaining, but seeking the consolations of religion. *Requiescat in pace!*"

CHAPTER III

"Then shook the hills with thunder riven,
Then rushed the steeds to battle driven,
And, louder than the bolts of heaven,
Far flashed the red artillery!"

Many of you have, no doubt, looked upon the field of battle where contending hosts have met in deadly strife. But there are those whose eyes have never gazed upon so sad a sight; and to such I may be enabled to present a picture that will at best give you but a faint idea of the terrible reality of a fiercely-contested field.

Imagine thousands upon thousands on either side, spreading over a vast expanse of ground, each armed with all the terrible machinery of modern warfare, and striving to gain the advantage of their opponents by some particular movement, studied long by those learned in the art of war.

Then comes the clang of battle; steel meets steel, drinking the blood of contending foes. The sabers flash and glitter in the sunlight, descending with terrible force upon devoted heads, which were once pillowed on the bosoms of fond and devoted mothers. Jove's dread counterfeit is heard on every hand; the balls and shells go whistling and screaming by, the most terrible music to ears not properly attuned to the melody of war. Thousands sink upon the ground overpowered, to be trodden under foot of the flying steed, or their bones to be left whitening the incarnadined field. Blows fall thick and heavy on every hand. The cries of the wounded and the orders of the commanders mingle together; and, to the uninitiated, all appears "confusion worse confounded."

But there is a method in all this *seeming* madness; and that which appears confusion is the result of well-laid plans. But as there is "many a slip 'twixt the cup and the lip," so there are slips in the actions of the best regulated armies. Gunpowder, shot, shell, and steel are not always to be implicitly relied upon: even they sometimes fail in carrying out what were conceded to be designs infallible; so true it is that "man proposes, *but God disposes*."

It has been my province to witness battles wherein Western men were the heroes; and that Western men will fight, has been pretty well authenticated during the present war. I have noticed the brave conduct of the gallant troops, the fighting boys of the various regiments of the West, and have never known them to falter in the hour of danger. They left their homes totally uneducated in warfare; they are now veterans—each a hero.

The conduct of the 2d Ohio at Perryville is spoken of thus by a correspondent:

"The brigade of Len Harris was in the center, and met the shock simultaneously with the left and right. The whole brigade was in the open fields, with the rebels in the woods before them. Long and gallantly did they sustain their exposed positions. An Illinois regiment, of Terrell's brigade, flying from the field, ran through this brigade, with terrible cries of defeat and disaster; but the gallant boys of the 2d Ohio and 38th Indiana only laughed at them, as, lying down, they were literally run over by the panic-stricken Illinoisans. Hardly had they disappeared in the woods in Harris's rear when the rebels appeared in the woods in his front. At the same time Rousseau came galloping along the line, and they received him with cheers, and the rebels with a terrible fire. Terrible was the shock on this part of the line, but gallant was the resistance. Up the hill came the rebels, and made as gallant a charge as ever was met by brave men. But, O! so terrible and bloody was the repulse! Along the line of the 2d Ohio and 38th Indiana and Captain Harris's battery, I saw a simultaneous cloud of smoke arise. One moment I waited. The cloud arose, and revealed the broken column of rebels flying from the field, but, in the distance, a second rapidly advancing. The shout that arose from our men drowned the roar of cannon, and sent dismay into the retreating, broken column."

In Major-General McCook's report of that battle, he says it was "*the bloodiest battle in modern times* for the number of troops engaged on our side," and "the battle was principally fought by *Rousseau's division*; and if there are, or ever were, better soldiers than the old troops engaged, I have neither seen nor read of them." Speaking of the new troops, General McCook points out those under the command of Colonel Harris, saying: "For instance, in the Ninth Brigade, where the 2d and 33d Ohio, 68th Indiana, and 10th Wisconsin fought so well, I was proud to see the 94th and 98th Ohio vie with their brethren in deeds of heroism." The 94th and 98th were new troops, and the example of the old soldiers in Colonel Harris's brigade, and the distinguished courage and good judgment of the Colonel, gave them confidence, and they stood in the storm like veterans.

General Rousseau's Report of the Battle

... "I then returned to Harris's brigade, hearing that the enemy was close upon him, and found that the 33d Ohio had been ordered further to the front by General McCook, and was then engaged with the enemy, and needed support. General McCook, in person, ordered the 2d Ohio to its support, and sent directions to me to order up the 24th Illinois also, Captain Mauf commanding. I led the 24th Illinois, in line of battle, immediately forward, and it was promptly deployed as skirmishers by its commander, and went gallantly into action, on the left of the 33d Ohio. The 2d Ohio, moving up to support the 33d Ohio, was engaged before it arrived on the ground where the 33d was fighting. The 38th Indiana, Colonel B. F. Scribner commanding, then went gallantly into action, on the right of the 2d Ohio. Then followed in support the 94th Ohio, Colonel Frizell. I wish here to say that this regiment, although new, and but few weeks in the service, behaved most gallantly, under the steady lead of its brave Colonel Frizell. Colonel Harris's whole brigade—Simonson's battery on its right—was repeatedly assailed by overwhelming numbers, but gallantly held its position. The 38th Indiana and 2d Ohio, after exhausting their ammunition and that taken from the boxes of the dead and wounded on the field, still held their position, as did also, I believe, the 10th Wisconsin and 33d Ohio. For this gallant conduct these brave men are entitled to the gratitude of the country, and I thank them here, as I did on the field of battle....

"I had an opportunity of seeing and knowing the conduct of Colonel Starkweather, of the Twenty-eighth Brigade, Colonel Harris, of the Ninth Brigade, and of the officers and men under their command, and I can not speak too highly of their bravery and gallantry on that occasion. They did, cheerfully and with alacrity, all that brave men could do...."

"I herewith transmit the reports of Colonels Starkweather, Harris, and Pope, and also a list of casualties in my division, amounting, in all, to 1,950 killed and wounded. My division was about 7,000 strong when it went into the action. We fought the divisions of Anderson, Cheatham, and Buckner.

"I am, very respectfully, your obedient servant,

"Lovell H. Rousseau."

It will not be amiss here to give a brief outline of the early history, coming down to a recent date, of the renowned hero, Major-General A. McD. McCook, United States Volunteers.

He was born in Columbiana County, Ohio, April 22, 1831. At the age of sixteen he entered the Military Academy at West Point, as a cadet. He graduated in July, 1852, and was commissioned Brevet Second Lieutenant, in the 3d Regiment United States Infantry. After being assigned to duty for a few months, at Newport Barracks, Ky., he was ordered, in April, 1853, to join his regiment, then serving in the Territory of New Mexico. Here he remained nearly five years, constantly on active duty in the field, and participating in all the Indian campaigns on that wild and remote frontier. His long services and good conduct were mentioned in General Orders by Lieutenant-General Winfield Scott. In January, 1858, he was ordered from New Mexico to West Point, and assigned to duty in the Military Academy, as instructor in Tactics and the Art of War. On the breaking out of the rebellion he was relieved from duty there, and ordered, in April, 1861, to Columbus, Ohio, to muster in volunteers. Before his arrival there he was elected Colonel of the 1st Ohio Volunteers, a three-months regiment, already on its way to the seat of war in Virginia; and hastening to join the command, to which he was elected without his knowledge or solicitation, soon had an opportunity of exhibiting those admirable qualities as a field-officer for which he has since become so justly distinguished. His coolness in the unfortunate affair at Vienna, and his consummate military skill in the management of his command at Bull Run, were universally commended. At the close of that eventful conflict he marched his regiment back to Centerville in the same good order in which it had left there, an honorable exception to the wide-spread confusion and disorder that prevailed elsewhere among the National forces.

When the three-months troops were mustered out of the service he received permission to raise the 1st Regiment Ohio Volunteers, a three-years regiment; but on the 3d of September, 1861, and before his command was ready to take the field, he was appointed Brigadier-General of Volunteers, and assigned to command the advance of the Federal forces then in Kentucky, at Camp Nevin. Here, and at Green River, he organized his splendid Second Division, with which he afterward marched to Nashville, and thence toward the Tennessee River.

On the 6th of April, 1862, alarmed by the sullen sound of distant artillery, and learning the precarious situation of Grant's army, he moved his division, over desperate roads, twenty-two miles, to Savannah, and there embarked on steamboats for Pittsburg Landing. After clearing a way with the bayonet through the army of stragglers that swarmed upon the bank of the river, soon after daylight on the morning of the 7th of April, the Second Division of the Army of the Ohio advanced through the sad scenes of our defeat the day before, and deployed, with stout hearts and cheers, upon the field of Shiloh. General McCook fought his troops that day with admirable judgment. He held them in hand; his line of battle was not once broken—it was not once retired; but was steadily and determinedly advanced until the enemy fled, and the reverse of the day before was more than redeemed by a splendid victory.

In the movement on Corinth, a few weeks after the battle of Shiloh, General McCook had the honor of being in the advance of General Buell's army corps, and his skirmishers were among the first to scale the enemy's works.

The rank of major-general of volunteers was soon after conferred upon him, in view of his distinguished services—a promotion not undeserved.

After the evacuation of Corinth, the command of General McCook was moved through Northern Alabama to Huntsville, thence to Battle Creek, where his forces remained for two months, in front of Bragg's army at Chattanooga. Upon the withdrawal of Buell's army from Alabama and Tennessee, General McCook moved his division, by a long march of four hundred miles, back to Louisville.

Here he was assigned to command the First Corps in the Army of the Ohio, and started on a new campaign, under Buell, in pursuit of Bragg. The enemy were met and engaged near Perryville, and two divisions of McCook's corps (one of them composed of raw recruits) bore the assault of almost the entire army of General Bragg. The unexpected and unannounced withdrawal of General Gilbert's forces on his right; the sad and early loss of those two noble soldiers, Terrell and Jackson, and the tardiness of reinforcements, made the engagement a desperate one, and resulted in a victory, incomplete but honorable, to the Union forces. After the battle of Chaplin Hills, Bragg's army, worn and broken, fled in dismay from Kentucky. The army corps of Major-General McCook was afterward moved to Nashville, and he assumed command of the Federal forces in that vicinity.

On the 6th of November, 1862, on the arrival of Major-General Rosecrans, who succeeded Major-General Buell in command, General McCook was assigned to command the right wing in the Department of the Cumberland. On the 26th of December, 1862, the Army of the Cumberland moved from Nashville to attack the enemy in position in front of Murfreesboro. General McCook commanded the right. On the evening of December 30 the two armies were in line of battle, confronting each other. Rosecrans had massed his reserves on the left, to crush the rebel right with heavy columns, and turn their position. Bragg, unfortunately, learning of his dispositions during the night, massed almost his entire army in front of McCook, and in the gray of the following morning, and before we had attacked on the left, advanced with desperate fury upon the right wing. Outnumbered, outflanked, and overpowered, the right was forced to retire, not, however, until its line of battle was marked with the evidences of its struggle and the fearful decimation of the enemy. To check the advancing rebel masses, already flushed with anticipated victory, the Federal reserves moved rapidly to the rescue. The furious onslaught of the enemy was resisted, and the right and the fortunes of the day were saved.

The rebels, whipped on the left and center, checked on the right, foiled in every attack, having lost nearly one-third of their numbers, fled from the field on the night of the 3d of January, and the victorious Union army advanced through their intrenchments into Murfreesboro. The great battle of Stone River, dearly won, and incomplete in its results, was yet a victory.

The right was turned and forced to retire in the first day's fight. Whether this was attributable to accidental causes, that decide so many important engagements, or to the superior generalship of the rebel commander, it is at least certain that generalship was not wanting in the disposition of the forces under General McCook; nor was courage wanting in his troops.

Major-General McCook now commands the Twentieth Army Corps.

CHAPTER IV

On the gory field of Murfreesboro, upon the ushering in of the new year, many a noble life was ebbing away. It was a rainy, dismal night; and, on traversing that field, I saw many a spot sacred to the memory of my loved companions of the glorious 6th Ohio. I incidentally heard of the death of a nephew in that fight. I thought of his poor mother. How could I break the news to her! Yes, there was I, surrounded by hundreds of dead and wounded, *pitying the living*. O, how true it is that—

Death's swift, unerring dart brings to its victim calm and peaceful rest, While those *who live* mourn and live on—the arrow in their breast!

With anxious haste I sought his body during that night. Many an upturned face, some with pleasing smile, and others with vengeance depicted, seemed to meet my gaze.

Stragglers told me to go further to the left. "There's where Crittenden's boys gave 'em h—l!" Just to the right of the railroad I found young Stephens, of the 24th Ohio. His leg was shattered. He called me by name, and begged me to get him some water, as he was perishing. I went back to the river, stripped three or four dead of their canteens, and filled them, and returned. He told me that young Tommy Burnett was only wounded. He saw him carried back. This relieved my anxiety. The next day the dead were buried. There, amid the shot and shell and other *debris* of the battle-field, the dead heroes of the 6th lie, until the last trump shall call.

A few days afterward I met one of the officers of that regiment. Of him I eagerly inquired as to its fate. A tear fell from his manly eye as he exclaimed, "O, sad enough, Alf! Our boys were terribly cut up; but they fought like tigers—no flinching there; no falling out of line; shoulder to shoulder they stood amid the sheeted flame; and, though pressed by almost overwhelming numbers, no blanched cheek, no craven look, not the slightest token of fear was visible. The boys were there to do or die. They were Ohio boys, and felt a pride in battling for their country and her honor." And when I asked of names familiar, the loss, indeed, seemed fearful. "What became," said I, "of Olly Rockenfield?" "Dead!" was the reply. "And George Ridenour?" "Wounded—can not live!"

Dave Medary, a perfect pet of the regiment, a boy so childlike, so quiet in his deportment, yet with as brave a heart as Julius Cæsar—Little Dave was killed! I saw his grave a few days after. It was half a mile to the left of the railroad; and, although it was January, the leaves of the prairie-rose were full and green, bending over him as if in mourning for the early dead.

Jack Colwell—few of the typos of Cincinnati but knew Jack, or Add, as he was frequently called—poor Jack died from want of attention! His wound was in the leg, below the knee. I saw him a week after the battle, and the ball was not yet extracted.

Adjutant Williams, Lieutenant Foster, Captain McAlpin, Captain Tinker, Lieutenant Schaeffer, young Montaldo, Harry Simmonds, A. S. Shaw, John Crotty, and many others, were wounded or killed in the terrific storm of shot and shell sent by the rebel horde under Breckinridge. At one time every standard-bearer was wounded, and for a moment the flag of the 6th lay in the dust; but Colonel Anderson seized it and waved it in proud defiance, wounded though he was. The Colonel soon found claimants for the flag, and had to give it up to those to whose proud lot it fell to defend it.

O! the wild excitement of a fight! How completely carried away men become by enthusiasm! They know no danger; they see none—are oblivious to every thing but *hope of victory*! Men behold their boon companions fall, yet onward they dash with closed ranks, themselves the next victims.

There are few in the Army of the Cumberland who have not heard of the 35th Indiana, commanded by Colonel Mullen, of Madison, and as fine an Irish regiment as ever trod the poetic sod of the Emerald Isle. On their march up from Huntsville, Alabama, toward Louisville, Kentucky, on the renowned parallel run between Buell and Bragg, the command were short of provisions. *Half-rations* were considered a rarity. Father Cony, who is at all times assiduous in his duties to his flock, had called his regiment together, and was instilling into their minds the necessity of their trusting in Providence. He spoke of Jesus feeding the multitude upon three barley loaves and five small fishes. Just at this juncture an excitable, stalwart son of Erin arose and shouted: "Bully for him! He's the man we want for the *quarter-master of this regiment!*"

Early in January General Rosecrans issued his orders that all the men that could possibly be spared from detail duty should be immediately placed into the ranks, and that negroes should be "conscripted" or captured to take their places as teamsters, blacksmiths, cooks, etc. By this means the Third Division of the Army of the Cumberland, then under General James B. Steadman, was increased eight hundred men—men acclimated—men who could shoulder a musket. This was all done in less than three weeks. The negroes were all taken from rebel plantations.

One morning Colonel Vandeveer, of the 35th Ohio, commanding the Third Brigade, sent an orderly to my tent to inquire if I would not like to accompany an excursion into the enemy's country. As items were scarce, I at once assented; and, although scarce daybreak, off we went. The Colonel informed me that, as I was a good judge of darkeys, General Steadman had advised my going with the party.

We called first at Mrs. Carmichael's, and got two boys, aged, respectively, fifteen and seventeen. Mrs. Carmichael begged, and, finally, wept quite bitterly at the prospect of losing her boys—said those were all she had left—(she had sent the others South). She plead with us not to take "them boys"—said "they wern't no account—couldn't do nothing nohow." But the *mother* of these boys told our men a different story, and begged us to take the boys, "For," said she, "dey does all de plantin' corn and tendin' in de feel. Dey's my chill'n, and if I never sees 'em agin, I want de satisfaction of knowin' *dey is free!*"

Mrs. Carmichael's supplications for the negroes not to be taken from her were quite pitiful. She said they had been *allers* raised *jest* like as they were her own flesh and blood, and she just *keered* for 'em the same. But, as Mrs. Carmichael had two sons in the rebel army, the boys were taken. Upon the first order to come with us they seemed delighted, which caused the mistress to become very wrathy. I told the boys to go to their cabin and get their blankets, as they would need them. Judge my surprise when this *kind-hearted* woman, who had just informed me that she had "allers treated them boys as if they were her own flesh and blood"—this woman seized the blankets from the half-naked boys, and fairly shrieked at them: "You nasty, dirty little nigger thieves! if them Yankees want to steal you, let 'em find you in blankets; *I'm not a-going to do it!*" I merely inquired if that was the way in which she treated *her other children*—those in the rebel *army?*

From thence we went to Mrs. Kidd's, who had a husband and two sons in the rebel service. On our approach she endeavored to secrete some of the blacks, *but they* wouldn't *"stay hid."* The cause of the visit was explained. The rebels had been driving most of the likely negroes South. They were using them against the Government; and it was thought, by some, that they might as well work for as *against* the Union. They were raising their crops, running their mills, manufacturing their army-wagons, etc., besides supporting the families of the rebels, thus placing every able-bodied white man of the South in the hands of the government. The Federal service needed teamsters and hospital nurses and cooks.

Mrs. Kidd seemed quite a reasonable woman—said she thought she understood the policy of the North, and that the South knew that *slavery* was their strength. I made the remark, that, probably, if her husband knew she would be left without help, perhaps he would be induced to return and respect the old flag that had at all times, while he was loyal to it, defended him.

This little speech on my part elicited a rejoinder from a young miss, a daughter of Mrs. Kidd, sixteen or seventeen years of age, who flirted around, and with a nose that reached the altitude of at least "eighty-seven" degrees, exclaimed—

"I don't want my par nor my brothers to come home not till every one of you *Yankees* is driven from our sile!"

Some of the boys were busy hunting for a secreted negro, one whom this young lady had stored away for safety. A soldier opened a smoke-house door, at which the young Secesh fairly yelled—

"There aint no nigger there! You Yankees haint a bit o' sense! You don't know a smoke-house from a hut, nohow!"

Supposing the negro, who we felt almost sure was there, might possibly have escaped, we were about retiring with those already collected, when I suggested, loud enough for any one to hear about the building, that the whole squad should pour a volley through that rickety old dormer-window that projected from the room, when, much to our astonishment, and amid roars of laughter, appeared a woolly head, white eye-balls distended, the darkey yelling loud and fast—

"Don't shoot, massa! don't shoot! here I is! I's a comin'! De missus made me clime on dis roof. I wants to go wid you folks anyhow!"

Mr. Crossman's plantation was then visited; but, as the rebels had driven him away because of his Unionism, and taken his horses, his property was undisturbed by us.

From thence we visited Nolinsville—met a gang of twenty "likely-looking boys," stout, healthy fellows, who had clubbed together to come to the Union camp. They told us the rebs were only four miles off, "scriptin' all the niggers dar was in de fields, and a-runnin' 'em South." These were added to our stock in trade.

On our way back, a couple of old, sour-looking WOMEN were standing on the steps that were built for them to *climb* a *fence*, who, seeing so many blacks, inquired what we were taking them for. "To work," was the reply. "The rebels were about to run them South, and we wanted them to work for us."

"Now who told you that?" they inquired.

"The negroes themselves, madam. Many of them came voluntarily, to escape being sent South."

"O, yes! you Federals git your information from the *niggers altogether.*"

"Yes, madam!" facetiously replied Captain Dickerson, of the 2d Minnesota Regiment, "that's a fact. All the *reliable* information does come from them."

On our homeward trip we called at what is known as "Kidd's Mills," between Concord Church and Nolinsville. There were there quite a number employed upon the lumber and grist. A selection was made from the lot. They *all* wanted to come, but some were too young, and others too *old.*

Old man Kidd said he had a "safeguard from the Gineral. The Gineral had been up to see his darters, Delilah and Susan, and give him a safeguard." Upon examination it was found to be a mere request. Requests don't stand in military (not arbitrary enough). Then the old man declared he had always been a Union man—"allers said this war wern't no good—that the South had better stand by the old flag."

I at once told him if *such was the case* he was all right—to just get his horse and come with me, and if he had *"allers"* been a *"Union man"* or a non-combatant, why, they would all be returned to him.

The negroes were grouped around with anxious faces, and with rather astonished looks; and, as Mr. Kidd went to the stable, a venerable, white-haired old darkey, who had been told to stand back—he was too old to join the Union teamsters—came forward, and begged to be taken. "Why, I does heap o' work. I tends dis mill; I drives a team fustrate. *Please take de ole man, and let him die free!*"

Another negro, too old to take, spoke up and said: "What was dat de old man Kidd told you?"

"Why," I replied, "he said he had always been a Union man."

"De Lor' bress my soul! Did he say dat *he* was a Union man?"

"Yes!"

"Well! well! well! Dat he was a Union man! Well! well! well! And he's gwine to de Gineral for to tell him dat; and dat ole man is a member ob de Church! Well! well! well! Why, look heah, my Men', when de rebs was here only a few weeks ago—when dey was here, dat ole man got on his white hoss, and took de seceshum flag, and rode, and rode, and waved dat rebel flag and shouted, and more dan hollered for Jeff Davis, and *now* he Union man! He wants de Gineral to gib up dese here colored people—*dat's what's de matter wid him!*"

In an hour after we arrived in camp, sure enough, the old Kidd and other parties were there, expecting or hoping to get their darkeys back; but General Steadman told them if the negroes *wished* to return, they could do so, but, if they chose rather to work for "Uncle Sam," why, his orders were to use them.

"Well, *Gineral*, you just tell my niggers that they can go home with me," said Kidd.

"O! they can if they want to." So, out goes Kidd, smiling as a "basket of chips."

"Boys, the Gineral says you can all go home *with me*."

"If you want to," was my addition *to his sentence*.

Not a negro stirred from the line. After a brief consultation, in an under tone, at which Kidd, I noticed, was becoming very impatient, Kidd broke the quietude by saying:

"Come on, boys—come, Jim."

Jim looked over to Bob and said: "Bob, what are you going to do?"

"Me! Ise gwine to stay for de Union!"

Old man Kidd looked beaten. "Well, Jim, what will *you* do?"

"O! I does what Bob does!"

This same old Kidd had been in the habit of going over the country enlisting recruits for the rebel service—telling them that he was an old man, or he would go himself; that the old folks expected to be taxed to take care of the soldiers' families; that if they wanted corn or any thing from his mill, while they were in the army, to come and get it. By such language he induced several men, who had only small families, to enlist. One of them was indebted to Kidd about thirteen dollars, and after he had been in the army a month or two, Kidd dunned him for the old bill, remarking:

"Well, John, you're in the army now, gittin' your regular pay now—guess you can pay that little bill now, can't you?"

CHAPTER V

Just after General Schofield took command of the Third Division, Roddy Patterson, aided by a division of infantry, made his appearance near our camp, and, as we were weak in numbers, fortifications were erected in every direction, trenches dug, and efforts made to place the troops in the best trim to give the rebs a "fine reception."

There was one splendid piece of timber-land that might possibly come in possession of the rebels and do us much mischief. General Schofield ordered it cleared, and soon twelve hundred axes were resounding through the vast forest, and Abe's rail-splitters were at work forming "abatis" from the fallen trees, while earthworks commanding the position were soon erected.

Captain Stinchcomb was the provost-marshal of the division, and old man Jordan was in the habit of going to him with all his grievances. The soldiers had made an awful gap in his *reserved* timber before he found it out; but, as soon as he did so, he made for head-quarters, and found the Captain at dinner.

Scene I—Act 1—Enter Old Man.

"Look a-heah, Gineral Stinchcomb, them boys of yourn is cuttin' all my timber down!"

Captain Stinchcomb, affecting great surprise, exclaimed, "Is it possible! is it possible!"

"Y-a-a-a-s; all my *resarve, too!* There! there! do you hear that? Them's trees a-fallin', and them's the boys yellin' as they fall."

"What are they cutting them for, Mr. Jordan?"

"God only knows! I don't. I think just for to be doin' mischief. *Nauen* else in this world."

"Why didn't you stop them?" inquired Stinchcomb.

"O! kase I was afeared. There! there! do you hear that agin? Them's my trees!"

"Well, you'd better go right down and order them to stop."

"O, no, Gineral. It wouldn't do a bit of good. Them there boys would *just cuss the life out of me.* They only laugh at me. Won't you please go and have it stopped? Won't you?"

Suffice it to say, when Captain S. got there *it was too late.*

There are many little incidents connected with the army, which, being jotted down in my "day-book," during service, belong to the public.

"Home Again" is a song ever joyous to the soldier, and I remember a little incident in relation to that song and a serenading party of "young and festive cusses" belonging to Uncle Sam's service.

There is residing near Murfreesboro a Secession family consisting of a rebel widow and four sprightly daughters.

Now, our "blue-coats" are proverbial for their gallantry in presence of the ladies, and the Secesh girls smile as benignly upon a Federal soldier, if he be good-looking, as they would upon the most ultra fire-eater of the South. The mothers don't like this—but mothers can't help themselves in many instances. Our boys will visit and enjoy a lively chat with the girls whenever occasion offers. A quartette, of fine vocal abilities, belonging to the gallant Rousseau's division, had practiced several beautiful ballads, preparatory to a grand serenade to the daughters of the buxom widow.

Night threw her mantle o'er the earth just as the serenaders started upon their expedition. Arriving in dew course of time, they commenced their melodies. The moon was peeping out from behind the far-distant hill as they commenced,

"Roll on, silver moon,"

at which I suggested to the party there should be a big premium, just now, on "*silver*" moons." The serenaders smiled grimly, in token of admiration of the "*goak*," and commenced—

"Thine eyes, like the stars that are gleaming,
Have entered the depths of my soul."

Now, the repetition of "my soul" sounded to me exactly like mice-hole, and I suggested the propriety of substituting a rat-hole, at which several became wrathy, and proposed a mustard-plaster for my head.

The young ladies, aroused from their nocturnal slumbers, glided like sylphs to the windows, and threw several bouquets to the "gallant choristers," after the reception of which, and sundry pressures to fond hearts of the "beautiful flowers," the quartette commenced the song of "Home Again," etc., and

"O, it fills my soul with joy, to meet my friends once more."

This brought the widow to the window, who, hastily flinging back the shutter, screamed out, at the top of her voice: "If it will give you Yankees any greater joy to get home than it will me, I hope to gracious you'll stop your confounded noise and go home and meet your friends, for you've got none here."

This was a bomb-shell thrown right at the party, and such a crouching down and gradual sliding off you can scarcely imagine. To be led, as 't were, to the seventh heaven of bliss by the fair daughters' presentation of beautiful bouquets, and then to have all their hopes blasted by the termagant voice of the mamma! If any of my readers ever visit Rousseau's division and inquire for the serenaders, my word for it, the gentlemen concerned will have no recollection of the serenade.

Colonel Loomis, whose name is now engraven in history, and whose battery is mentioned with pride everywhere in the Army of the Cumberland, was, during the Virginia campaign, *Captain* Loomis. He was late Chief of Artillery upon Rousseau's staff. Captain Loomis, with his train, arrived in Cincinnati one Sunday morning, on his way to the Army of Virginia. Upon each caisson and every piece of artillery was plainly painted "Coldwater Battery."

Services in a church on Sixth Street were just concluded, and the warlike array attracted the congregation's attention, and the rather splendid figure of the young though "venerable-looking" Captain Loomis demanded a large share of attention. The pastor of the church introduced himself, spoke with admiration of the fine appearance of the Captain's men, etc., and, with a hearty pressure of the hand, remarked:

"Captain Loomis, yours is a noble motto; stick to that, stick to that, my young soldier. You have many hardships to undergo, but your glorious motto of Cold Water will carry you safely through."

Loomis, for the first time, caught the idea of the parson, but was too courteous to undeceive the preacher by informing him that his battery was raised in the town of Coldwater, Michigan. I have spent many a pleasant hour with the Captain, but never could "see" the "cold water" part of his battery.

A very pretty and pathetic little poem was handed me by one of Secessia's daughters, upon a prolific theme, entitled

The Dying Soldier

My noble commander! thank God, you have come;
You know the dear ones who are waiting at home,
And O! it were dreadful to die here alone,
No hand on my brow, and my comrades all gone.

I thought I would die many hours ago,
And those who are waiting me never could know
That here, in the faith of its happier years,
My soul has not wandered one moment from theirs.

The dead were around; but my soul was away
With the roses that bloom round my cottage to-day.
I thought that I sat where the jessamine twines,
And gathered the delicate buds from the vines.

And there—like a bird that had folded its wings,
At home, 'mid the smile of all beautiful things,
With sweet words of welcome, and kisses of love—
Was one I will miss in yon heaven above.

By the light that I saw on her radiant brow,
She watches and waits there and prays for me now.
My captain, bend low; for this poor, wounded side
Is draining my heart of its last crimson tide.

Some day, when you leave this dark place, and go free,
You will meet a fair girl—she will question of me!
She has kissed this bright curl, as it lay on my head;
When it goes back alone, she will know I am dead.
And tell her the soul, which on earth was her own,
Is waiting and weeping in heaven alone.

My Mother! God help her! Her grief will be wild
When she hears the mad Hessians have murdered her
child;
But tell her 'twill be one sweet chime in my knell,
That the flag of the South now waves where I fell!

It is well, it is well, thus to die in my youth,
A martyr to Freedom and Justice and Truth!
Farewell to earth's hopes—precious dreams of my heart—

My life's going out; but my love shall depart,
On the wings that my soul has unfurled,
Going up, soft and sweet, to that beautiful world.

A Joke on an "Egyptian" Regiment

A well-known commander was drilling a brigade at "Kripple Kreek," a short time since, and in it was a slim portion of the "1159th" Illinois. Quite a large number of this regiment have deserted upon every occasion offered, the men generally being very inattentive. The commanding officer of "all that is left of them" was severely censured, the other day, for dereliction of duty. The General swore by the Eternal he wished the Colonel of the "1159th" would *"go home* and join his regiment."

CHAPTER VI

It is well known by all that General Turchin has been fully vindicated. Captain Heaton, of Columbiana County, who was an eye-witness of his trial, and who knew the noble Russian, said to me, in speaking of this gallant soldier, "He looked like a lion among a set of jackals!" General Turchin was basely persecuted. He came out of the ordeal unscathed. The correspondent of the *Gazette*, who was in Huntsville, gave an account of affairs under Rousseau, who was as rigid in the punishment of rebels as Mitchel was before him. The court-martial convened to try Turchin for *punishing traitors* bid fair to last for months, under Buell's management.

Mrs. Turchin, before the arrest of her husband, had been making the campaign of Northern Alabama in his company, enduring, with the utmost fortitude, and for weeks together, all the hardships incident to a soldier's life. To ride on horseback, forty or fifty miles per day, was to her a mere matter of amusement, and in the recent march of the 19th Illinois, from Winchester to Bellefonte, she is said to have taken command of the vanguard, and to have given most vigorous and valuable directions for driving off and punishing the infamous bushwhackers who infested the road. These and similar things had so much excited the admiration of Colonel Turchin's men, that they would have followed his gallant lady into the field of battle with all the enthusiasm that fired the hearts of the French chivalry when gathered around the standard of the Maid of Orleans. As soon as Colonel Turchin was arrested, Mrs. Turchin suddenly disappeared. The next that was heard from her she was in Washington City; and now the story goes, that when she left the South she hastened to Chicago, enlisted the sympathies of noble-hearted men in the cause of her husband, prevailing upon a delegation of noble Illinoisans to accompany her to Washington, and, with their assistance, secured the confirmation of the Colonel as a brigadier-general of volunteers. Truly, in the lottery matrimonial, Colonel Turchin had the fortune to draw an invaluable prize.

All that has been alleged against Generals Turchin and Mitchel authorizing the sacking of Athens, Alabama, appears to have reacted; and, except General Rousseau, they were the most popular officers in that region.

The 18th Ohio was stationed at Athens, and encamped upon the fairgrounds. Here they were assailed by Scott's rebel cavalry. They resisted for some hours, when, learning through their scouts that an overwhelming force of the enemy were advancing against them, they thought best to retire, which they did in good order. As they passed through the town, on their way to Huntsville, some rash, inconsiderate rebel sympathizers jeered at and insulted them, cheering lustily for Jeff Davis and the Southern Confederacy. One or two of them, also, seized their guns, and when the rebel forces made their appearance, joined them in pursuit of our soldiers. A feeling of vindictive wrath sprang up in the minds of the boys of the 18th, and when they met the 19th Illinois and other troops, who, under command of Colonel Turchin, were coming to the rescue, they naturally magnified their own loss, and told the rescuers exaggerated stories of the manner in which they had been treated by the citizens of Athens.

Under those circumstances the whole force re-entered the town, driving the rebels before them, and, in the midst of great excitement, vowing vengeance. Then came the inevitable result: some good soldiers were carried away into acts of unwarrantable violence, and a few unprincipled scoundrels seized upon the opportunity to plunder, pilfer, and steal. But the mass of the forces entered the place under the impression (as appears from the testimony before the court-martial) that it was to be sacked and burned, as a just and proper military punishment. This impression was, unfortunately, not corrected by Colonel Turchin, because it was, in all probability, unknown to him. It arose, no doubt, from the fact that a general order had been issued, or, as reported, was about to be issued, denouncing, in severe terms, all citizens who should fire upon, or in any way molest our troops, and threatening both them and their property with destruction. Such a proclamation or order was, in fact, issued about this time.

Notwithstanding it was generally understood that the plundering of Athens was permitted, at least three-fourths of the soldiers voluntarily abstained from laying their hands upon a single dollar's worth of private property.

Now, as to the outrages themselves, I unhesitatingly pronounce that they have been greatly exaggerated. To say that the town was in any way "ruined" is simply an exhibition of ignorance on the part of those who are not acquainted with the facts, and a falsehood on the part of those who are.

Some three or four stores were broken into, and the most valuable part of the merchandise abstracted; the contents of the apothecary's shop were badly injured, and articles of value were taken from at least a dozen houses; some thousands of dollars' worth of horses, mules, and "niggers" were taken out of the town and suburbs; two or three scoundrels abused the persons of as many colored women; and this was the extent of the "ruin" inflicted upon Athens. I visited it more than a month ago. I saw no sign of "ruin," dissolution, or decay, and I am too good a friend of the Athenians not to say that I consider their beautiful town as being to-day the most flourishing in all North Alabama; and if a citizen from any other place, especially from Huntsville, should go to Athens and say otherwise, nothing but the presence of the military would prevent him from getting a thrashing upon the spot.

It is an old and trite saying, that "children and fools always tell the truth." Captain Moar and Lieutenant Wood, of General Steadman's staff, went out with a full expedition. It was under Colonel Bishop, of the 2d Minnesota; but these staff officers preceded the party. We arrived at the proposed field, where we were to bivouac for the night. A house was near, and Colonel Moar proposed to go there and order supper. There were four females in the house. All pretended to be glad to receive us. We brought them sugar and coffee, articles they had not enjoyed for over a year. While supper was preparing, Lieutenant Wood, seeing a very pretty little girl, said to her, "Come here, sissy."

The child reluctantly advanced, and as the Lieutenant placed her upon his knee, the little innocent looked up and said, "I Hate Yankees!"

The mother tried to catch the eye of the child.

Lieutenant Wood said, "O, no, you don't!"

"Yes, I do," reiterated the child.

"Why, sissy, what makes you hate Yankees?"

"'Cause mother told me I must," was the child's reply.

The mother blushed crimson, and said, very confusedly, "Why, Hattie! I Never!"

Picket Talk

I have often heard pickets chaff one another. Just after the capture of New Orleans, one of our boys, on picket duty, as light dawned, discovered a rebel just lighting his breakfast-fire up a ravine. Our picket called out to the rebel to stop building fires and come over and take breakfast with him. The rebel replied:

"No, I shan't, You haven't got any coffee."

"Yes, I have," says the Union soldier.

"Well, you haven't any sugar?"

"Yes, we have. We've got *Orleans*."

The man who makes the assertion that our boys in the field, when called upon to vote on resolutions, are influenced by fear of officers, *is most grossly mistaken*. Why, your American soldier is the most independent "cuss" in the world; and if a regiment is in line, and asked to vote, you may rest assured they vote as they please, and are governed by the dictates of their own consciences. The great address that was sent from the army was voted upon in this way: The regiments were drawn up in line, the address read, and the color-bearers were asked, "Do you indorse the address to which you have listened?" From every one came the hearty "I do!" when the colors were ordered two paces front. The regiments then voted on the address, the "ayes" stepping out in line with the colors, and, if there had been any "noes," they were to stand fast; but I have yet to hear of the man who did so. They rallied on their colors to a man, and stood with an unbroken front.

During the fight this side of Chapel Hill, Captain Kirk, one of the General's aids, seeing two rebels a little way off, on a by-road, put spurs to horse and gave chase. We all watched him very eagerly until he ascended the hill, when three more rebs joined the two, and made a stand. Kirk, thinking discretion the better part of valor, reined in his horse, when, to the infinite amusement of the staff, young Lu. Steadman (a son of the General, and, though but sixteen years of age, a gallant boy) exclaimed: "Father, father, look yonder; *Kirk has formed a line of battle!*" It is scarcely necessary to say that Kirk soon changed his base on a *double-quick*.

CHAPTER VII

Army of the Cumberland, Third Division,
Camp near Triune, Tenn., *May 2, 1863.*

"What will become of all of us women?" said an excited female to Colonel Vandeveer, one morning. "The States-rights men 'scripted all the young men, and you are drivin' all the old away. What will we ladies do?"

"Import Yankees," was the gallant Colonel's reply.

"We are raising a big stock especially for this market, and can spare any quantity."

"O! but Yankees don't suit us; we'd rather have our own people," was Secesh's reply.

"O! if that's the case, you women had better use your influence to get the traitors to lay down their arms and return to their homes, and behave themselves as honest men should, and that will end this little dispute, and you can have all the men you want."

"Well, Colonel, we are all tired of this war, and would be mighty glad to know our kinfolks were on their way home; but it will be mighty grindin' to 'em to have to come back and acknowledge that they couldn't lick you Yankees."

Deserters from the rebel army, I am told by citizens, are fast making their appearance wherever they can get the protection of our forces, and as we advance they will no doubt increase.

The provost-marshal of the division was kept busy administering the oath to those who came in from the surrounding country to Triune. Many very laughable incidents occurred at the swearing-in.

One long, lean, lank specimen of the rebel order came up to Captain Stinchcomb, who was proposing the oath.

"Hallo, mister, are you the captain of these ridgements around here? Dr. Wilson, my neighbor over across Spring Bottom, said I must come over to the feller what swored in folks, and get the Constitution, and keep it as long as you folks staid around here."

Wouldn't Go Round

Captain Airhardt, who was well known as the Topographical Engineer of this division, and one of the best-natured men in the world, was engaged in strengthening the fortifications around the camp near Triune, and in doing so had occasion to use some fifty men from the 2d Minnesota. As the boys had worked faithfully for four hours, the Captain thought he would issue a ration of whisky to each, and, not having any himself, he borrowed some from General Steadman's tent, without leave, from a keg the General had been keeping for his own medical purposes. He drew off about a gallon. The boys were drawn up in line, and the Captain commenced the issue, and as each man received his portion he was ordered to fall out. They did so, however, seeking the first opportunity to retire to the other end of the line, and again resume a position in the ranks. The Captain went after reinforcements of the *creature comfort* from the before-mentioned keg, and the *reinstated* members of the ditch-diggers were again ready for active service.

This state of things continued as long as the whisky lasted, and as the Captain handed the last ration, he looked at the few remaining boys, whom he supposed would have to go without any, and expressed his sorrow that he *hadn't enough to go round*. The fact was, every body had had at least three drinks.

I spent a very pleasant evening among a party of ladies who reside near our camp. Our officers are very attentive to them, and the ladies seem thankful for the protection. The house was furnished in elegant style. We had music, songs, and an elocutionary entertainment; every thing passing off pleasantly. As I am above suspicion myself, I may remark that I fear for the hearts of several of this brigade. Mine is already engaged; had it not been, I could not swear to the consequences of that visit. One really pretty specimen of Secesh sang "The Bonnie Blue Flag," by particular desire. She acknowledged she used to go it strong for dissolution, but let us hope she is becoming enlightened.

Major Boynton and the Chicken

Miss Mollie Jordan is a peculiar specimen of *ye Southern maiden*. I heard a good story illustrative of her rebellious nature some time ago:

Our troops were then stationed at Concord Church, and, in their peregrinations for fodder, came out this way, and, among other things, took off several contrabands belonging to Miss Mollie. Some time afterward she rode into camp and inquired for Colonel Vandeveer, and riding right up to him, she said, "How do, Colonel?" The Colonel tipped his hat, *a la militaire*, in token of recognition. "Colonel, you've been out our way and stole all my niggers, and I've just ridden into camp to see if you would be magnanimous enough to lend me my blacksmith to shoe this horse?"

The Colonel assisted her in alighting; had her boy hunted up, and the horse shod.

Dinner being ready, the lady was invited to partake of the repast; and, as she noticed a chicken upon the table almost as large as a turkey, she looked across at the Colonel, and then at the good-looking Major Boynton, and inquired whom she was dining with.

"O, with the Major, Miss. Why did you ask?" said the Colonel.

"I merely wished to know who stole my chickens; for those were particular pets of mine, and the only ones of that breed in the country."

The reader can imagine the laugh that took place at the Major's expense. As a matter of course, neither the Major nor the Colonel knew any thing as to where the servant-man had *bought* the fowls.

The Tennessee cavalry were out again yesterday, with Colonel Brownlow, and touched up the Alabamians. They brought in six prisoners. The rebels massed their men and undertook to charge us, but our Tennessee boys stood their ground, and the rebels backed out. They outnumbered us three to one; but they were not aware of that, or perhaps they would have given us fits. Now Brownlow is a daring, dashing fellow, and, in fact, all the officers and men seem made of the same material.

I suppose you will begin to think I've got cavalry on the brain, I talk so much of those boys; but they, at present, are the only ones out this way doing the fighting. When this bully division of infantry does go in, you can depend upon it somebody will get hurt.

All the regiments are quartered in elegant little pup-tents, as they call them. These tents are handsomely sheltered with evergreens and various bushes, presenting a picturesque appearance. The Lancaster, Chillicothe, and Cincinnati boys are vieing with each other as to who shall have the neatest camp.

A chicken-fight is to take place this evening between two game-cocks. One is owned by the fat boy of the 35th, the other by the new grocery-keeper of this brigade—he with the yellow vest and spectacles. Spectacles can whip fat boy, sure, so I must hurry up to see it done. We are striving our best to break up this love of cruel sports, but fear our efforts will be fruitless.

The weather is delightful; garden truck is progressing finely; the wheat and oat-fields are waving delightfully, while the corn is becoming like a man drinking whisky—*elevated*. With the above horrid joke I close.

Yours, dismally, till I see my love,

ALF.

Reminiscence of Camp Life in Virginia, in 1861

Camp Beverly, Va., *July 31, 1861.*

A soldier's life becomes irksome when he is encamped for any great length of time at any one point. A change of scenery, or the busy bustle of a march, wearisome though it be, makes the hours pass lightly. This is our eighth day at this place, and beautiful though the surroundings are, yet they begin to weary the eye. The boys want action, and if no prospect of a fight is here, they wish for still further progress.

The chief product of this never-ending and infernal mountainous region seems to be rain and ignorant people. It rains from Monday till Saturday, and commences fresh on Sunday; and if you put a question of the most commonplace order, the only answer you are likely to receive is the vacant stare of those you speak to. The first relief to this monotony occurred a few days since. Captain Bracken, editor of the Indianapolis *Sentinel*, who is in command of a splendid cavalry company, sent me an invitation to accompany him upon a scouting excursion, as a number of houses in the vicinity needed a little examination; so, accompanied by his two lieutenants and our gallant Major, Alex. Christopher, together with the ever-affable Andy Hall, the scouts, mounted upon as fine horses as could be selected by Captain Bracken, started jovially on duty. *"Now up the mead, now down the mead,"* and then over hill and dale they sped. Soon the outer pickets were passed, and we were in the enemy's country, where, 'tis said, the faster your horse travels the less likelihood there is of being shot by guerrillas. In the course of the afternoon we visited several houses, at one of which quite a quantity of contraband stuff was found, *which was placed in our canteens.*

RUNAWAY SCRAPE IN VIRGINIA.

At dusk we commenced a homeward tramp; and having to pass a house in which I had previously enjoyed the hospitality of its inmates, I alighted to refresh myself with a cool drink of water, the balance of the party going on. I had but just mounted my horse, when he took fright, and in a moment he was beyond control. Your humble servant clung with tenacity to the brute, and although I told him to "whoa," he wouldn't do it. Now he takes a by-road; away he flies with lightning speed; 'tis getting dark, and the *fool horse* is running further and further from camp. I tried kicking the animal so as to induce him to believe that it was me that was forcing him to his utmost speed, but 't was no go. Then, as I came near falling, I "*affectionately*" threw my arms around his neck, thinking, if life was spared, what a fine item this runaway would make. In vain I tried kicks, seesawing, jerks, coaxing, whoaing; in despair, I gave a loose hold of the reins to the runaway, hoping he would get tired, endeavoring, however, to keep him in the middle of the road. He jumped ditches, turned curves, until I began to think I would make a good circus performer, and eventually hire out to John Robinson, if safely delivered from this perilous expedition. At last he took me off my guard: turning abruptly to the left on a by-road, your correspondent went to the right, heels up in the air for a brief space—in fact, a balloon ascension; the balloon's burst was the next vivid thing in my mind, for I remembered scratching in the air, and then an almost instantaneous collision with mother Earth, alighting upon the right side of my head, from which the blood gushed in a slight attempt at a deluge. As luck would have it, some friendly folks came to my rescue, and bathed my head with camphor; I remounted, and, in a few minutes, met my companions, who were in search for me. They wet my lips with some of that stuff in the canteens. On arriving at camp, and sending for a surgeon, my wounds were dressed. A broken bone in my right hand, a terrific black eye and disfigured forehead, a sprained leg and battered side were the result of my excursion. This is the first letter I have been able to write since.

Last Saturday the whole regiment was in the finest spirits at seeing among us the kindly face of Cincinnati's universally-beloved citizen, Larz Anderson, and it did one good to see the hearty shake of hands our gallant officers and men gave him. He leaves for home to-day, laden with, no doubt, messages of love to many. God bless and speed him on his journey.

Captain Burdsall arrived to-day from Cheat Mountain. His command will remain here a few days, acting as mounted scouts. The Captain received a serious kick from his horse a week or two ago, and has been confined to his bed ever since. This company has been a very valuable auxiliary to the brigade, both at Cheat River Mountain and this place. We are sorry to hear of their intended return to Cincinnati in a few weeks.

The battle-field of Rich Mountain is about four miles from this place, and to-day I met with an old veteran, upon whose ground they fought. He is a thorough Union man, and was a prisoner in the hands of the Secession party. The rebels, to spite the old veteran, dug a trench around his house, for burying their dead, only eighteen inches below the surface. They also ruined his well by throwing in decayed horse-flesh—in fact, ruined his old homestead, by cutting down his fruit-trees, and various other specimens of Vandalism.

An incident occurred during the preparation for that battle worth mentioning. Mr. — —, an old man of this town, a Representative in the Legislature, one who was elected as a Union candidate, and then basely betrayed his constituents, and afterward was re-elected as a Secessionist— this man, on the eve of the battle, having partaken freely of liquor, heard of the advance of our army, and, mounting his horse, rode hastily to the rebel camp, to inform them of the intended attack. He passed the outer pickets, but was halted by a full company of Georgians, who, hearing of the advance of our men, had been thrown out to reconnoiter. He, much frightened, supposing he was mistaken and was in the Union men's camp, begged them not to shoot, exclaiming, "*I am a Union man.*" Scarce had the lying words passed his lips when a dozen balls pierced his body.

An announcement, made last night, that the rebels were advancing upon this post, put the boys in excellent humor. Every piece was put in order, and preparations made for a warm reception of the rebel gentry. Extra pickets were sent out by Colonel Bosley, who has entire command of this post, Captain Wilmington being field-officer of the day. The *guests*, however, did not arrive, thus greatly disappointing the boys, who had a magnificent *banquet* in store for them. The bill of fare consisted of

> Bullet Soup—with Gunpowder Sauce;
>
> Bayonets—drawn from Scabbards;
>
> Minié Muskets—nicely *ranged*;
>
> Twelve Six-pound Dumplings—U. S. on the margin;
>
> 2,600 Harper's Ferry Clickers;

besides numerous little delicacies in the way of Colt's "Revolving Pudding-hitters" and "*Derangers*," lightning-powder, Bowies, slashers, etc.

But as they refused the banquet, why, we will keep it, for the time being, ready for them in case of an intended *surprise party.*

A serenade in camp is sweet music, indeed. Last night the Guthrie Serenading Club, consisting of E. P. Perkins, W. B. Sheridan, Charlie Foster,

Captain Wilmington, Zeke Tatem, W. Craven, and S. B. Rice, gave the denizens of this town and camp a taste of their quality. The hills resounded with sweet sounds.

"Music soft, music sweet, lingers on the ear."

Captain Pic Russell had an acquisition to his company a few evenings since—in fact, a Secession emblem: a snake seven feet long—a regular "black sarpent"—quietly coiled himself in the Captain's blanket. He was, as soon as discovered, put to death. This region, of country abounds in serpents, the rattlesnake being a prolific article.

I must close, as the mail is about to start.

Yours, Alf.

CHAPTER VIII

Fun in the 123d Ohio

One of the boys furnished me with a copy of his experiences of camp, entitled "*Ye Chronicles of ye One Hundred and Twenty-third Regiment.*"

1st. Man that is born of woman, and enlisteth as a soldier in the One Hundred and Twenty-third Ohio, is few of days and short of rations.

2d. He cometh forth at reveille, is present also at retreat, yea, even at tattoo, and retireth, apparently, at taps.

3d. He draweth his rations from the commissary, and devoureth the same. He striketh his teeth against much hard tack, and is satisfied. He filleth his canteen with apple-jack, and clappeth the mouth thereof upon the bung of a whisky-barrel, and after a little while goeth away, rejoicing in his strategy.

4th. Much soldiering has made him sharp; yea, even the seat of his breeches is in danger of being cut through.

5th. He covenanteth with the credulous farmer for many turkeys and chickens; also, at the same time, for much milk and honey, to be paid for promptly at the end of each ten days; and lo! his regiment moveth on the ninth day to another post.

6th. His tent is filled with potatoes, cabbage, turnips, krout, and other delicate morsels of a delicious taste, which abound not in the Commissary Department.

7th. And many other things not in the "returns," and which never will return; yet, of a truth, it must be said of the soldier of the One Hundred and Twenty-third, that he taketh nothing that he can not reach.

8th. He fireth his Austrian rifle at midnight, and the whole camp is aroused and formed in line of battle, when lo! his mess come bearing in a nice porker, which he solemnly declareth so resembled a Secesh that he was compelled to pull trigger.

9th. He giveth the provost-marshal much trouble, often capturing his guard, and possesseth himself of the city.

10th. At such times "lager" and pretzels flow like milk and honey from his generous hand. He giveth without stint to his own comrades; yea, and withholdeth not from the One Hundred and Sixteenth Ohio Volunteer Infantry, or from the lean, lank, expectant Hoosier of the Eighty-seventh Indiana.

11th. He stretcheth forth his hand to deliver his fellow-soldiers of the One Hundred and Sixteenth from the power of the enemy; yea, starteth at early dawn from Petersburg, even on a "double-quick" doth he go, and toileth on through much heat, suffering, privation, and much "vexation of spirit," until they are delivered. Verily I say unto you, after that he suffereth for want of tents and camp-kettles. Yea, on the hights of Moorfield his voice may be heard proclaiming loudly for "hard tack and coffee," yet he murmureth not.

12th. But the grunt of a pig or the crowing of a cock awakeneth him from, the soundest sleep, and he goeth forth until halted by the guard, when he instantly clappeth his hands upon his "bread-basket," and the guard, in commiseration, alloweth him to pass to the rear.

13th. No sooner hath he passed the sentry's beat than he striketh a "bee-line" for the nearest hen-roost, and, seizing a pair of plump pullets, returneth, soliloquizing: "The noise of a goose saved Rome; how much more the flesh of chickens preserveth the soldier!"

14th. He even playeth at eucher with the parson, to see whether or not there shall be preaching in camp on the following Sabbath; and by dexterously drawing from the bottom a Jack, goeth away rejoicing that the service is postponed.

15th. And many other things doeth he; and lo! are they not recorded in the "morning reports" of Company B? Yea, verily.

A Thrilling Incident of the War

Captain Theodore Rogers, son of the Rev. E. P. Rogers, of New York City, formerly of Albany, N. Y., enlisted in May, 1861. After a varied experience he returned home, and, on the 7th of January, 1862, was married, in Cazenovia, New York, to the adopted daughter of H. Ten Eyck, Esq., a young lady who, we may be allowed at least to say, was every way worthy of the hand of the gallant soldier. The bridal days were passed in the camp, where a few weeks of happiness were afforded them.

Six months roll away, and the battle at Gaines's Mills opens. Mr. Rogers, having left home as first lieutenant, was, on account of his superior qualities as a soldier and as a man, promoted to the office of captain. His indefatigable efforts to discharge the duties of his position seriously impaired his health, and, previous to the battle referred to, he was lying sick in his tent. But the booming of the enemy's cannon roused the spirit of the soldier, and he forgot himself in his desire to win a victory for his country.

An account of the last scene is given by an officer in the rebel army, and, coming from such a source, its accuracy can not be questioned. Colonel McRae, while passing through Nassau, N. P., on his way to England, sought an introduction to a lady, who, he was informed, was from Albany. Finding that she knew Dr. Rogers and his family, she writes that his whole face lighted up, and he said: "O, I am so glad! I have been longing for months to see some one who knew the family of the brave young soldier who fell before my eyes."

He then said: "It was just at evening on Friday, June 27, at the battle of Gaines's Mills, as your army was falling back, I was struck with the appearance of a young man, the captain of a company, who was rushing forward at the head of his men, encouraging them, and leading them on, perfectly regardless of his own life or safety. His gallantry and bravery attracted our notice, and I felt so sure that he must fall, and so regretted the sacrifice of his life, that I tried hard to take him prisoner. But all my efforts were vain; and when at last I saw him fall, I gave orders at once that he should be carried from the field. It was the last of the fight, and in a few moments General Garland (also of the Confederate army) and I went in search of him, and found him under the tree whither I had ordered him to be carried."

Here the voice of the Colonel trembled so that he was hardly able to proceed. Recovering himself, he added: "I took from his pocket his watch, some money, and three letters—one from his wife, another from his father, and the third from his mother. As General Garland (who has since been killed) and I read the letters, standing at the side of the youthful husband and son, we cried like children—tears of grief and regret for the brave and honored soldier, and at the thought of those who would mourn him at home."

The Colonel said: "Tell his wife and father and mother that, though he was an enemy of whom we say it, he died the bravest and most gallant man that ever fell on the battle-field—encouraging and leading his men on, going before them to set the example. Tell them, also, that we saw him laid tenderly in his grave, (by himself,) and that, when this hateful war is over, I can take his wife to the very spot where her husband lies."

Colonel McRae was very anxious to know whether the letters and watch had been received by his wife, as he said that he gave them into the hands of Colonel T— —, of the 23d Regiment, who had promised to send them by a flag of truce.

From all that could be gathered, the lamented youth never spoke a word after receiving his death-wound.

While in the Army of Virginia I obtained the following facts in regard to the shooting of Colonel (now General) Kelley. A Staunton (Virginia) paper contained the following boastful article:

"Colonel Kelley, the commandant of a portion of Lincoln's forces at Philippa, was shot by Archey McClintic, of the Bath Cavalry, Captain Richards. Leroy and Foxall Dangerfield, (brothers,) and Archey McClintic, soldiers of the Bath Cavalry, were at the bridge, when a horse belonging to their company dashed through the bridge without its rider, whereupon these soldiers attempted to cross the bridge for the purpose of seeing what had been the fate of the owner of the riderless horse, when they were met by a portion of the enemy, led on by Colonel Kelley. As they met, Archey McClintic shot Colonel Kelley with a pistol. Seeing that they would be overcome by the number of the enemy, this gallant trio wheeled and retreated through the bridge. As they were retreating, they heard the enemy exclaim, 'Shoot the d—d rascal on the white horse!' meaning McClintic, who had shot Colonel Kelley. They fired, and broke the leg of Leroy P. Dangerfield. As McClintic was able to unhorse the colonel of a regiment with an old pistol, we hope that no soldier will disdain to use the old-fashioned pistol. They are as good as any, if in the proper hands."

From the same paper I cut the following:

"We have been informed that the gallant men who were under the command of Captain J. B. Moomau, in the precipitate retreat from Philippa, positively refused, after going a mile or two, to retreat any further. They were told that, if they would not retreat any further, they had better send a flag of truce to the enemy and surrender. It was proposed to decide the matter by a vote, when the men *unanimously* voted that they would *rather die than surrender*. The word 'surrender' does not belong to the vocabulary of the brave men of our mountains. They are as heroic as Spartans. They are willing to *die*, if needs be; but surrender, *never!* Though the enemy were constantly firing Minié muskets at them, they were not at all alarmed, and, being true republicans, they were resolved to take the vote of the men before they would agree to send a flag of truce, or think for a moment of surrendering. Who ever heard of a vote being taken under such circumstances? They were flying before the superior and overwhelming force of the enemy, yet they were sufficiently calm and self-composed to get through with the republican formality of taking the vote of the company. The men then under the command of Captain Moomau, of Pendleton, were his own company and some fifty belonging to the company of Captain Hull, of Highland, who had become separated from the other portion of their own company. Such soldiers will never be conquered—they may be killed, but they will never surrender."

A few days afterward these "never-surrender" Spartan chaps were brought into camp, the most hang-dog looking set of villains I ever met.

CHAPTER IX

Our Hospitals

I have visited many of the hospitals, both on the field and those located in cities where every convenience obtainable for money was profuse. Those in Nashville, Gallatin, and Louisville were, at all times, in the most perfect order. Still, in the field, and often in cities, cut off as Nashville and Murfreesboro sometimes are, the men suffer from the want of many little things. Miss Louisa Allcott, of Boston, who has been kindly administering to the wants of the sick and wounded in the hospitals, says:

One evening I found a lately-emptied bed occupied by a large, fair man, with a fine face, and the serenest eyes I ever met. One of the earlier comers had often spoken of a friend who had remained behind, that those apparently worse wounded than himself might reach a shelter first. It seemed a David and Jonathan sort of friendship. The man fretted for his mate, and was never tired of praising John, his courage, sobriety, self-denial, and unfailing kindliness of heart—always winding up with—"He's an out-and-out fine feller, ma'am; you see if he aint." I had some curiosity to behold this piece of excellence, and, when he came, watched him for a night or two before I made friends with him; for, to tell the truth, I was afraid of the stately-looking man, whose bed had to be lengthened to accommodate his commanding stature—who seldom spoke, uttered no complaint, asked no sympathy, but tranquilly observed all that went on about him; and, as he lay high upon his pillows, no picture of dying statesman or warrior was ever fuller of real dignity than this Virginia blacksmith.

No Hope

A most attractive face he had, framed in brown hair and beard, comely-featured and full of vigor, as yet unsubdued by pain, thoughtful, and often beautifully mild, while watching the afflictions of others, as if entirely forgetful of his own. His mouth was firm and grave, with plenty of will and courage in its lines, but a smile could make it as sweet as any woman's; and his eyes were child's eyes, looking one fairly in the face, with a clear, straightforward glance, which promised well for such as placed their faith in him. He seemed to cling to life as if it were rich in duties and delights, and he had learned the secret of content. The only time I saw his composure disturbed was when my surgeon brought another to examine John, who scrutinized their faces with an anxious look, asking of the elder: "Do you think I shall pull through, sir?" "I hope so, my man." And, as the two passed on, John's eyes followed them with an intentness which would have won a clearer answer from them had they seen it. A momentary shadow flitted over his face; then came the smile of serenity, as if, in that brief eclipse, he had acknowledged the existence of some hard futurity, and, asking nothing, yet hoping all things, left the issue in God's hand, with that submission which is true piety.

At night, as I went my rounds with the surgeon, I happened to ask which man in the room probably suffered the most, and, to my great surprise, he glanced at John.

"Every breath he draws is like a stab; for the ball pierced the left lung, broke a rib, and did no end of damage here and there; so the poor lad can find neither forgetfulness nor ease, because he must lie on his wounded back or suffocate. It will be a hard struggle, and a long one, for he possesses great vitality; but even his temperate life can't save him. I wish it could."

"You don't mean he must die, Doctor?"

"Bless you, there is not the slightest hope for him, and you'd better tell him so before long—women have a way of doing such things comfortably; so I leave it to you. He won't last more than a day or two at furthest."

I could have sat down on the spot and cried heartily, if I had not learned the propriety of bottling up one's tears for leisure moments. Such an end seemed very hard for such a man, when half a dozen worn-out, worthless bodies round him were gathering up the remnants of wasted lives, to linger on for years, perhaps burdens to others, daily reproaches to themselves. The army needed men like John, earnest, brave, and faithful, fighting for liberty and justice, with both heart and hand—a true soldier of the Lord. I could not give him up so soon, or think with any patience of so excellent a nature robbed of its fulfillment, and blundered into eternity by the rashness or stupidity of those at whose hands so many lives may be required. It was an easy thing for Dr. P— — to say, "Tell him he must die," but a cruelly hard thing to do, and by no means as "comfortable" as he politely suggested. I had not the heart to do it then, and privately indulged the hope that some change for the better might take place, in spite of gloomy prophesies, so rendering my task unnecessary.

A Short and Simple Story

After that night, an hour of each evening that remained to him was devoted to his ease or pleasure. He could not talk much, for breath was precious, and he spoke in whispers; but from occasional conversations I gleaned scraps of private history, which only added to the affection and respect I felt for him. Once he asked me to write a letter, and, as I settled with pen and paper, I said, with an irrepressible glimmer of female curiosity, "Shall it be addressed to mother or wife, John?"

"Neither, ma'am: I've got no wife, and will write to mother, myself, when I get better. Did you think I was married because of this?" he asked, touching a plain gold ring he wore, and often turned thoughtfully on his finger when he lay alone.

"Partly that, but more from a settled sort of look you have—a look young men seldom get until they marry."

"I don't know that; but I'm not so very young, ma'am—thirty in May, and have been what you might call settled these ten years, for mother's a widow. I'm the oldest child she has, and it wouldn't do for me to marry till Lizzie has a home of her own, and Laurie has learned his trade; for we're not rich, and I must be father to the children, and husband to the dear old woman, if I can."

"No doubt you are both, John; yet how came you to go to the war, if you felt so? Wasn't enlisting as bad as marrying?"

"No, ma'am, not as I see it; for one is helping my neighbor, the other pleasing myself. I went because I couldn't help it. I didn't want the glory or the pay; I wanted the right thing done, and the people said the men who were in earnest ought to fight. I was in earnest, the Lord knows; but I held off as long as I could, not knowing what was my duty. Mother saw the case, gave me her ring to keep me steady, and said 'Go;' so I went."

A short story, and a simple one; but the man and the mother were portrayed better than pages of fine writing could have done it.

A Soldier's Pride

"Do you ever regret that you came, when you lie here suffering so much?"

"Never, ma'am. I haven't helped a great deal, but I've shown I was willing to give my life, and perhaps I've got to; but I don't blame any body, and if it was to do over again, I'd do it. I'm a little sorry I wasn't wounded in front. It looks cowardly to be hit in the back; but I obeyed orders, and it don't matter much in the end, I know."

Poor John! it did not matter now, except that a shot in front might have spared the long agony in store for him. He seemed to read the thought that troubled me, as he spoke so hopefully when there was no hope, for he suddenly added:

"This is my first battle—do they think it's going to be my last?"

"I'm afraid they do, John."

It was the hardest question I had ever been called upon to answer; doubly hard with those clear eyes fixed upon mine, forcing a truthful answer by their own truth. He seemed a little startled at first, pondered over the fateful fact a moment, then shook his head, with a glance at the broad chest and muscular limbs stretched out before him.

"I'm not afraid; but it is difficult to believe all at once. I'm so strong, it does not seem possible for such a little wound to kill me."

The Last Letter

"Shall I write to your mother now?" I asked, thinking that these sudden tidings might change all plans and purposes; but they did not: for the man received the order of the Divine Commander to march with the same unquestioning obedience with which the soldier had received that of the human one, doubtless remembering that the first led him to life, the last to death.

"No, ma'am—to Laurie, just the same; he'll break it to her best, and I'll add a line to her, myself, when you get done."

So I wrote the letter, which he dictated, finding it better than any I had sent, for, though here and there a little ungrammatical or inelegant, each sentence came to me briefly worded, but most expressive, full of excellent counsel to the boy, tenderly bequeathing "mother and Lizzie" to his care, and bidding him good-by in words the sadder for their simplicity. He added a few lines, with steady hand, and, as I sealed it, said, with a patient sort of sigh, "I hope the answer will come in time for me to see it." Then, turning away his face, he laid the flowers against his lips, as if to hide some quiver of emotion at the thought of such a sudden sundering of all the dear home ties.

Those things had happened two days before. Now John was dying, and the letter had not come. I had been summoned to many death-beds in my life, but to none that made my heart ache as it did then, since my mother called me to watch the departure of a spirit akin to this, in its gentleness and patient strength. As I went in, John stretched out both his hands.

"I knew you'd come! I guess I'm moving on, ma'am."

He was, and so rapidly that, even while he spoke, over his face I saw the gray veil falling that no human hand can lift. I sat down by him, wiped the drops from his forehead, stirred the air about him with the slow wave of a fan, and waited to help him die. He stood in sore need of help, and I could do so little; for, as the doctor had foretold, the strong body rebelled against death, and fought every inch of the way, forcing him to draw each breath with a spasm, and clench his hands with an imploring look, as if he asked, "How long must I endure this, and be still?" For hours he suffered, without a moment's respite or a moment's murmuring. His limbs grew cold, his face damp, his lips white, and again and again he tore the covering off his breast, as if the lightest weight added to his agony; yet, through it all, his eyes never lost their perfect serenity, and the man's soul seemed to sit therein, undaunted by the ills that vexed his flesh.

Soldierly Sympathy

One by one the men awoke, and round the room appeared a circle of pale faces and watchful eyes, full of awe and pity; for, though a stranger, John was beloved by all. Each man there had wondered at his patience, respected his piety, admired his fortitude, and now lamented his hard death; for the influence of an upright nature had made itself deeply felt, even in one little week. Presently, the Jonathan who so loved this comely David came creeping from his bed for a last look and word. The kind soul was full of trouble, as the choke in his voice, the grasp of his hand betrayed; but there were no tears, and the farewell of the friends was the more touching for its brevity.

"Old boy, how are you?" faltered the one.

"Most through, thank heaven!" whispered the other.

"Can I say or do any thing for you, anywheres?"

"Take my things home, and tell them that I did my best."

"I will! I will!"

"Good-by, Ned."

"Good-by, John; good-by!"

They kissed each other tenderly as women, and so parted; for poor Ned could not stay to see his comrade die. For a little while there was no sound in the room but the drip of water from a pump or two, and John's distressful gasps, as he slowly breathed his life away. I thought him nearly gone, and had laid down the fan, believing its help no longer needed, when suddenly he rose up in his bed, and cried out, with a bitter cry, that broke the silence, sharply startling every one with its agonized appeal, "For God's sake, give, me air!"

It was the only cry pain or death had wrung from him, the only boon he had asked, and none of us could grant it, for all the airs that blow were useless now. Dan flung up the window; the first red streak of dawn was warming the gray east, a herald of the coming sun. John saw it, and, with the love of light which lingers in us to the end, seemed to read in it a sign of hope, of help, for over his whole face broke that mysterious expression, brighter than any smile, which often comes to eyes that look their last. He laid himself down gently, and stretching out his strong right arm, as if to grasp and bring the blessed air to his lips in fuller flow, lapsed into a merciful unconsciousness, which assured us that for him suffering was forever past.

As we stood looking at him, the ward-master handed me a letter, saying it had been forgotten the night before. It was John's letter, come just an hour too late to gladden the eyes that had looked and longed for it so eagerly — yet he had it; for after I had cut some brown locks for his mother, and taken off the ring to send her, telling how well the talisman had done its work, I kissed this good son for her sake, and laid the letter in his hand, still folded as when I drew my own away.

On my visit to the hospital at Gallatin, I was called to the bedside of a dying boy, who belonged in Columbus, Ohio. There I met Dr. W. P. Eltsun, Dr. Armington, Dr. Landis, and other surgeons, all working faithfully for the suffering men; but Death had marked this boy for his own. I took his almost pulseless hand in mine, wiped the cold sweat from his brow, and, as I did so, he murmured, in a soft tone — a tone of sweet sadness — and with a half vacant stare, "Mother, is that you? O, how long I've waited for your coming! Tell sister I'm better now. Good-by, Charlie. Halt! who goes there?" and then a sudden start seemed to bring him to a realization of his situation, and he quietly gazed at me for a moment, called me by name, and said, "Alf, will you write a letter for me to-morrow?" This I promised, should he be able to dictate to me what I should write. In a few minutes he again called the sweet name of "Mother! Mother!" and with the words "good-by" upon his lips, and a smile of joy beaming on his face, he fell into that sleep that knows no waking.

There were three ministering angels, who had left all the luxuries of a home, attending in this hospital. They had volunteered as nurses, and had come from Indianapolis, to render all the aid they could to our country's noble defenders. Indiana should remember the names of Miss Bates, Miss Cathcart, and Mrs. Ketchum.

The Ensign-Bearer

Written Expressly for Mr. Alf. Burnett, by Miss Cora M. Eager.

Never mind me, Uncle Jared, never mind my bleeding breast; They are charging in the valley, and you're needed with the rest; All the day through, from its dawning till you saw your kinsman fall, You have answered fresh and fearless to our brave commander's call, And I would not rob my country of your gallant aid to-night, Though your presence and your pity stay my spirit in its flight.

All along that quivering column, see the death-steeds trampling down Men whose deeds this day are worthy of a kingdom and a crown. Prithee, hasten, Uncle Jared—what's the bullet in my breast To that murderous storm of fire, raining tortures on the rest? See, the bayonets flash and falter—look I the foe begins to win! See, see our faltering comrades! God! how the ranks are closing in!

Hark! there's muttering in the distance, and a thundering in the air, Like the snorting of a lion just emerging from his lair; There's a cloud of something yonder, fast unrolling like a scroll; Quick, quick! if it be succor that can save the cause a soul! Look! a thousand thirsty bayonets are flashing down the vale, And a thousand hungry riders dashing onward like a gale.

Raise me higher, Uncle Jared; place the ensign in my hand; I am strong enough to wave it, while you cheer that flying band. Louder! louder! shout for Freedom, with prolonged and vigorous breath; Shout for Liberty, and Union, and—the victory over death! See! they catch the stirring numbers, and they swell them to the breeze, Cap, and plume, and starry banner, waving proudly through the trees.

Mark! our fainting comrades rally—mark! that drooping column rise; I can almost see the fire newly kindled in their eyes. Fresh for conflict, nerved to conquer, see them charging on the foe, Face to face, with deadly meaning, shot, and shell and trusty blow; See the thinned ranks wildly breaking; see them scatter toward the sun! I can die now, Uncle Jared, for the glorious day is won.

But there's something, something pressing with a numbness on my heart, And my lips, with mortal dumbness, fail the burden to impart. O, I tell you, Uncle Jared, there is something, back of all, That a soldier can not part with when he heeds his country's call. Ask the mother what, in dying, sends the yearning spirit back Over life's broken marches, where she's pointed out the track?

Ask the dear ones gathered nightly round the shining household hearth, What to them is brighter, better than the choicest things of earth? Ask that dearer one, whose loving, like a ceaseless vestal flame, Sets my very soul a-glowing at the mention of her name; Ask her why the loved, in dying, feels her spirit linked with his In a union death but strengthens? she will tell you what it is.

And there's something, Uncle Jared, you may tell her, if you will, That the precious flag she gave me I have kept unsullied still; And—this touch of pride forgive me—where Death sought our gallant host, Where our stricken lines were weakest, there it ever waved the most; Bear it back, and tell her, fondly, brighter, purer, steadier far, 'Mid the crimson strife of battle, shone my life's unsetting star!

But, forbear, dear Uncle Jared, when there's something more to tell, And her lips, with rapid blanching, bid you answer how I fell; Teach your tongue the trick of slighting, though 'tis faithful to the rest, Lest it say her brother's bullet is the bullet in my breast. But, if it must be that she learn it, despite your tender care, 'T will soothe her bleeding heart to know my bayonet pricked the air.

Life is ebbing, Uncle Jared; my enlistment endeth here; Death, the conqueror, has drafted—I can no more volunteer. But I hear the roll-call yonder, and I go with willing feet Through the shadows to the valley where victorious armies meet. Raise the ensign, *Uncle Jared*—let its dear folds o'er me *fall*; Strength and Union for my country, and *God's* banner over *all*.

CHAPTER X

SPORTS IN CAMP.

Army of the Cumberland,
Camp near Triune, Tenn., *May 12, 1863.*

There are, at all times, sunny sides as well as the dark and melancholy picture, in camp life. Men whose business is that of slaughter—men trained to slay and kill, will, amid the greatest destruction of life, become oblivious to all surrounding scenes of death and carnage.

I have seen men seated amid hundreds of slain, quietly enjoying a game of "seven-up," or having *a little draw.* Yet let them once return to their homes, and enjoy the society and influence of the gentler sex, and they will soon forget the excitement and vices of camp, and return to the more useful and ennobling enjoyments of life.

Yesterday a lively time, generally, was had in camp. After the drilling of the division, a grand cock-fight occurred on the hill. Some of the boys, who are regular game-fanciers, brought some splendid chickens, and, as a consequence, a good deal of money changed hands. The birds fought nobly: three were killed, one of them killing his opponent the first round, and instantly crowing, much to the amusement of the Sports. This fighting with gaffs is not a cruel sport, as one or the other is soon killed.

Snakes are not so prevalent in these parts as they were when we first came: then it was not uncommon to find a nice little "garter" quietly ensconced in one's pocket, or in your pantaloon leg, or taking a nap in one corner of your tent.

A prize-fight occurred in the division a few days ago. A couple of sons of *Ethiopia*, regular young bucks, feeling their dignity insulted by various epithets hurled at each other, from loud-mouthing adjourned to fight it out in the woods—a big crowd following to enjoy the fun. A ring was soon formed, and at it they went, *a la* Sayers and Heenan. Umpires were improvised for the occasion, and time-keepers, etc., chosen.

The first clash was a *butter* and a *rebutter*, their heads coming together, fairly making the *wool* fly. This was round first.

Round 2d.—35th Ohio darkey came boldly to the scratch; as he only weighed sixty-five pounds more than his opponent, and with the *slight* difference of one foot six inches higher, he pitched in most valiantly, and received a splendid hit on the sconce, which made him feel as if a *flea* bit him. After full ten minutes skirmishing, during which time neither struck the other, both retired to the further *corner* of the *ring*, until time was called.

Round 3d.—Minnesota Ethiopian, who had been weakening in the pulse for some time, came up shaky, and was received with laughter by his opponent; but the little fellow hit out splendidly, and launched an eye-shutter at the stalwart form of the 35th darkey. First blood claimed for the 2d Minnesota.

Round 4th was, per agreement, a rough and tumble affair, as the spectators were growing impatient; and such "wool-carding" was never before exhibited. Both fought plucky; but the 2d Minnesota having but just recovered from a *sick of fitness*, as he said, was about being overpowered, when the officer of the day interfered; and thus ended the dispute for the time. Betters *drew* their money, as the fight was a *draw*.

Ball in Camp

Last night we had a fancy-dress ball, a *recherché* affair, a fine dancing-floor having been laid down in Company I's ground. A first-rate cotillion band was engaged, and played up lively airs. Your correspondent had a special invitation to be present, and enjoyed the party amazingly.

The belles of the evening were Miss Allers, the Widow Place, Miss Stewart, Miss Austin, and Miss Dodge, all of Minnesota.

Miss Dodge wore an elegant wreath of red clover, mingled with beech-leaves, and was dressed in red and white—the red being part of a shirt, kindly furnished by one of the friends of the lady; the white was expressly manufactured by the Widow Place, dressmaker and milliner for this regiment.

Miss Stewart is a beautiful creature, of a bronzed hue, from excessive exposure to the sun. She also wore a wreath of young clover, mingled with bunches of wheat.

Miss Allers was rather undignified in her actions; her dress we thought too short at the bottom, and too high in the neck; however, Miss A. was dressed in Union colors, having an American flag for an apron, and blue and red dress, with a neat-fitting *waste*—of materials.

But the one in whom we felt the deepest interest was the Widow. She had all the grace and elegance of a hippopotamus, and her style was enchanting. She wore a low-necked dress, with a bouquet of cauliflowers and garlick in her bosom, a wreath of onion-greens in her hair, full, red dress, and elaborate hoops, which continually said, "Don't come a-nigh me." Her bashful behavior was the talk of the evening, and the gay Widow and your correspondent, when upon the floor, were the cynosure of all eyes. The dance continued until the Colonel ordered a *double tattoo* sounded, so that we could hear it. Several intruders were put out, for conduct unbecoming gentlemen. The ball was strictly *private*, as no *commissioned* officers were allowed to participate.

However, the officers were truly amused at the fun, and, as women have, ere this, been dressed in *men's* clothes, there is no reason the boot shouldn't, this time, be on the other leg.

Miss Austin's dance of the Schottische, with double-soled military boots, was excellent. Miss Austin belongs in Louisville, and has long been known as a female *auctioneer*.

The 9th Ohio band has arrived, and the boys are delighted. This is a new band, all Cincinnati musicians, and they are truly welcome to the camp.

Boys want to hear from home as often as possible. It will be well for the girls to bear this in mind, and write often. Letters of love, we may say, alphabetically speaking, are X T Z to those who get them.

Anecdote of the 63d Ohio and Colonel Sprague

The 63d boys love Colonel Sprague; they are not exactly afraid of him, but many a one would rather be whipped, any day, than take a reprimand from him. For instance: several nights ago one of the men, instigated by the love of good eating, and not having the fear of God before his eyes, attempted to pinch, as they say in the 63d, a can of fruit at the sutler's tent.

But, unluckily for him, the sutler saw him, sprang out of bed, caught him by the collar and took him prisoner. As soon as the sutler got hold of him he began to address him in language more forcible than polite. "You d—d thief, I'll pay you for this; I'll take you before the Colonel, and, if I had my boots on, I'd take it out in kicking you."

"I'll tell you what," said the soldier, "I'll wait here till you put your boots on, and you may kick me as much as you please, if you won't take me before the Colonel."

The following exquisite poem was handed me by Colonel Durbin Ward, of the 17th Ohio. I wish I knew the author. They are beautiful lines:

The Soldier's Dream of Home

You have put the children to bed, Alice—
Maud and Willie and Rose;
They have lisped their sweet "Our Father,"
And sunk to their night's repose.

Did they think of me, dear Alice?
Did they think of me, and say,
"God bless him, and God bless him,
Dear father, far away?"

O, my very heart grows sick, Alice,
I long so to behold
Rose, with her pure white forehead,
And Maud, with her curls of gold;
And Willie, so gay and sprightly,
So merry and full of glee—,
O, my heart yearns to enfold ye,
My smiling group of three.

I can bear the noisy day, Alice—
The camp life, gay and wild,
Shuts from my yearning bosom
The thoughts of wife and child;
But when the night is round me,
And under its starry beams
I gather my cloak about me,
And dream such long, sad dreams!

I think of a pale young wife, Alice,
Who looked up in my face
When the drum beat at evening
And called me to my place.
I think of three sweet birdlings,
Left in the dear home-nest,
And my soul is sick with longings,
That will not be at rest.

O, when will the war be over, Alice?
O, when shall I behold
Rose, with her pure white forehead,
And Maud, with her curls of gold;
And Will, so gay and sprightly,
So merry and full of glee,
And more than all, the dear wife
Who bore my babes to me?

God guard and keep you all, Alice;
God guard and keep me, too,
For if only one were missing,
What would the others do?
O, when will the war be over,
And when shall I behold
Those whom I love so dearly,
Safe in the dear home-fold?

THE WIFE'S REPLY
Dedicated to the Author of "The Soldier's Dream of Home"

You say you dream of us, Willie,
When fall the shades of night,
And you wrap your cloak around you
By the camp-fire's flickering light;
And you wonder if our little ones
Have bowed their curly heads,
And asked a blessing for you,
Before they sought their beds!

It was but this very night, Willie,
That our Willie came to me,

And looking up into my face,
As he stood beside my knee,
He said, "Mamma, I wonder
When will this war be o'er,
For O, I long so much to see
My dear papa once more."

My heart was full of tears, Willie,
But I kept them from my eyes,
And the answer that I made him
Opened his with sad surprise—?
"Suppose he should *never* come, Willie!"
"But, mamma, I *know* he will,
For I pray to Jesus every night
To spare my father still."

I clasped him in my arms, Willie,
I pressed him to my breast;
His childish faith it shamed me,
And my spirit's vague unrest;
And I felt that our Heavenly Father,
From his throne in the "City of Gold,"
Would watch you and guard you and bring you
Safe back to the dear home-fold.

We think of you every night, Willie;
We think of you every day;
Our every prayer wafts to Heaven the name
Of one who is far away.
And Rose, with her pure white forehead,
And Maud, with her curls of gold,
Are talking in whispers together,
Of the time when they shall behold

The father they love so dearly;
And Willie, with childish glee,
Is bidding me "not to forget to tell
Papa to remember me."
So we think of you every night, Willie
By the camp-fire's fitful gleams,
Until the war shall be over,
Let us mingle still in your dreams.

A. L. Y.

CHAPTER XI

The Atrocities of Slavery

A late number of the *Atlantic Monthly* gives the following in relation to General Butler and his administration in Louisiana:

Among the many personal anecdotes are the following, which are almost too horrible to be published, but for the impressive lesson they convey. One of the incidents was related more briefly by the General himself, when in New York, in January last. We quote from the writer in the *Atlantic*.

Just previous to the arrival of General Banks at New Orleans, I was appointed Deputy Provost-Marshal of the city, and held the office for some days after he had assumed command. One day, during the last week of our stay in the South, a young woman of about twenty years called upon me to complain that her landlord had ordered her out of her house, because she was unable longer to pay the rent, and she wished me to authorize her to take possession of one of her father's houses that had been confiscated, he being a wealthy rebel, then in the Confederacy, and actively engaged in the rebellion.

The girl was a perfect blonde in complexion; her hair was of a very pretty light shade of brown, and perfectly straight; her eyes a clear, honest gray; and her skin as delicate and fair as a child's. Her manner was modest and ingenuous, and her language indicated much intelligence.

Considering these circumstances, I think I was justified in wheeling around in my chair, and indulging in an unequivocal stare of incredulous amazement, when, in the course of conversation, she dropped a remark about having been born a slave.

"Do you mean to tell me," said I, "that you have negro blood in your veins?" And I was conscious of a feeling of embarrassment at asking a question so apparently preposterous.

"Yes," she replied, and then related the history of her life, which I shall repeat as briefly as possible:

"My father," she commenced, "is Mr. Cox, formerly a judge of one of the courts in this city. He was very rich, and owned a great many houses here. There is one of them over there," she remarked, naively, pointing to a handsome residence opposite my office in Canal Street. "My mother was one of his slaves. When I was sufficiently grown, he placed me at school, at the Mechanics' Institute Seminary, on Broadway, New York. I remained there until I was about fifteen years of age, when Mr. Cox came on to New York and took me from the school to a hotel, where he obliged me to live with him as his mistress; and to-day, at the age of twenty-one, I am the mother of a boy five years old, who is my father's son. After remaining some time in New York, he took me to Cincinnati and other cities at the North, in all of which I continued to live with him as before. During this sojourn in the Free States I induced him to give me a deed of manumission; but on our return to New Orleans he obtained it from me and destroyed it. At this time I tried to break off the unnatural connection, whereupon he caused me to be publicly whipped in the streets of the city, and then obliged me to marry a colored man; and now he has run off, leaving me without the least provision against want or actual starvation, and I ask you to give me one of his houses, that I may have a home for myself and three little children."

Strange and improbable as this story appeared, I remembered, as it progressed, that I had heard it from Governor Shepley, who, as well as General Butler, had investigated it, and learned that it was not only true in every particular, but was perfectly familiar to the citizens of New Orleans, by whom Judge Cox had been elected to administer justice.

The clerks of my office, most of whom were old residents of the city, were well informed in the facts of the case, and attested the truth of the girl's story.

I was exceedingly perplexed, and knew not what to do in the matter; but, after some thought, I answered her thus:

"This department has changed rulers, and I know nothing of the policy of the new commander. If General Butler were still in authority, I should not hesitate a moment to grant your request; for, even if I should commit an error of judgment, I am perfectly certain he would overlook it, and applaud the humane impulse that prompted the act; but General Banks might be less indulgent, and make very serious trouble with me for taking a step he would perhaps regard as unwarrantable."

I still hesitated, undecided how to act, when suddenly a happy thought struck me, and, turning to the girl, I added—

"To-day is Thursday: next Tuesday I leave this city With General Butler for a land where, thank God! such wrongs as yours can not exist; and, as

General Banks is deeply engrossed in the immediate business at head-quarters, he will hardly hear of my action before the ship leaves—so I am going to give you the house."

I am sure the kind-hearted reader will find no fault with me that I took particular pains to select one of the largest of her father's houses, (it contained forty rooms,) when she told me that she wanted to let the apartments as a means of support for herself and her children.

My only regret in the case was that Mr. Cox had not been considerate enough to leave a carriage and a pair of bays on my hands, that I might have had the satisfaction of enabling his daughter to disport herself about the city in a style corresponding to her importance as a member of so respectable and wealthy a family.

And this story, that I have just told, reminds me of another, similar in many respects.

One Sunday morning, late last summer, as I came down-stairs to the breakfast-room, I was surprised to find a large number of persons assembled in the library. When I reached the door, a member of the staff took me by the arm and drew me into the room toward a young and delicate mulatto girl, who was standing against the opposite wall, with the meek, patient bearing of her race, so expressive of the system of oppression to which they have been so long subjected. Drawing down the border of her dress, my conductor showed me a sight more revolting than I trust ever again to behold. The poor girl's back was flayed until the quivering flesh resembled a fresh beefsteak scorched on a gridiron. With a cold chill creeping through my veins, I turned away from the sickening spectacle, and, for an explanation of the affair, scanned the various persons about the room.

In the center of the group, at his writing-table, sat the General. His head rested on his hand, and he was evidently endeavoring to fix his attention upon the remarks of a tall, swarthy-looking man who stood opposite, and who, I soon discovered, was the owner of the girl, and was attempting a defense of the foul outrage he had committed upon the unresisting and helpless person of his unfortunate victim, who stood smarting, but silent, under the dreadful pain inflicted by the brutal lash.

By the side of the slaveholder stood our Adjutant-General, his face livid with almost irrepressible rage, and his fists tight-clenched, as if to violently restrain himself from visiting the guilty wretch with summary and retributive justice. Disposed about the room, in various attitudes, but all exhibiting in their countenances the same mingling of horror and indignation, were other members of the staff—while near the door stood three or four house-servants, who were witnesses in the case.

To the charge of having administered the inhuman castigation, Landry (the owner of the girl) pleaded guilty, but urged, in extenuation, that the girl had dared to make an effort for that freedom which her instincts, drawn from the veins of her abuser, had taught her was the God-given right of all who possess the germ of immortality,—no matter what the color of the casket in which it is hidden. I say "drawn from the veins of her abuser," because she declared she was his daughter; and every one in the room, looking upon the man and woman confronting each other, confessed that the resemblance justified the assertion.

After the conclusion of all the evidence in the case, the General continued in the same position as before, and remained for some time apparently lost in abstraction. I shall never forget the singular expression on his face. I had been accustomed to see him in a storm of passion at any instance of oppression or flagrant injustice; but on this occasion he was too deeply affected to obtain relief in the usual way. His whole air was one of dejection, almost listlessness; his indignation too intense, and his anger too stern, to find expression even in his countenance.

Never have I seen that peculiar look but on three or four occasions similar to the one I am narrating, when I knew he was pondering upon the fatal curse that had cast its withering blight upon all around, until the manhood and humanity were crushed out of the people, and outrages such as the above were looked upon with complacency, and the perpetrators treated as respected and worthy citizens, and that he was realizing the great truth, that, however man might endeavor to guide this war to the advantage of a favorite idea or a sagacious policy, the Almighty was directing it surely and steadily for the purification of our country from this greatest of national sins.

But to return to my story. After sitting in the mood which I have described at such length, the General again turned to the prisoner, and said, in a quiet, subdued tone of voice—

"Mr. Landry, I dare not trust myself to decide to-day what punishment would be meet for your offense, for I am in that state of mind that I fear I might exceed the strict demands of justice. I shall, therefore, place you under guard for the present, until I conclude upon your sentence."

A few days after, a number of influential citizens having represented to the General that Mr. Landry was not only a "high-toned gentleman," but a person of unusual "AMIABILITY" of character, and was, consequently, entitled to no small degree of leniency, he answered that, in consideration of the prisoner's "high-toned" character, and especially of his "amiability," of which he had seen so remarkable a proof, he had determined to meet their views, and therefore ordered that Landry give a deed of manumission to the girl, and pay a fine of five hundred dollars, to be placed in the hands of a trustee for her benefit.

Beauties of the Peculiar Institution—A Few Well-substantiated Facts

A Mr. P——, deceased, of Gallatin, Tenn., for years a slave-trader, had children both by his wife and her body-servant, a beautiful mulatto woman—thus making, generally, the additions to his family in *duplicate*. One of his illegitimate daughters—a beautiful, hazel-eyed mulatto girl—is now the waiting-maid of his widow. This bright mulatto girl is married to a slave belonging to a prominent member of Congress from Tennessee, and has a son, a particularly apt and intelligent boy, whom the rebel women used to send around the camps, head-quarters, and street corners, to obtain the latest news, and report the same to them. Although but eight years old, he was too shrewd to remain quietly a slave. When the daughter of a Federal officer opened a little school, to teach a few contrabands, he came, and learned very rapidly. But his intellectual growth was suddenly stopped by the interference of his *grand*mother, who followed him to the school one day, and dragged him from the room in a perfect rage, threatening to kill him if he ever dared enter a *free*-school again, at the same time declaring to him that "he was not President Lincoln yet."

Another instance: The wealthy and prominent Colonel G——, of Gallatin, Tenn., a very *respectable* and *high-toned* gentleman, who is reputed a *kind-hearted* and benevolent man, *remarkably lenient* toward his slaves, whose praise is in the mouths of our Northern soldiers for his kind hospitalities, finding that his slaves, in view of the coming difficulties, did not increase fast enough for profit, called them all together on the 1st of January, 1862, and said to them: "Now, wenches, mind, every one of you that aint 'big' in three or four months, I intend to sell to the slave-trader." He afterward chuckled over it, adding that it "brought them to terms." Comment needless.

In the fall of 1861, in Piketon, Ky., at the headwaters of the Big Sandy, were two families—one known as the Slone family, the other as the Johnson family. The slaves of the former were all liberated about seventeen years before, by a will, stipulating that they should remain with his wife and work the plantation while she lived. Mrs. Slone died about two years after her husband, and not only emancipated these slaves, according to the last will and testament of her deceased husband, but, as they had taken more care of the old lady in her declining years than her sons, she thought it but equitable and right to disinherit the sons and leave the remnant of a once large estate, reduced to $9,000, to the slaves. But the gloating avarice of her gambling sons, backed by a vile public sentiment, prompted these unnatural sons to attempt to break the wills of their father and mother. After litigating the case about twelve years, and having been defeated in the highest courts in Kentucky, they went back and set up a claim of $2,000 against their father's estate, when these despoiled slaves had to deposit the last of their estate as security, having been for more than twelve years thus harassed and perplexed by vexatious lawsuits. When the Union army under General Nelson came into that country, and had that trumpeted battle at Ivy Mountain, and our troops reached Prestonburg, twenty-five miles from Piketon, these hunted and plundered ones concluded that *now* was the time for them to escape to the "promised land." They gathered together their little *all*, cut fifty or sixty saw-logs, made a raft, loaded their worldly goods on it, and floated down the river. When they reached Prestonburg, General Nelson had them arrested, cut their raft to pieces, and sent them back to Piketon. Afterward, when our troops, under the intrepid Garfield, moved up the river, and made their head-quarters at Piketon, these tormented and persecuted ones were told that now they might avail themselves of the Government boats to go down the river and leave the land of their tormentors.

The Johnson family slaves were liberated, at the death of their owner, by a will, the writer and executor of which had run off into the rebel army, carrying it with him. A distant relative of Mr. Johnson, a worthless, shiftless, ignorant fellow, moved upon the plantation, and claimed not only the property, but the slaves. "When our troops were about leaving Piketon, the most intelligent of the Slone family asked of Captain H— —, A. A. Q. M., the privilege of using a push-boat to transport the family down the river. Consent was given them, and, the next morning, the *two* families gathered together, the old and young, men and women and children, numbering fifty-nine souls, and started down the river. Colonel C— —, commanding the post, had them arrested, and ordered them back. One of his own officers represented to him that these people had an order for the boat from General Garfield, and, becoming alarmed, he let them go upon their way. Soon, however, the biped hounds were on their track, in hot pursuit. Two slaves, married into these families, had escaped and followed this boat-load. Although their villainous masters had fought in the rebel army, they were furnished with passes to pursue their fleeing slaves, under the protection of the United States arms. These pursuers, weary and exhausted, stopped at a slave-trader's above Paintsville, where a large bend in the river enabled them to gain several miles by a cross cut, took horses, and arrived at foot of Buffalo Shoals just as the boat-load of fifty-nine frightened souls were going over it. They at once leveled their rifles, and ordered the boat to lie-to, supposing their slaves were aboard. They did so, and occupied a small vacant hut on the bank of the river, awaiting a Government boat that would be down on the following morning. Early the next morning, (Sunday,) two lewd fellows of the baser sort, pursuing them in a skiff, landed at the place of rendezvous, and were about to rush into the cabin, when the leader of the negroes stopped them, saying:

"Porter and Radcliff, *you can't enter here*; we have none of your slaves."

But the boldest of these desperadoes, tiger-like, crouched on his hands and knees, and got in the rear of the cabin. Then, suddenly rushing upon the old man, said, "Damn you, I'll shoot you any way," and fired, the ball lodging in the abdomen. He continued to fire, indiscriminately, into the group of women and children, hitting one girl in the knee, and a younger child on the side of the head. Then these cowardly miscreants rushed away, but not until a ball from the rifle of one of these freedmen took effect in the thigh of Radcliff. These men seemed to love the negro so well that they were not willing to let even freedmen leave the State, if they have but the least taint of African blood in their veins; and now they stand as sentinels around the tottering bastile, lest some of the victims escape.

Another instance: In Hospital No. 2, in Gallatin, there is now at work a girl eighteen years of age, of pure Anglo-Saxon blood. This girl's reputed mother says, that when her own child was born, it was taken away from her, and this white child put in its place. She is satisfied it was the illegitimate child of her master's daughter, which she had *by her own father*.

In September, 1862, at Stevenson, Alabama, in collecting contrabands to work on the fortifications, we found a *white man*, sixty-three years old, who had all his life been compelled to herd with negroes. He had been forced to live with four different black women as his wives, by whom he had twenty-eight children. Colonel Straight, of the 51st Indiana Regiment, saw one of the old man's daughters, and said she was as white and had as beautiful blue eyes as any girl he ever saw in his own State. His was the same sad story—that he was an illegitimate son of his master's daughter, in Virginia; was taken to the slave-pen, where, with one hundred and twenty-seven others, he was raised for the market. We started him to Governor Morton, of Indiana, as a specimen of the men made chattels, and for which the South was fighting. He was captured on his way North. This is wickedness, "naked, but not ashamed."

We copy the following from the Montgomery (Alabama) *Advertiser*:

One Hundred Dollars Reward—Or Fifty Dollars if arrested in the State, will be paid for the arrest and confinement in jail, so that I may get him, of my boy Lewis, who left home on Sunday, the 14th inst. Lewis is about five feet, seven inches high, *light complexion, nearly white*, spare made, well dressed, wore mustache and goatee, quick to reply when spoken to, has "traveled," and *may attempt to pass for a white person*; he may endeavor to get to Richmond, where his mother and family reside.

WILLIAM FOSTER.

Tuskegee, Ala., *June 14, 1863.*

We suppose that this "nearly white" slave, who, it is suspected, will try to "pass for a white person," is William Foster's grandson, or perhaps his own offspring. Foster, no doubt, thinks that the negro is indebted to slavery for his moral and religious training. We advise the conservative journals to copy the above advertisement, and comment indignantly on the practice of amalgamation. The occasion will be a good one; and we assure them that the instances are as plenty as blackberries in Dixie.

At Athens, Alabama, in the summer of 1862, when that noble, earnest, and efficient officer, General Turchin, was court-martialed because he *hurt* the rebels of that State, General G— — was invited to make his head-quarters at Dr. Nicklin's, one of the largest slaveholders in that part of the State, a devoted member of the Methodist Episcopal Church, and really a highly cultivated and courteous gentleman. One day he charged the General with being *radical*. The General said, "No, I'm only a Republican; but I have a most radical commissary on my staff." The next day the radical commissary was invited to the house by Mrs. N— —, who said she "wanted to see a Yankee who would not deny being an Abolitionist." While at dinner the Doctor proposed to investigate the causes of our wide differences. Captain H— — remarked at the same time:

"Would it not be better, while enjoying your hospitalities, to talk upon subjects of agreement?"

"No," said the Doctor; "we arrive at truth only by comparing notes."

"Then," the Captain said, "I must be a freeman, and talk from my own platform."

"Certainly," was the answer.

"Then," said the Captain, "you are on trial. You must give a reason for the hope within you. We charge you with having commenced a wicked and causeless war. And now give us your reasons for it."

"Well, in the first place, the Abolitionists are fighting against the Bible, and against God. The Bible, an express revelation from Heaven, says, 'When these servants, or slaves, are to be procured of the heathen round about you, of them shall ye buy, and they shall be your possession forever.' That settles the question of *moral* right; and in relation to the political question, you were for excluding us from the territories, when they were manifestly ours equal with yours. We had the same right there with our property that you had. Equality of rights was the cardinal principle of our Government. In your political action you strike a blow at the very foundation of our Government—equality of rights."

To which Captain H—— replied: "Though not much of a theologian, I have, nevertheless, looked into the Levitical law, and found a paragraph like the following: 'He that stealeth a man, or selleth him, or if he be found in his hands, shall surely be put to death.' Let us analyze this 'stealeth a man'—the *foreign* slave-trader—'and selleth him'—the American slave-seller, or, 'if he be found in his hands'—the American slaveholder. If you will show me how any of these can escape punishment, then I will pursue the Biblical argument. In regard to the political question, the citizen of Ohio and the citizen of Alabama are treated just alike. A citizen of Ohio can take his household goods, merchandise, and cattle into the territories. A citizen from Alabama has the *same* right, but he can not take his slave; nor yet can a citizen of Ohio. Hence, they *have* equal rights."

At the close of the discussion the Doctor said, that "his neighbors were greatly alarmed when the Union army came into the district, for fear the slaves would leave them; but I said to my slaves, 'If you prefer to go away and leave me, do so: come and tell me; don't sneak away at night with your little bundle, but come right up and tell me, "We want to leave," and I will give you five dollars, and let you go, with this condition, that you never show your faces around my plantation.'"

Captain H—— looked as though it were doubtful, but said nothing. About a week afterward, the Doctor said to the General—

"I want you to take a ride with me over to the plantation. You Northern men don't know how well our slaves love us. Whenever I go to see them, they run out to meet me; inquire after my wife and children with as much interest as *your* children would inquire after you."

The General said he "would be glad to avail himself of the opportunity to see the workings of their system," and started off with the Doctor.

On the way down, the Doctor remarked that he "had another reason for wishing him to go down;" that "there were three cases of insubordination, and I want to show you *my mode* of controlling slaves. When I told your Abolition commissary, Captain H——, the other day, how I managed my boys, I saw he did not believe one word I said. Now I want you to see for yourself; then you can convince him."

Arriving at the plantation, sure enough, the slaves came out, and made special inquiries about his wife and family. The General said that the saddest sight of all was, that all these women and *children* gave promise to increase the number of slaves—girls eleven years old were among these.

The Doctor called up the culprits and addressed the principal offender. "Aleck," said he, "unless you submit to the mild punishment of our plantation discipline, all order and discipline will be lost. You know my rule. I have told you before, whenever you are not satisfied, just say so, and I will let you go. What do you say, Aleck, Bob, and Dick?"

Bowing very low, the darkeys said, "Well, den, massa, gib us de fibe dollars and we go."

He turned pale, and, being utterly dumfounded, after regaining himself, and *not giving* them the money, said, "Be off, then!" He had too much of the Southern chivalry to back out, and came away a wiser if not a better man, but said "nary word" about convincing the Abolition commissary.

CHAPTER XII

Triune, Tenn., *April 29, 1863.*

The last letter I wrote you was from the Missouri army. I am so continually *flying* around that I have won the cognomen of "the kite." It is astonishing what a charm there is in camp life; boys that have been away but a short time feel a craving to once more resume their duties among their comrades. With me 'tis a great pleasure to get back to the familiar faces of this splendid division.

Our new commander, General Schofield, is fast winning the devotion of his troops; his policy in Missouri meeting the cordial approbation of men and officers here. Leniency is played out; nothing but the most extreme rigor of military law will bring these traitors to a realization of the villainous stand they have taken. Nothing but the driving of every enemy from our lines, as we go, will bring the misguided citizen to his senses. The men and women, who have been allowed so many privileges, have all along been acting as spies. A few days since, a little boy, only eight years of age, was caught going over to his "uncle Palmer's;" he said his mother wanted him to go over and get a chicken, as the "sogers" ate all theirs up, and his mother was sick. The picket was about to let the child pass, on such an errand as that, and being such a small specimen of humanity. The lieutenant of the guard questioned the child closely, but could not glean any information of importance. As the child started off, down the road, he again called him, and, upon searching, found in the heel of his little stocking, *sewed in*, a full description of the entire camp and fortifications. The boy knew nothing of this, but was merely an instrument in the hands of the parents. As a matter of course the house was immediately searched, but the whole mystery is solved in the fact that several of the Secesh *dam-sells* were quite favorites in camp.

General Schofield is driving all known sympathizers beyond his lines, and permitting none but the undoubted Union men to remain.

A few nights since, as I was about retiring beneath the umbrageous shade of a lovely maple, a voice from above shouted, "Is 'Alf' here?"

"Yes, sir," was the response.

The voice emanated from the epigastrium of a huge fellow-wanderer in this wilderness, who was mounted upon a fiery steed.

"You are sent for by the commanding officers of the First Brigade, and I have orders to take you there, *peaceably*, if I can; *forcibly*, if I must."

As our camp was just getting wrapped in the arms of "Murphy," and not wishing to disturb them in their slumber, I consented to go. It was about a mile, over hill, through woods and thicket, to their camp. I preferred walking; but the gentle persuader on the horse induced me to "double up," and, after various efforts, I succeeded in mounting. I told the driver I was a poor rider, and convinced him of it before long. As the horse objected to my being placed so far back on his haunch, and I couldn't get forward, there naturally arose a dispute, which eventuated in the horse running off with both of us. After being duly deposited on the ground, the horse seemed delighted, and expressed his pleasure by kicking up his heels. After various vicissitudes, I was safely deposited at the head-quarters of the First Brigade, under the command of Colonel Connell.

Upon the announcement that "Alf" had "arriv," I heard the stentorian lungs of Colonel Durbin Ward ask: "Dead or alive?"

With fear and trembling I entered the tent, and found Colonel Connell, with nearly all his officers. I think Byron says something about there being

"A sound of revelry by night."

Well, so there was. Byron can prove it by me. O, shades of the "vine-clad hills of Bingen," but the "Isabella" was profuse! I remember being kept busy for two hours telling yarns and riddles, and the next day was accused of borrowing a horse and leading him home. My medical adviser, Dr. Wright, of the 35th Ohio, kept with me until the roads forked, and then he *deviated*.

Yesterday I paid a visit to the lamented Bob McCook's "Old Ninth" Regiment. The men are in splendid condition—the pride of the division. They are noted as the most ingenious battalion in the Army of the Cumberland. They have improvised a turning-shop, and manufacture chessmen, checkers, and every variety of specimens in that line. They have a flying-Dutchman, revolving swing, quoits, bag races, etc., while the lovers of horse-racing and cock-fighting can be duly amused every day in the week by members of the different regiments, each tenacious of the fair fame of his favorite battalion. Last night a fine game-cock, belonging to the 2d Minnesota, whipped one owned by the 35th Ohio, and, as a matter of course, the 2d Minnesota are in high glee, "crowing" over their chicken.

The 2d Minnesota, the 35th Ohio, and 9th Ohio Regiments are wedded. Each will vie with the other for the laurels in case of a fight. We have here, close at hand, the 17th, 31st, and 34th Ohio, besides those already mentioned. Our force is adequate for all the rebels dare send against us.

The voice of the boys is universally for the Union, against all traitors, whether those who openly meet them in the field, or the more dastardly coward that remains at home and backbites, and aids the enemy by words of comfort, and spreading dissensions in the rear.

The soldiers are unanimous upon the war question. They want no milk-and-water policy, and all they ask is, that the friends at home will back them in the field. Let all, whether Democrat, Republican, Abolitionist, or Pro-slavery, *unite* upon the *Union*. Let us have the Government sustained, regardless of all else. People at home have no right to dictate to our leaders what policy they should pursue. They are presumed to know what is best. If slavery falls, why sympathize with the owners? What claims have they upon your sympathies? A strange change has come over the people since former years. One party accused the other, and all who were opposed to slavery, as having "nigger on the brain." Now it is reversed. The rebel sympathizer, the ultra pro-slavery man, is the individual who is now troubled with this complaint.

Let us hope our whole people will be thoroughly united at the coming elections, and let their motto be: "We are unalterably opposed to the secession of one inch of the territory of the American Union." Then I, for one, and I know it is the universal feeling of this entire division, will not care if the man who comes in on that platform be Democrat, Whig, or Republican; he should have the support of all true lovers of his country.

Women in Breeches

Whether the women in modern times have taken the cue from the poet's words,

"Once more unto the *breech*, dear friends,"

and merely added the plural, making it "breeches," I know not; but the present war for the Union has elicited much enthusiasm among the gentler sex, causing them, in many instances, to lay aside their accustomed garb, and assume the exterior of the sterner portion of creation; in proof of which the following story of the war is given:

A young woman arrived in Chicago from Louisville, Ky., whose history is thus related in the *Post* of that city:

"She gave her name as Annie Lillybridge, of Detroit, and stated that her parents reside in Hamilton, Canada. Last spring she was employed in a dry-goods store in Detroit, where she became acquainted with a Lieutenant

W——, of one of the Michigan regiments, and an intimacy immediately sprang up between them. They corresponded for some time, and became much attached to each other. Some time during last summer, Lieutenant W—— was appointed to a position in the 21st Michigan Infantry, then rendezvousing in Ionia County. The thought of parting from the gay lieutenant nearly drove her mad, and she resolved to share his dangers and be near him. No sooner had she resolved upon this course than she proceeded to the act. Purchasing male attire, she visited Ionia, enlisted in Captain Kavanagh's company, 21st Regiment. While in camp she managed to keep her secret from all; not even the object of her attachment, who met her every day, was aware of her presence so near him.

"Annie left with her regiment for Kentucky, passed through all the dangers and temptations of a camp life, endured long marches, and sleeping on the cold ground, without a murmur. At last, the night before the battle of Pea Ridge, (or Prairie Grove,) in which her regiment took part, her sex was discovered by a member of her company; but she enjoined secrecy upon him, after relating her previous history. On the following day she was under fire, and, from a letter she has in her possession, it appears she behaved with marked gallantry, and, with her own hand, shot a rebel captain, who was in the act of firing upon Lieutenant W——. But the fear of revealing her sex continually haunted her. After the battle, she was sent out, with others, to collect the wounded, and one of the first corpses found by her was the soldier who had discovered her sex.

"Days and weeks passed on, and she became a universal favorite with the regiment, so much so that her Colonel (Stephens) frequently detailed her as regimental clerk, a position that brought her in close contact with her lover, who, at this time, was either major or adjutant of the regiment. A few weeks subsequently she was out on picket duty, when she received a shot in the arm that disabled her, and, notwithstanding the efforts of the surgeon, her wound continually grew worse. She was sent to the hospital at Louisville, where she has been ever since, until a few weeks ago, when she was discharged by the post surgeon, as her arm was stiffened and rendered useless for life. She implored to be permitted to return to her regiment; but the surgeon was unyielding, and discharged her. Annie immediately hurried toward home, and, by the aid of benevolent strangers, reached this city. At Cincinnati she told her secret to a benevolent lady, and was supplied with female attire. She declares that she will enlist in her old regiment again, if there is a recruiting officer for the 21st in Michigan. She still clings to the lieutenant, and says she must be near him if he falls or is taken down sick; that where he goes she will go; and when he dies, she will end her life by her own hand."

Another Incident of the War

A few weeks since, a captain, accompanied by a young soldier, apparently about seventeen years of age, arrived in this city, in charge of some rebel prisoners. During their stay in the city, the young soldier alluded to had occasion to visit head-quarters, and at once attracted the attention of Colonel Mundy, as being exceedingly sprightly, and possessed of more than ordinary intelligence. Being in need of such a young man at Barracks No. 1, the Colonel detailed him for service in that institution. He soon won the esteem of his superior officers, and became a general favorite with all connected with the barracks. A few days ago, however, the startling secret was disclosed that the supposed young man was a young lady, and the fact was established beyond doubt, by a soldier who was raised in the same town, with her, and knew her parents. She "acknowledged the corn," and begged to be retained in the position to which she had been assigned; having been in the service ten months, she desired to serve during the war. Her wish was accordingly granted, and she is still at her post.

We learned the facts above stated, and took occasion to visit the barracks, and was introduced to "Frank Martin," (her assumed name,) and gleaned the following incidents connected with her extraordinary career during the past ten months:

Frank was born near Bristol, Penn., and her parents reside in Alleghany City, where she was raised. They are highly respectable people, and in very good circumstances. She was sent to the convent in Wheeling, Va., at twelve years of age, where she remained until the breaking out of the war, having acquired a superior education, and all the accomplishments of modern days. She visited home after leaving the convent; and, after taking leave of her parents, proceeded to this city, in July last, with the design of enlisting in the 2d East Tennessee Cavalry, which she accomplished, and accompanied the Army of the Cumberland to Nashville. She was in the thickest of the fight at Murfreesboro, and was severely wounded in the shoulder, but fought gallantly, and waded Stone River into Murfreesboro, on the memorable Sunday on which our forces were driven back. She had her wound dressed, and here her sex was disclosed, and General Rosecrans made acquainted with the fact. She was accordingly mustered out of service, notwithstanding her earnest entreaty to be allowed to serve the cause she loved so well. The General was very favorably impressed with her daring bravery, and superintended the arrangements for her safe transmission to her parents. She left the Army of the Cumberland, resolved to enlist again in the first regiment she met.

Negro Sermon delivered at Triune, Tenn

CAMP NEAR TRIUNE, TENN., *May 16, 1863.*

Last Sunday week there was a grand revival meeting of the numerous contrabands, at the Brick Church, near the village. The house was crowded by the most fashionable black belles in the county, many of them dressed *"a la mode."* An old man arose, and stated that he had formerly been a *circus* preacher, and "done been ober de country from station to station, preachin' de gospel," and he now felt like "talkin' to de brudders and sistern." He commenced his discourse:

"MY BELUBED BREDERN—I haben't got no Bible. De rebels, when dey squatulated from dis place, done toted dem all off wid 'em. Derefore, I am destrained to make a tex' myself, and ax you,

"'WHAR DO YOU LIB?'

"Is your dwellin' in de tents of wickedness? Now, my belubed bredern, de world am a whirlin' and a whirlin', jest as it allers hes bin. Dish here world nebber stan' still for de Yanks or for de rebs, but keeps on its course jest de same, and why shouldn't you do so likewise?

"If de Lord is a smilin' on us dark sheep ob de flock, and Fader Abraham has got his bosom ready for to *deceib* us, why should we not be *preparred* for de glory ob dat day?

"My tex' *requires* ob you, *'Whar do you lib?'*

"Is you strollin' round, wid no hope of de future freedom starrin' you in de face? Massa Linkum has done tole you, dat if you work for de salvation ob de Union, dat you shall be saved, no matter what de Legislatur' ob Kaintuck may say to de reverse contrary dereof—*dat is*, if de *Union* be saved *likewise*; and Massa Linkum is de man what will stand up to de rack; so, derefore, I ax you, *'Whar do you lib?'*

"De good book done tole you dat you can't serb two masters; but dat is a passenger ob Scriptur' I nebber could understan' wid all my larnin', for de most ob us has been serbin' a heap o' masters durin' dis comboberation ob de white folks, wherein we colored gemmen is interested; derefore I ask, agin and agin, de momentus question ob *'Whar do you lib?'*

"Now, my brudders, I is perfec'ly awar dat many ob you don't lib much, but dat you jest 'sassiate round;' you isn't de right stripe; *you don't lib nowhar.*

"Wharfor is dis state ob society, after all de white folks am a doin for you?

"Look aroun' an' aroun' you, an' see de glorious names oh our colored bredern what is fitin' an a fitin' for you in de army. Dars Horace Greeley and Fred Douglass; dars Jack Mims and Wendal Phlips; dars Lennox Ramond and Lloyd Garrison. De last-mentioned colored pusson is a tic'lar friend ob mine, and is named after a place whar dey now is trainin' a lot ob our race. De Garrison was named after de garrison.

"Den dars Mrs. Beechum Sto; look at dat lady; isn't she going from de camp to de camp just like de Martingale—what de English people had in de las' war in Florence; and don't dey call her de Florence Martingale ob dis hemisphere?

"Be ye also ready to answer de question as to 'Whar do you lib?'

"So dat de glorification ob Uncle Abraham Linkum shall resound ober de earth, and we darkeys no longer hab to hoe de corn, but lib foreber on de fat ob de lan'. Brudder Jerry will please pass aroun' de hat."

CHAPTER XIII

Letter from Cheat Mountain

CAMP OF 6TH OHIO, AT ELKWATER, VA., 1861.

The trees begin to look barren, the bronzed hue of the surrounding hills admonishing us that October, chill and drear, is upon us. Every thing in nature is cheerless, and, adding to nature, man has, with despoiling hands, laid waste the country for miles about our present location. Pen can not describe the devastation of an army: orchards are swept away; of fences scarce a trace is left; houses are converted into stables, fodder-cribs, and store-houses; corn-fields are used as pastures; forests must fall to supply our men with fire-wood; in fact, with the soldier nothing is sacred. And why should any thing be sacred in this "section," where traitors have been fostered, and where every vote cast was for secession? Let them reap the harvest they themselves have sown.

The farmers come daily into camp, whining because our men cut down their sugar-trees, or "find" a few cabbages or apples; but, as the Colonel is aware that the boys must be kept in fire-wood, he is heedless of their whimperings.

The cold is telling fearfully upon the men at night, and I fear, if a supply of clothing is not soon forthcoming, much suffering will be the consequence. It is a burning disgrace to somebody, that such things should be, and it is galling to our regiment to see Indiana troops, just mustered into service, passing our encampment with large, heavy overcoats, and every thing about them denoting comfort and an attention to their wants. The cold frosts are beginning to leave their imprints; already snow is capping the mountain-tops, and God help us if we get winter-bound in this "neck of woods." Some few are glorying in the thought of the fine deer and bear hunts they will have. The latter I can't *bear* to think about, and the former a man must be *der*anged to think of catching upon, these mountains.

The paymaster has been disbursing his funds for the past three days, and the boys are all in excellent spirits. Theodore Marsh and Leonard Swartz will go home heavily laden with the hard earnings of this regiment.

How many hearts will be gladdened by the receipt of the little pittances sent, and how loth many will be to use the money when they remember the toil endured to obtain it! But let the friends rest assured that the *money* was not thought of. A purer, a more noble thought and higher aim animated the breasts, of those who have so nobly suffered—a determination to see their country's honor maintained.

Our pickets have scoured the country around, far and near, but no signs of the enemy can be found. There is no doubt but that they have retired for the winter. There will, however, be plenty left to guard the interests of the Federal army until spring, when, no doubt, the campaign will be opened with vigor, if not sooner settled.

In the reconnoissance by our regiment, a week since, traces of Captain Bense and his party were found in the Secession camp; several of Hall & Cobb's (our sutlers) checks being found in their camp, and a prisoner, afterward brought in, said they had been forwarded to Richmond, Va.

A rumor that this regiment is to be immediately ordered to Cincinnati set the boys fairly dancing; but Madame Rumor is so frequent a visitor that the more sensible scarcely noticed her arrival. The most authentic rumor is, that Colonel Bosley is to be made a brigadier-general. "We shall see what we shall see."

The sky is threatening, and dark as midnight, the air intensely cold, and we are hourly expecting a regular old snow-storm. Chestnuts, fine and ripe, are abundant; there are hundreds of bushels all over these hills, while wild grapes are as abundant as hops in Kent.

Yesterday, a wild-cat was shot and brought into camp by one of the 3d Ohio boys. He was about three feet in length, and a "varmint" I shouldn't like to meet on a dark night.

Yours, Alf.

The Women of the South

A great deal has been written about them, and there is no doubt but they are a thousandfold more bitter than the men. They were, and many are yet, perfectly venomous; and the more ignorant, the more spiteful they seem. The following act was blazoned forth as wonderfully heroic in its character, just after our forces occupied Philippa, Beelington, and Beverly:

"The two noble heroines, Misses Abbie Kerr and Mary McLeod, of Fairmont, Marion County, who rode from their home to Philippa, a distance of thirty-odd miles, to apprise our forces there of the approach of the enemy, arrived in Staunton by the western train, on Wednesday night last, and remained till Friday morning, when they went to Richmond. While here they were the 'observed of all observers,' and were received with a cordial welcome. Great anxiety was manifested by all to hear a detailed account of their interesting adventures from their own lips.

"They left Fairmont at six o'clock on Sunday morning, and hastened, without escorts, to Philippa. They had not gone a great distance before they found that a shoe of one of the horses needed fixing. They stopped at a blacksmith's shop for that purpose, and while there a Union man came up and questioned them very closely as to who they were, and on what mission they were going. Miss McLeod replied to his interrogatories, telling him that their surname was Fleming, and that they were going to Barbour County, to see their relations. Their interrogator seemed to be very hard to satisfy, and it taxed the ingenuity of Miss McLeod to improvise a story which would succeed in imposing upon him. As soon as the horse-shoe had been fixed, they again proceeded upon their way, but had not gone far before their evil genius, their interrogator at the blacksmith's shop, dashed by them on horseback. They perceived that his suspicions had not been allayed, and that he was going on in advance of them to herald the approach of spies. They allowed him to pass out of sight, in advance, and then destroyed the letters they had in their possession, that the search of their persons, to which they then anticipated they would be required to submit, might not betray them. When they arrived at the village of Webster, they found it in commotion, and many persons were anxiously awaiting their arrival, in the eager hope of capturing the spies.

"They were there subjected to a rigorous cross-examination. The heroines were calm and self-possessed—answering questions without hesitancy, and expressing a perfect willingness to have their persons searched by any lady who might be selected for that purpose. They were allowed to pass on, after being detained for some time, though there were some in the crowd who were very much opposed to it. As soon as they got out of sight of that village they rode very rapidly, for fear they might still be arrested by some of those who were so much opposed to allowing them to proceed. They arrived at Philippa about two o'clock in the afternoon of the same day, and told Colonel Porterfield that the enemy would attack his camp that night or the next morning.

"These ladies then went to the house of a Mr. Huff, about a mile and a half from Philippa, where they stayed all night. The next morning they heard the report of the firing at Philippa, and, in disguise, accompanied by a countrywoman, returned to Philippa, on foot, to see what had been the result. They moved about among the enemy without being detected or molested in the least degree. Going into one of the houses, they found

James Withers, of the Rockbridge Cavalry, who had concealed himself there to prevent the enemy from capturing him. These ladies immediately told him that they would effect his rescue, if he would trust to them. He very readily consented; whereupon these ladies disguised him as a common countryman, by furnishing him with some old clothes; they then gave him a basket of soap, with a recipe for making it, that he might pass as a peddler of that necessary article. With these old clothes, and a basket of soap on his arm, and gallantly mounted upon a mule, accompanied by his guardian angels, he passed safely through the crowds of the enemy, and was brought by them, safe and sound, into the camp of his friends at Beverly, after a circuitous and hard ride over precipitous mountains, where persons had seldom, if ever, ridden before. His fellow-soldiers and friends rejoiced greatly when he arrived, for they thought that he was either killed or taken prisoner by the enemy; they rejoiced that the supposed 'dead was alive,' and the 'lost was found.' He is now known in our camp as the 'peddler of soap.' The heroic conduct of these ladies will live in history, and they will become the heroines of many a thrilling story of fiction, in years to come."

We have no doubt but that their names will live in history. Benedict Arnold is still in the memory of every American, loathed and despised, as Davis and his crew will eventually be, without doubt.

Gilbert's Brigade

In May last, the 124th Ohio was near Franklin, Tenn., a part of General Granger's division, and belonging to Gilbert's brigade. Friend "Esperance," in writing about the regiment, says: "We are encamped near Franklin, in a beautiful situation as regards the view of the country; and in a military point of view it is excellent, being surrounded with sufficient elevations of land to enable our fortifications to sweep the whole country in every direction. The brigade is composed of the 113th, 124th, 125th, and the 121st Ohio Volunteers, and the 78th Illinois. The 124th Ohio was organized in Cleveland, but contains two companies from Cincinnati—company G, under the command of William A. Powell, of your city, and company I, under the command of Captain J. H. Frost, also of Cincinnati. Captain Powell has been in the service ever since the commencement of the war; he has served in Virginia and Maryland, also in Missouri, in General Fremont's Body-guard. He was again in Maryland last summer, at Cumberland, in command of a company in the 84th Ohio Volunteer Infantry, and is, in all respects, strictly a military man, very generally liked by his company, and respected by his superior officers. Captain Frost has also been in the service before, and is much liked by his men, and esteemed by all who know him here. The health of the regiment is good, and of the two companies from Cincinnati especially so.

"With regard to the army of General Rosecrans, it is by us considered invincible. General Rosecrans is looked upon as a host in himself. Every soldier appears anxious to meet the enemy; the idea of a defeat never seems to enter into their imagination, but all are enthusiastic in their expectation of being able to restore the South and South-west of our common country to subjection to the Constitution, and obedience to the laws."

A chaplain of an Indiana regiment recently married one of the Hoosier boys to a Tennessee girl, and concluded the ceremony by remarking, the *oath* was binding for three years, or *during the war!*

CHAPTER XIV

Confessions of a Fat Man—home-guard

THE FAT VOLUNTEER.

The moment the flag was threatened, large bodies of men were called upon to rally to its defense. Being large and able-bodied, I enrolled with the home-guard. The drill was very severe in hot weather, and I wanted an attendant, a fan, and pitcher of ice-water.

I am constantly reminded that one of the first requirements of a soldier is to throw out his chest and draw in his stomach. Having been burned out several times, while occupying an attic, I have had considerable practice in throwing out my chest; but by what system of practice could I ever hope to draw in my stomach? I can't "dress up;" it's no use of my trying. If my vest buttons are in a line, I am far in the rear. If I toe the mark, a fearful bulge indicates my position. Once we had a new drill-sergeant, who was near-sighted. Running his eye along the line, he exclaimed sharply:

"What is that man doing in the ranks with a base drum?"

He pointed at me; but I hadn't any drum; it was the surplus stomach, that I couldn't, for the life of me, draw in. I am the butt of numberless jokes, as you may well suppose. They have got a story in the Guards, that, when I first heard the command "order arms," I dropped my musket, and, taking out my notebook, began drawing an *order* on the Governor for what arms I needed. They say I ordered a Winans steam-gun, with a pair of Dahlgren howitzers for side arms! Base fabrication! My ambition never extended beyond a rifled cannon, and they know it!

Although, in respect to size, I belong to the "heavies," my preference is for the light infantry service. My knapsack is marked "Light Infantry!" One evening the spectators seemed convulsed about something, and my comrades tittered by platoons, whenever my back was turned. It was a mystery to me till I laid off my knapsack. Some wretch had erased the two final letters, and I had been parading, all the evening, labeled, "Light Infant!"

The above is one of the thousand annoyances to which I am subjected, and nothing but my consuming patriotism could ever induce me to submit to it. I overheard a spectator inquire of the drill-sergeant one day:

"Do you drill that fat man all at once?"

"No," he returned, in an awful whisper; "*I drill him by squads!*"

I could have *drilled* him, if I had had a bayonet.

Specifications have been published in regard to my uniform, and contractors advertised for; the making will be let out to the lowest bidder. In case the Guards are ordered to take the field, a special commissary will be detailed to draw my rations.

That reminds me of a harrowing incident. On last night's drill an old farmer, who dropped in to see us drill, took me aside, and said he wanted to sell me a yoke of powerful oxen.

"My ancient agriculturist," said I, smiling at his simplicity, "I have no use for oxen."

"Perhaps not at present," quoth he, "but if you go to war you will want them."

"For what?" said I, considerably annoyed.

"Want 'em to *draw your rations!*"

The Guards paid me a delicate compliment at their last meeting: elected me *Child* of the Regiment, with the rank of a First *Corpulent*. I was about to return thanks in a neat speech, when they told me it was no use; that a reporter, who was present, had got the whole thing in type—speech and all—and I could read it in the evening paper. I got his views, and held my own.

Yours for the Union, including the Stars, also the Stripes.

FAT CONTRIBUTOR.

"What are you going to do, you bad woman's boy?" said Mrs. Wiggles, as her youngest son passed through the kitchen into the garden.

"Down with the Seceshers!" he shouted; and she looked out just in time to see the top of a rose-bush fall before the artillery-sword of her son, that the youngster held in his hand.

"You had better go to Molasses Jugtion, if you want to do that," she said, restraining his hand as 't was lifted against a favorite fuschia, that she had trained with so much care.

"Dear me!" she murmured, half to herself; "what a terrible thing war is, when children show signs of such terrible consanguinity!"

The Negro on the Fence

"Hearken to what I now relate,
And on its moral meditate."

A Wagoner, with grist for mill,
Was stalled at bottom of a hill.
A brawny negro passed that way,
So stout he might a lion slay.
"I'll put my shoulder to the wheels,
If you'll bestir your horse's heels."
So said the African, and made
As if to render timely aid.
"No," cried the wagoner, "stand back!
I'll take no help from one that's black;"
And, to the negro's great surprise,
Flourished his whip before his eyes.
Our "darkey" quick "skedaddled" thence,
And sat upon the wayside fence.
Then went the wagoner to work,
And lashed his horses to a jerk;
But all his efforts were in vain;
With shout, and oath, and whip, and rein,
The wheels budged not a single inch,
And tighter grow the wagoner's pinch.

Directly there came by a child,
With toiling step, and vision wild,
"Father," said she, with hunger dread,
"We famish for the want of bread."
Then spake the negro: "If you will,
I'll help your horses to the mill."
The wagoner, in grievous plight,
Now swore and raved with all his might,
Because the negro wasn't white;
And plainly ordered him to go
To a certain place, that's down below;
Then, rushing, came the wagoner's wife,
To save her own and infant's life;
By robbers was their homestead sacked,
And smoke and blood their pillage tracked.

Here stops our tale. When last observed,
The wagoner was still "conserved"
In mud, at bottom of the hill,
But bent on getting to the mill;
And hard by, not a rod from thence,
The negro sat upon the fence.

A Camp Letter of Early Times

Our camp is alive; our camp is exuberant; our camp is in a *furore*. "Who's that man with 'Secesh' clothes?" says one; and "Who's that big-faced, genial, good-natured looking feller?" says another. "Are they prisoners?" "Maybe it's the paymaster; and that short, chunky man is here to watch the other feller, and see that the money is paid all on the square." "No, it aint one nor t' other—'tis Cons Millar, the ever-vigilant and hard-working Cons, of the *Commercial*; and the good-natured looking feller is Invisible Green, or, as he is familiarly called, Bill Crippen, of the *Times*." They have brought sunshine into camp, for a merrier set of soldiers the sun never shone on than are the Guthrie Grays to-night. Cons has just had supper, and Bill is "spreading devastation" over the table of Captain Andrews. They have both been up inspecting intrenchments, which are *in statu quo*, the brave Lee having retreated some sixteen miles, or, more politely speaking, "fallen back." So I suppose we will soon have to creep up on the gallant gentleman once more, and see if he can not be induced to fall still further back.

The news of the gallant conduct of our Cincinnati boys at the late fight under Rosecrans sent a thrill of pleasure to the hearts of all our men, and a feeling of envy that we were not with them to share the glory of that day. Colonel Lytle, Stephen McGroarty, and the other brave fellows' names, are on the lips of all, and a fervent "God bless them" is frequently uttered. Our encampment now may be said to extend over four miles, a brigade of twelve thousand; and I can assure you they make a formidable appearance. Three splendid batteries, three or four fine cavalry companies, and any quantity of men, are yet on the way.

One of the best Secesh tricks I have heard of was attempted, a short time since, by a rebel telegrapher. When Lee was about to advance upon this point, wishing to ascertain the number of troops here, he sent out this operator, with pocket implements, to attach to our wires. So, carefully picking his way through the woods, Mr. Operator came upon a secluded part of the road; climbing the pole, he attached his battery, and "click, click, click," he inquires of our operator at head-quarters, "How many troops have you altogether, that can, at any pressing event, be sent to aid us if we attack Lee?" Just as he concluded the query, one of the ever-vigilant pickets of the Indiana regiments, who infest the woods and roads in every direction, espied the gentleman, and brought him into camp with his non-confiscated horse. A minute more and the fellow, doubtless, would have been fully informed, as he had guarded against cipher-telegraphing by telegraphing that the cipher-operator was out, and the general wanted an immediate answer.

Our boys continue to scour the woods, and constantly are finding Secesh documents. The following *beautiful poem* is from the pen of Miss M. H. Cantrell, of Jonesboro, Tennessee, and was found in the pocket of a "Secesher," who had invaliantly fled, dropping his overcoat and love-epistles. It is entitled:

Sweetharts Against War

O Dear! its shameful I declare
To make the men all go
And leive so manny sweetharts here
Wit out a single bough.

We like to see them leave 'tis true,
And wold not urge them stay;
But what are we poor girls to do
When you are all away?

We told you we cold spare you here
Before you had to go,

But Bless your Harts, wernt aware
That we would miss you sow.

We miss you all in manny ways,
But troth will ware out;
The gratest things we miss you for
Joy going withe out.

On Sunday when we go to church,
We look in vane for sum
To mete us smilin on the porch,
And ask to see us home.

And then we dont enjoy a walk
Since all the bows have gone;
For what the good to us plain talk
If we must trip alone?

But what the use talkin thus
We will try to beecontent
And if you cannot come to us
A message may bee cent.

And that one comfort any way
Although we are Apart,
There is no reason why we may
Not open hart to hart.

We trust it may not ever come
To any War like test,
We want to see our Southern home
Secured in peaceful rest.

But if the blood of those we love
In freedoms cause must floo,
With fervent trust in Lov Above
We bid them onward go.

Written By your friend,
M. H. Cantrell.

I inclose you the original document. I suppose the aforesaid lovyer did "onward go," and, no doubt, is still going, if he has not already reached the town of Jonesboro, and met his gal upon "the porch" as she returned from church.

Snake-hunting has given way to trout-fishing. As a matter of course, the noise of camp has driven all trout four miles from our present abode; but scarcely a day passes but our men return with a nice string of these delicious denizens of the brooks hereabouts.

I have often, heretofore, thought I would like much to be a cavalry soldier, but I'll swear I wouldn't like to be a cavalry horse; for, of all the hay-forsaken, fleshless-looking animals eyes ever gazed upon, the horses out here take the premium. Well, 'pon my word, I took Captain Bracken's horse (the roan I once rode) a quart of oats, sent from Beverly; well, the horse wouldn't eat them; he didn't know what they were! and I had to break or smash some of them so that he might smell the "aroma," to facilitate his knowledge, and he was too weak to inhale air enough to inflate his nostrils, so that he could smell the dainty meal I had in my kindness brought him. Captain Bracken promised to have them parched and made into a tea for the animal.

September 30.—What a jump of time! Well, I'll tell you the cause. The morning I intended to post this letter the entire regiment was ordered to make an advance upon Mingo Flats, a Secession hole fifteen miles from this place. They were accompanied by Howe's battery and an Indiana regiment. The boys were not more than fairly started when a terrific rain-storm set in. O! what a pitiless, deluging rain! The very thought of that *sprinkle* of twenty hours of unceasing torrent makes me, even now, feel as if I should forever have an antipathy against drinking water. Onward the boys trudged, seemingly not caring a cuss if school kept or not. The Elkwater soon assumed a rather formidable appearance; night came on, and with it an increase of the flood. We stood up against trees to rest; some crawled in fence-corners; a few, more lucky, found an old log stable and a smoke-house; these were quickly filled from "pit to dome," as Fred Hunt would say, for some slept on rafters, cross-beams, etc. Still it poured down; still the fountains of heaven gushed *forth*, fifth, tenth, or twentieth; anyhow, it continued to rain, and at daybreak it rained yet, and the regiment moved on to Mingo Flats; drove in the rebel pickets; heard the Secesh varmints beat the long roll; knew they were scared; *and still it rained!* Colonel Sullivan, of the Indiana regiment, was in, command: sent out a big gun; boys went on a big hill; found the enemy were eight or ten thousand strong; big gun ordered back, and as we only had two thousand men, remembered the axiom about "discretion being the better part of valor;" obeyed the aforesaid axiom. *Still, recollect, it kept raining in torrents*; dripping down Quarter-master Shoemaker's pants into his boots; running over Colonel Anderson's back. Major Christopher looked dry, in order to get a drink: but that was a failure. Captain Westcott looked sad; in fact he said it was the wettest time he ever knew or heard tell of—wondered if old Noah ever explored these big hills.

Captain Russell picked out a fine hill to locate upon, if this really intended to be another deluge. Captain Clark observed he was fond of *heavy wet*. Jules Montagnier said it was *due* time to *dry up*. *Still it rained*. The regiments were ordered to fall back. Well, the mud was so infernal slippery it was very easily done; some fell forward in the vain endeavor to fall back. After killing seven or eight poor, pauper-looking, "Secesh varmints," the boys set fire to Marshall's store, the enterprising proprietor being away from his business—a very notorious Secessionist, having donated $25,000 to the C. S. A. The building made a *beautiful* fire, and our boys brought away a fine lot of saws, augers, and various other articles of *dry goods*. The loss of the augers, Colonel Anderson says, will be a great *bore* to Marshall. *Please don't forget how infernal hard it was raining all this time.*

Well, they reached the first ford on their return trip; a sad misnomer now, for it was an unfordable ford. The water of old Elkwater was rearing and plunging, and furiously wild. Every mountain (and there are myriads) was sending out its wet *aid* to swell the raging torrent; the regiment, at this time, only three miles from the Secessionists. A bold front had to be put on, as it was a sure thing, if the rebels found out the weakness of our force, we were goners. There was no doubt, however, but that they were terribly frightened, as they had heard we were twenty thousand strong. Anxiously the boys waited the falling of the mighty waters. *It had now rained twenty-six hours.* Large trees came whistling by with lightning speed; the river seemed wild with delight, and the waves clapped their hands, leaping higher and higher; but, *as you know,* (no reflection meant,) Mr. Editor, a drunken man will get sober if not supplied with more liquor, so the river will *subside* if not furnished with the "aqueous fluid."

Colonel Anderson was the first to cross the stream. His horse plunged in boldly, but was within an ace of being carried away by the still almost resistless current. There goes "Shoemaker," the easy, good-natured "Ned," as he is called. Yes, sure enough, there he does go, for his horse has plunged, and the torrent is too wild, for they are both beyond their depth, and the horse is going down, down. Every eye is bent upon "Shoe." He is carried further and further. He grasps a tree and pulls himself up, looking the picture of despair. The major says, "H-o-l-d, b-o-y-s! d-o-n't b-e i-n t-o-o m-u-c-h h-u-r-r-y;" but they, eager to get back, walked a foot-bridge of rough timber and old logs, very narrow. Several crossed upon this, Captain Russell making a very narrow escape with his life. Colonel Anderson, perceiving the danger, ordered that no more should cross, threatening to shoot the first man who should disobey the order. This, as a matter of course, was done to deter the men from hazarding their lives needlessly. Colonel Anderson had but just given the order, when Frank Guhra, a private in Captain Clark's company, made the attempt, reached the middle of the stream, lost his balance, fell, and in a moment was whirled out of sight, the current running at the rate of twenty miles an hour. Several lost their guns. It was three or four hours before they succeeded in crossing.

Upon their return to camp an unwelcome sight was presented; the water had swept nearly every thing away. The tents had been, many of them, three and four feet in water; some had to take to trees to save life. The water had subsided, leaving a nasty slime, a foot thick, all over the camp-ground. Camp-kettles, knapsacks haversacks, and numerous floatable, light articles, had passed down stream—Captain Wilmington losing every thing. I saw the Captain trying to borrow a pair of pantaloons, he running around in his drawers. An old resident of this locality (Mr. Stonnicker) says this is the biggest flood ever known in this region. By the by, Mr. Stonnicker has a beautiful daughter, Miss Delilah, who seems to be fairly "the child of the regiment," especially of the officers. I will not mention names, as the wives at home would be jealous.

I see you talk of sending out a gentleman to take money home to the families of the volunteers. But cuss the paymaster, "or any other man." Why don't the paymaster come? Send *me* some papers. I can't get any without a peck of trouble.

CHAPTER XV

The Winter campaign in Virginia

Your correspondent has been sick. Your correspondent has been in bed; has had the rheumatism in his back, neck, arms, legs, toes; is down with the mountain-fever; tries in vain to sleep; howling dog, belonging to Captain Russell's "brigade," keeps up such an infernal howling it makes me mad: wish Russell had to eat him, hair and all. It was raining when I last wrote; think we had just been flooded out. Well, the very next day we were again ordered over that Godforsaken road, when the clouds again blackened up, and five hundred men tramped it. What have the Sixth done that the heavens should open their floodgates? All I wonder is, how the boys stand it. But they do bear up under it nobly, remembering the Shakspearian passage, slightly altered:

> "The same clouds that lower upon the house of Abe Lincoln
> Look frowningly upon Jeff Davis."

The boys are truly "ragged and sassy;" very many are shoeless, and with a flag of truce protruding from the rear. The service in these woods wears out more clothing than ordinary service should. Some of the boys are careless, but many are, helplessly, nearly naked. Our officers have used every exertion to get apparel, but the apparel is, like a paymaster, "hard to get hold of." Our men have been sorely tantalized by seeing regiment after regiment of the Indiana troops paid off, before their very eyes. In fact, they have been running round camp, with five, ten, and twenty-dollar gold pieces, shaking them in our faces. Add Colwell—Corporal Add—paid an Indiana boy of the 17th Regiment three slices of bacon and half a pound of coffee just for the privilege of hefting and rubbing his eye with an *eagle*. Colwell is a good printer; Colwell is a good writer; and, last and best of all, he can eat more gingerbread than any other one man in the army: he wants Wash Armstrong to send him a box of the article.

Since the accidental shooting of Lieutenant Moses Bidwell, by Adams, of the 17th Indiana, we have had another accident. Mr. Hopkins has had his collar-bone broken, and his shoulder-blade thrown completely out of place, by the falling of a tree.

We are having jovial times out here, rain or shine. A convocation of good fellows met at Captain Abbott's quarters, 3d Ohio. Captain Abbott is from Zanesville. Captain McDougal of Newark, Captain Dana of Athens, Captain Rossman of Hamilton, Lieutenants House and Swasey of Columbus, Lieutenants Bell and Dale of Newark, not forgetting Miles—the smiling, good-natured Miles—of the 17th Indiana, Quarter-master Shoemaker, Andy Hall, J. W. Slanker, W. B. Sheridan, and Self, all of the 6th Ohio, made up the party. The landlord filled his flowing bowl, and stories, songs, and recitations were the order of the evening, and the

"Glow-worm '*began*' to show the matin to be near"

ere we started to separate.

Miles invited those who would, to go over to his palace, and promised us a sardine supper; accordingly, but few refused the invitation. Now, Miles had a *jug of oil*, just from the Thurston House, Paris, *Bourbon* County, Ky. This oil was put to good use; and soon a *box* of herring was opened, and the oil again distributed, and then some speeches were made.

The meeting was called to order by the fat Quarter-master, Shoemaker.

A motion was made that we adjourn and go to Cincinnati. This was voted down. Motions were continually made to take a drink. These were carried, every *pop*, by *Sherry*, your correspondent being the only one having the moral courage to vote in the negative.

Now, Miles is from Columbus; a jolly, good fellow, and, when the time for retiring arrived, proffered me his bed, provided I would notice him in my next letter. This I promised, and accepted his hospitality. The party dispersed, and Miles was soon in the arms of Morpheus; he had fallen asleep making an eloquent appeal to the *chair*. I had just got into a nice doze, when I was aroused by the sound of a voice.

"Gen'l'men, you're all my frens, every one of you. But, gen'l'men, I invite you, freely, to my sardines. You, 'specially, Ned Shoemaker; 'specially you, Andy Hall, and all of you.

"The country is a momentous question," — —

Here I ventured to inquire of him as to whom he was addressing his conversation?

"Why, my frens," replied he. "Isn't that Ned Shoemaker?" pointing to a barrel, upon the top of which was my hat; "and are not those my companions," pointing to a pile of cheese-boxes, herring-kegs, etc., that were strewn around.

He was much astonished when I assured him his friends had *departed* an hour since, at least.

Didn't Know of the Rebellion

Going out with a party of scouts, one day, in Virginia, we espied, away up a little ravine, a log-house, completely isolated. Anticipating a good, substantial meal, we rode up to the domicile, where an old woman, with a face with all the intelligence of a pig beaming from it, came to the door, looking the very picture of consternation. We dismounted, and asked for something to eat.

"What! wittles?" exclaimed the horrible-looking creature. "Whar did you come from? And what be sogers doin' on here?"

"Well, I came from Indianapolis," said Captain Bracken, "and am after something to eat. Are there any Secesh in these parts?"

"Any what?"

"Secesh."

"Why, gracious, what's them?"

"Are you and your folks for the Union?"

"Why, sartain; thar's the old man neow."

Just at this moment there came a gaunt-eyed, slim-livered, carnivorous, yellow-skinned, mountain Virginian—no doubt belonging to one of the first families, as his name was Rhett.

"Look-a-hear," continued the old woman; "this ere soger wants to know if you be for Union?"

The old man looked, if any thing, more astonished than the old woman at the soldier. In the course of conversation we asked the man, "What he thought of the war?"

"What war?" exclaimed the old fellow; "the Revolution?"

"Yes. The rebellion, we call it."

"Ah! we gin the Britishers fits, didn't we?"

It was evident the man knew nothing of the rebellion going on.

When asked if he heard the fight, the other day, only six miles from his house, he opened his eyes widely, and said he "heard it '*thunderin*'" mighty loud, but couldn't see no clouds, and didn't know what to make *on it.*"

The fact was, these people live up in this place; raise what little will keep them from year to year; never read a paper, ('cause why, they can't); and they scarcely ever visit anybody.

There are many cases of this kind within a few miles of this place, where as much *pent-up* ignorance is displayed. If North Carolina is any worse, in Heaven's name send no more money to *distant heathen*, but attend to those at home.

General William H. Lytle,

Of whom our city has cause to be justly proud, has won for himself a name, engraven on the scroll of honor, as one of our country's heroes. A brief mention of his military career may be summed up as follows:

He was, during the Mexican campaign, on General Scott's line, and, although but a mere youth, he commanded an independent company of volunteer infantry, from Cincinnati, that was afterward attached to the 2d Ohio, on Scott's line, and commanded by Colonel William Irwin, of Lancaster, Ohio. They were stationed most of the time at the "Rio Frio," keeping open the line of communication between the cities of Puebla and Mexico. Brigadier-General Robert Mitchell, of Kansas, and Brigadier-General McGinnis, of Iowa, were captains in the same regiment. At the termination of that war General Lytle studied and entered into the practice of the law.

In 1857 he was elected Major-General of the First District of Ohio Volunteers. On the 19th of April, 1861, he was ordered by the Governor of Ohio to organize a camp for four regiments of infantry, and the day after receiving this order General Lytle took into Camp Harrison the 5th and 6th Ohio Infantry, and shortly after the 9th and 10th Ohio. The latter regiment tendered him the colonelcy, which was accepted; and he led it through the Virginia campaign, under McClellan and Rosecrans, up to the date of Carnifex Ferry, where he was wounded, September 10, 1861. Recovering from his wounds, he reported for duty in January, 1862, and was placed by General Buell in command of the Camp of Instruction at Bardstown, Ky., relieving General Wood. In March he was relieved, and reporting at Nashville, was placed in command of Dumont's brigade, Major-General O. M. Mitchel's division, at Murfreesboro, and made, with General Mitchel, the campaign in Northern Alabama, and conducted the evacuation of Huntsville, August 31, 1862, under orders from Major-General Buell. He commanded the Seventeenth Brigade up to the battle of Chaplin Hills, where he was again wounded, October 8, 1862. During the following winter he was promoted to Brigadier-General, dating from November 29, 1862, and reported for duty to the Army of the Cumberland in the spring of 1863, and was assigned to the command of the First Brigade, Third Division, of the Twentieth Army Corps.

A Tribute To the Tenth Ohio

When Colonel Mulligan was in Cincinnati, he and the noble William H. Lytle were invited to the dedication of the Catholic Institute. It was the 22d of November, 1861. Lytle had just recovered from his Carnifex Ferry wound. The Colonel was called upon for a speech. He said:

"When I go back and tell my men how, for their sakes, you have received me to-night, *they will feel very proud.* They often think of you, my fellow-citizens; and the brother, mother, wife, or sister, among you, in spirit visits the soldier as he rests in his chill tent at night.

"It does not become me to speak of my own regiment, for I know that he who putteth his armor on can not boast as he that puts it off. But, as it is distant, and can not hear my words, I may say this much: the Tenth has been ever true to the motto inscribed upon its flag—'God and the Union.'"

The Colonel paid a feeling tribute to John Fitzgibbons, the dead color-bearer of the Tenth, and hoped that the memory of his deeds, of Kavanagh, and others, who fell on the field in defense of their country, might inspire their countrymen to rise and avenge them.

Drilling

Sweet Amy asked, with pleading eyes,
"Dear Charley, teach me, will you,
The words I've heard your captain say?
I should so like to drill you!"

"What! little one, you take command!
Well, Amy, I'm quite willing;
In such a company as yours,
I can't have too much drilling.

"Stand over, then, and sing out clear,
Like this: 'Squad! stand at ease!'"
"O, Charles! you'll wake papa, up stairs;
Don't shout like that, love, please."

"Now, stand at ease, like this, you see!
And then, I need scarce mention,
The next command you have to give,
Is this one: 'Squad! attention!'

"Now, Amy, smartly after me;
(You're sure, dear, it won't bore you?)

'Forward, march! Halt! Front! Right dress!'
There, now, I'm close before you.

"'Present arms!'" "Well, it does look odd."
"You don't believe I'd trifle!
We hold our arms out, just like this,
In drill without the rifle.

"Now say, 'Salute your officer!'"
"O, Charles! for shame! how can you?
I thought you were at some such trick,
You horrid, naughty man you."

Charles "ordered arms" without command;
She smoothed her ruffled hair,
And pouted, frowned, and blushed, and then
Said softly, "*As you were!*"

A Black Nightingale's Song

Shortly after our troops occupied one of the towns in Virginia, a squad occupying a tent near a dwelling heard delightful music. The unknown vocalist sang in such sweet, tremulous, thrilling notes, that the boys strained their ears to drink in every note uttered.

On the following day they made some excuse to visit the house, but no one was there. Once they observed a sylph-like form, but she was not the person; and so they lived on, each night hearing the same divine music.

One night, when they were gathered together, the voice was again heard. "By Jove!" said one, "I'm bound to find out who that is; she must be discovered." A dozen voices took up the remark, and a certain nervous youth was delegated to reconnoiter the place. He crept on tiptoe toward the dwelling, leaped the garden-wall, and finally, undiscovered, but pallid and remorseful, gained the casement. Softly raising his head, he peeped within. The room was full of music; he seemed to grow blind for a moment, when lo! upon the kitchen-table sat the mysterious songster, an ebony-hued negress, scouring the tinware, and singing away. Just as he was peering through the window, the ebony songster discovered him. The soldier's limbs sank beneath him, and the black specimen of humanity shouted:

"Go 'way dar, you soger-man, or I'll let fly de fryin' pan at your head! You musn't stan' dar peekin' at dis chile."

The soldier left, his romantic vision dispelled.

OUR HOOSIER BOYS
Dedicated To The Brave Soldiers Of Indiana

From East to West your camp-fires blaze,
Hoosier boys! our Hoosier boys!
On Vicksburg's hights our flag you raise,
Hoosier boys! our Hoosier boys!
And on Virginia's trait'rous soil,
In answer to your country's call,
The echoes of your footsteps fall,
Hoosier boys! our Hoosier boys!

While Southern suns upon you beat,
Hoosier boys! our Hoosier boys!
You sternly march the foe to meet,
Hoosier boys! our Hoosier boys!
Two winters, numbered with the past,
Have o'er you swept with stormy blast,
Since home's dear walls inclosed you last;
Hoosier boys! our Hoosier boys!

By Richmond's fields, baptized with blood,
Hoosier boys! our Hoosier boys!
By precious dust 'neath Shiloh's sod,
Hoosier boys! our Hoosier boys!
By every martyred hero's grave,
By sacred rights they died to save.
We'll cherish in our hearts the brave
Hoosier boys! our Hoosier boys!

While yet a vacant place is here,
Hoosier boys! our Hoosier boys!
From hearts and homes will rise the prayer,
Hoosier boys! our Hoosier boys!
"God bless our gallant men and true,
And let foul treason meet its due!"
That faithful hearts may welcome you
Home again, our Hoosier boys!

CHAPTER XVI

Old Stonnicker and Colonel Marrow, of 3d Ohio

A Peculiar specimen of the "genus Virginia" had a great deal of trouble while our army was encamped at Elkwater. Stonnicker's fences and sugar-camp were used for fire-wood, corn-field for fodder, apple-trees stripped.

Stonnicker's family were sick. One of his oldest gals had the "soger's fever." He "guessed she must o' cotched it from either the 3d Ohio or 17th Ingeeana Regiment, as the officers kept a comin' there so much."

One day he sent for Colonel Marrow, and the Colonel obeying the summons, Stonnicker said:

"Colonel, one of my children is dead, and I haven't any thing to bury the child in."

The Colonel, a kind-hearted gentleman, had a neat coffin made; lent the old man horses and an ambulance, and attended personally to the burial, at which the old man took on "*amazingly.*"

An hour or two after the funeral, old Stonnicker strolled up to the Colonel's quarters.

"Colonel," said he, as the tears rolled down his cheeks; "Colonel, what shall I do?"

The Colonel, thinking he was mourning over the loss of his lately-buried child, replied:

"O, bear up under such trials like a man."

"Wal, I know I orto; but, Colonel, can't you do something for me? It is too bad! I feel so miserable! Boo-hoo-hoo-hoo-hoo!"

"O, come, be a man," said the Colonel; "any thing I can do for you shall be done, willingly."

"O, Colonel! I knowed it; I knowed it. My old woman allers said you was a fust-rate feller; and, Colonel, ef you'll only pay me for them two stacks of hay your men took from my field, I shall be mighty glad, for I want the money."

It is needless to say that the Colonel's sympathies instantly ceased, and, turning on his heel, he might have been heard to say, "O, d——n you and your hay."

General Garnett and His Dogs

It was said by the boys that at the battle in which General Garnett was killed, a favorite dog of his was with him on the field. During the three months following I saw not less than fifty dogs, each one said, positively, to be the identical dog belonging to the rebel general.

Are You the Col-o-nel of this Post?

I was seated one day in the telegraph office at Beverly. Prince was the telegrapher, and he was communicating with some female at Buckhannon, telling her to come over on the next train. While enjoying a lump of white sugar dissolved in hot water, sent by Uncle Peter Thomson, especially to cure my cold, a big, brawny Irishman entered the office, and, as I was rigged out in the Secession uniform of Captain Ezzard, of the Gate City Guards, Atlanta, Georgia, I was mistaken for a general by the said Irishman, who accosted me much after this style:

"Good mornin' to ye, sur. And how are yees dis mornin'?"

"Good morning, sir," said I.

"Sure, sir," said he; "are you the Col-o-nel of this post? for it was him I was towld to ax for—for a pass to get to see my wife, who lives five miles away from here, adjoining the white church, forninst the first woods to the right as you go to Huttonsville."

As soon as he finished his speech I informed him I was not the Col-o-nel, but that Colonel William Bosley was the gentleman he must see. I told him, moreover, that "the Colonel was a very cross man; very strict in his discipline: if he didn't approach him "just so," he would very likely refuse any pass, and kick him into the bargain."

"Thank you, sur; thank you, sur. O, but I'll approach him right. Never fear me!"

I pointed him to the marquee, in front of which was a large stake, or post, for hitching horses.

"There," said I, "you see; that's the post."

"Well, sur; plaise to tell me what I must do?"

"You must go three times round the post; make your bow; place your hands behind you; walk to the entrance of his tent, and inquire, 'If he commands that post?' Tell him you want to see your wife, and the pass, no doubt, will be given you."

The Irishman did as requested. Colonel Bosley said he knew there was a joke up, and humored it; and after putting all sorts of grotesque questions to the man, he was allowed to go on his way, rejoicing.

High Price of Beans in Camp—a Little Game of "Draw"

Beans were excessively high, one season, in our army. I have seen Charley Brutton and Lieutenant Southgate and Captain Frank Ehrman, and other officers, pay as high as five cents apiece for them. Brutton said he intended to make bean-soup of his. Often, while I stood looking at parties around a table, I heard remarks like these:

"Ten beans better than you."

I suppose he meant that his ten beans were better than his opponent's ten beans. Then some one of the party, seated at the end of the table, would say:

"I see them ten beans."

Well, so did I, and everybody else about there. We couldn't help but see them. Why, therefore, need he make so superfluous a remark? Then the other would say:

"I call you."

But I didn't hear him *call*. All he would do was, to lay his beans on the pile in the middle of the table, and soon they all spread out some pictures and dots that were printed on white pasteboard. Then *one man* reaches out his hand and *draws* over the beans to his side; and he smiles complacently, and all the others look beat and crabbed. And this they call a little game of *draw*.

Charley Clark and Captain Westcott say 'tis a bad practice; *and they ought to know.*

Profanity in the Army

It is astonishing how rapidly men in the service become profane. I never before appreciated the oft-quoted phrase, "He swears like a trooper." Young men whom I have noticed, in times gone by, for their urbanity and quiet demeanor, now use language unbecoming gentlemen upon any occasion. But here it is overlooked, because "*everybody does it;*" but, to my mind,

"'Tis a custom more honored in the breach than the
observance."

Gambling, too! O, how they take to it! "O, it's just for pastime," says
one. Yes; but it is a pastime that will grow and grow, and drag many a one to
ruin. Among the many ways that the boys have of evading the law against it
in camp is, going off into the woods and taking a "quiet game," as they term
it. Chuck-a-luck, sweat-cloth, and every species of device for swindling are
resorted to by the baser sort.

CHAPTER XVII

Hard on the Sutler—spiritualism Tried

The officers of some regiments will drink—that is, they can be *induced*.

There was a sutler, a great devotee to the modern science—if science it can be called—of spiritualism. The officers found this out, and determined to play upon his credulity. The quarter-master was quite a wag, and lent himself to the proposed fun. His large tent was prepared: holes were made in it, and long black threads attached to various articles in the apartment, and one or two persons stationed to play upon these strings.

The party met as per agreement; every thing was arranged; the credulous sutler present. While enjoying the evening, the crowd were surprised to see things jumping around; a tumbler was jerked off a table, no one near it; clothing lifted up from the line running through the length of the tent. Some one suggested "spirits." All acknowledged the mystery, while some would, and others would not, accept the spiritual hypothesis as a correct solution. The matter must be tested, and the sutler was appointed chief interrogator.

"If," said he, "there are really spirits, why can they not prove it, by knocking this candlestick from my hand?"

"Why can't they?" echoed others.

And, sure enough, no sooner said than done, and done so quickly that no one but the performer was the wiser, whose knuckles, he said, pained him for a week afterward. Another of the party said to the spirit, "Fire a pistol."

Bang! was the reply.

The sutler became terrified. Again it was agreed that they should try questioning by the rapping process. The sutler proceeded:

"Are there any spirits present?"

Rap! rap! rap!

"Is it the spirit of a deceased relative?"

Rap! rap! rap!

"Whose relative is it? The Quarter-master's?"

Rap.

"The Adjutant's?"

Rap.

"Mine?"

Rap! rap! rap!

Here the sutler was requested to ask if there was anybody in the room who had committed any crime. The question was asked, and

Rap! rap! rap! was the reply.

"Is it the Quarter-master?"

Rap.

"Is it the Colonel?"

Rap!

"Is it the Adjutant?"

Rap!

"Is it the Surgeon?"

Rap!

"Is it m-m-e?"

Rap! rap! rap!

"O yes; I know it!" exclaimed the conscience-stricken sutler. (The first case of the kind I ever knew.) "O yes; I confess I was a Methodist class-leader, and now, here I am, drinking whisky, and selling it, and getting three prices from the boys for every thing I sell. O! I'll go and pray!" And he accordingly departed. The sutler reported, in the morning, that he had prayed, and felt much relieved. It so wrought upon his mind that the joke had to be explained to him, to prevent his being driven to distraction.

A Specimen of Southern Poetry

From the appended exquisite gem of "Southern poetry," it will be seen that they wish to raise the black flag. Well, *why don't they raise it?* Let us hope that for every black flag they raise, Uncle Abraham will raise a *black regiment*. It is from the Chattanooga *Rebel*, and is entitled

The Black Flag

Raise now the sable flag! high let it wave
O'er all Secessia's hills and flowery vales,
And on its sable folds the motto trace,
"For victory or death!" The hated foe
Have gathered in our lovely land, and trod,
With desecrating steps, our State's proud Capital.
They've pillaged in our cities, burned our homes,
Exiled our stanch, true-hearted patriots,
Arrested loyal citizens, and sent
Them to those hungry bastiles of the North,
The ignominious "Chase" and "Johnson's Isle."
Our clergy—God's anointed—who refused
To take a black, obnoxious oath, to perjure
Their own souls, they placed in "durance vile."
The noble daughters of the "sunny South,"
Whose hearts were with their country's cause, they forced
To yield obedience to their hated laws,
Nor heeded cries of pity; whether from
Matron staid, beseeching them to leave her,
For her little ones, her own meat and bread;
Or from the bright-eyed boy, with manly grace,
Who brooks, with sorrowing looks, the insults she
Is forced to bear, and dares not to resent;
Or from the gray-haired sire, whose cord of life
Is nearly loosed, who, in enfeebled tones,
Prays them to cease their vexing raids, and let
An old man die in peace. Nor will they list
To maiden fair, whose virtue is their goal.
They've desolated every home where once
Abundance bloomed, and with the weapons of
A warrior (?)—fire and theft—have laid our homes
In ashes, plundered their effects, and sworn
Th' extermination of Secessia's sons.
Then raise the ebon flag! with Spring's warm breath
Let it unfurl its night-like folds, and wave
Where noble "Freeman" fills a martyr's grave.
Then strike! but not for booty, soldiers brave;
Fight to defend your liberties and homes—
The joy it gives to see the Vandals fall,
And catch the music of their dying groans.

Go! burn their cities, scourge their fertile lands;
Teach them retaliation; plow their fields,
And slay by thousands with your iron hail;
Scorn every treaty, every Yankee clan.
Defy with Spartan courage. *Vengeance* stamp
Upon your bayonets; and let the hills and
Vales resound with *Blood*—your battle-cry.

Singular

Civilians are often puzzled, in reading reports of battles, to understand how it is that a thousand troops in a body can "stand the galling fire of the enemy" for an hour or more, and come out with but two or three killed and half a dozen wounded; or how they can "mow down the enemy at every shot" for a long time, and yet not kill over a dozen or so of them. Every thing that is done now-a-days is a complete "rout;" all the enemy's camp equipage, guns, ammunition, etc., are taken. Will somebody wiser than I am please explain?

The Modern Troubadour

A Camp Song.

Gaily the bully boy smoked his cigar,
As he was hastening off for the war;
Singing—"To Secesh land, thither I go:
Rebuels! rebuels! fight all you know!"

'Lize for the bully boy gave nary weep,
Knowing full well he'd his promise keep,
And make her his little wife; so this was her song—
"Bully boy! bully boy! come right along!"

In Camp, Near Tennessee Line,
October 7, 1862.

At five o'clock this morning struck tents at camp, a few miles this side of Bowling Green, and were on the march for "any place where ordered." I am thus indefinite, because the publication of the "ultimate destination" is contraband news. Yesterday we were encamped in a wildly picturesque part of Kentucky—*intensely* rocky—abounding in caverns and subterranean streams; to-day we marched through what has been a delightful country, beautifully rolling land, and highly-cultivated farms; but now, what a sad picture is presented! Scarce a fence standing; no evidences of industry; all is desolation, and the demon of devastation seems to have stalked through the entire State with unchecked speed—houses burned, roads neglected, farms destroyed, in fact, nothing but desolation staring you in the face, turn which way you will.

Early this morning the road was very dusty, but by nine o'clock we had a splendid representation of "Bonaparte crossing the Alps," minus the Alps, and nothing but active marching kept the boys from feeling the extra keenness of old Winter's breath. Still, the boys trudged merrily on, feeling confident the present march is not to be fruitless in its results, as preceding ones have been. This campaign now presents an active appearance, every thing indicating a head to conceive and the will to do.

At three o'clock to-day we passed through the neat-looking town of Franklin. It looks very new, most of the houses being substantial bricks. Here we met General Fry, the man who *slewed* Zollicoffer. The General is of plain, unostentatious appearance, a keen eye, lips compressed, the whole countenance denoting determination and quickness of perception.

General Steadman Challenged by a Woman

Riding along to-day with General Steadman, who, in his province as commander of this brigade, had called at the dwellings on the road-side, to see about the sick soldiers left in the houses, the General knocked at a door, and a voice within yelled "Come in." Obeying the injunction, he opened the door, and inquired how many men were there, and, also, if they had the requisite attention shown them. After a few minutes' talk with the soldiers, General Steadman entered into conversation with Mr. Reynolds, the owner of the property, who, among other things, asked the General when he thought the war would end; to which the General replied:

"Not till the rebels lay down their arms, or the Secessionists get perfectly tired of having their country devastated."

This reply brought in a third party—old Mrs. Reynolds, a regular spitfire, a she-Secessionist of the most rabid, cantankerous species—a tiger-cat in petticoats. This she specimen of the "Spirit of the South," of the demon of desolation, had bottled up her venom during the conversation of her son, but could hold in no longer; her *vial* of wrath "busted," the cork flew out, and the way she came at the General was a caution to the wayfarers over this road, at any rate.

"O, yes! and that's all you nasty Yankees come here for, is, to destroy our property, invade our sile, *deserlatin'* our homes. This 'ere whole war is nothing but a Yankee speculation, gotten up by the North, so that they can steal niggers and drive us from our homes."

"Well, madam, as it is not my province to quarrel with a woman, I shall not talk to you. You get excited, and don't know what you're talking about."

"O! but I'll talk to *you* as much as I please. You're all a sneaking set of thieves. You can just take yourself out of my house, you dirty pup. You're drunk."

The General very placidly listened to the old termagant, and merely remarked, "It was too cold to go out of the house just then; he guessed he'd warm himself first."

"Get out, quick," said she, opening the door. "I'll let you know I'm a Harney. Yes, I'm a grand-daughter of General Harney, of Revolutionary fame."

"Well, madam, I have before told you I don't want to quarrel with a woman, but if you have any of the male Harneys about the house, who will give me the tenth part of the insolence that I have listened to from the lips of 'one old enough to know better,' I will soon show him of what mettle I'm made."

"Jeemes, give me your six-shooter," fairly shrieked the old woman; "I'll soon show him. *I'll fight you at ten paces, sir!*"

The General laughed at her last remark; seeing which, she became perfectly furious. Her sons and daughters begged her to desist from such talk; but the more they cried "Don't," the less she "*don'ted.*"

The family, by this time, had been made aware that it was a real General at whom this insolence of tongue was being hurled, and the tribulation of the son was great. The General, after thoroughly warming himself, quietly walked out with his staff. The son followed to the door, making all sorts of apologies for his mother—that she had been sick, was peevish, and, at times, out of her head. I suggested to him, that I didn't think she would *be so apt to go out of her head if John Morgan had come along*, instead of a Union man.

Lucky for that house and its inmates that the 9th Ohio, or any of General Steadman's command, were not apprised of the proceedings. The General, in the kindness of his heart, and for the sake of the soldiers quartered there, placed a guard around her house, to prevent her being troubled in the least while the regiments were passing.

CHAPTER XVIII

Going into Battle

Many wonder if men wear their coats and knapsacks, and carry blankets, when going into battle. That depends upon circumstances. Sometimes, when marching, they find themselves in battle when they least expect it. Upon such occasions, soldiers drop every thing that is likely to incommode them, and trust to luck for the future.

Many wonder if regiments fire regularly, in volleys, or whether each man loads and fires as fast as he can. That, also, depends upon circumstances. Except when the enemy is near, the regiments fire only at the command of their officers.

You hear a drop, drop, drop, as a few of the skirmishers fire, followed by a rattle and a roll, which sounds like the falling of a building, just as you may have heard the brick walls at a fire.

Sometimes, when a body of the enemy's cavalry are sweeping down upon a regiment to cut it to pieces, the men form in a square, with the officers and musicians in the center. The front rank stand with bayonets charged, while the second rank fires as fast as it can. Sometimes they form in four ranks deep—the two front ones kneeling, with their bayonets charged, so that, if the enemy should come upon them, they would run against a picket-fence of bayonets. When they form this way, the other two ranks load and fire as fast as they can. Then the roar is terrific, and many a horse and rider go down before the terrible storm of leaden hail.

Letter To the Secesh

My Dear Rebs: Having just learned that Vicksburg has gone up—Port Hudson caved—Jackson surrendered—Bragg unwell—I thought I would ask you a few questions, for instance:

How are you, any how?

How does "dying in the last ditch" agree with your general health?

How is the Constitution down your way?

Do you think there is any Government?

How is King Kotting?

Is Yancey well and able to hold his oats?

Has Buckner taken Louisville yet?

I understand Tilghman *has quit* hanging Union men.

Is Floyd still *rifling* cannon, and other small arms?

How is the Southern heart?

Are you still able to whip five to one?

What is your opinion of the Dutch race?

When will England and France recognize you?

What have you done with the provisional government of Kentucky?

Where is the Louisville-Bowling-Green-Nashville-Atlanta *Courier* published now? Say—

What do you think of yourselves any how?

A prompt answer will relieve many anxious hearts.

Yours, in a horn, A Lincoln Man.

General Garfield, Major-General Rosecrans's Chief of Staff

The rather brilliant career of the General is worthy of a more extended notice than I have room for.

General Garfield was born in Cuyahoga County, Ohio, in 1831. It is said that, in his early love of freedom, he formed a strong attachment for horses, and, to gratify this feeling, he ran away from home and became a driver on the canal. Possessing remarkable endurance, and great strength, with no small amount of combative spirit, he soon became a "shoulder-hitter," whipping all opponents who were any way near his own age, and becoming a terror to the quarrelsome rowdies who had previously ruled the ditch.

During the hight of his wild career he attended a revival meeting, became converted, found new and wealthy friends, who supplied him with funds to attend college, and, in 1856, he graduated at William's College, Massachusetts, with the highest honors.

Returning to Ohio, he at once settled as a clergyman and president of the college at Hiram, Portage County. He here became very popular as an eloquent divine, as a lecturer before lyceums, and as a profound scholar. The success of his school was without a precedent. Two years ago he was elected, by an immense majority, as a member of the State Senate. At the first call for troops, he at once entered the field, and rallied round him some of the ablest boys to be found in the State.

General Garfield is what would be called, by ladies, a really handsome man; has large, blue eyes, an expressive mouth, the outlines of which denote good nature. It was prophesied at once, after his enlistment, that, "Let Rev. Mr. Garfield have a chance at the rebels, and he would die in the field, or win a victory." He has, at all times, so far, been on the winning side.

Humphrey Marshall—the barn-door of the Southern Confederacy—it is said, once beat General Garfield, during the early Kentucky campaign. Marshall was in a trap, and, wanting a little time, called upon Garfield with a white flag, who was commanding a brigade, and asked—

"Is there no way to settle this without fighting?"

"No, sir," said Garfield, "none but to fight—*somebody* has got to get hurt."

But Marshall didn't see it in that light—retired to consult—and, in the mean time, beat a hasty retreat, and thus beat *Garfield*.

General Lew Wallace

General Lew Wallace was formerly colonel of the 11th Indiana (three-months men,) known as Zouaves, who were noted for their daring bravery and dash. When the regiment returned to Indiana to be reorganized for the war, General Wallace remained quiet a few days, when the trouble in Missouri aroused his energies, and he issued a spirited call to his fellow-citizens, which was responded to with the greatest enthusiasm. They flocked to his standard, and were sent to the Department of Missouri, and thence to Paducah, after which he was promoted to a generalship in the division of General C. F. Smith.

General Wallace made himself a legion of friends in his able management of affairs during the memorable siege of Cincinnati by the rebels. At a public meeting in Columbus, Ohio, a *Flagg* was raised, and the following war poem recited:

The Siege of Cincinnati

Who saved our city, when the foe
Swore in his wrath to lay it low,
And turned to joy our tears of woe?

Lew Wallace.

Who taught us how to cock the gun,
And aim it straight, and never run,
And made us heroes, every one?

Lew Wallace.

And told us how to face and wheel,
Or charge ahead with pointed steel,
While cannon thundered, peal on peal?

Lew Wallace.

Who, when all in bed did sleep,
About us watch and ward did keep,
Like watch-dog round a flock of sheep?

Lew Wallace.

Who made us all, at his commands,
With fainting hearts and blistering hands,
Dig in the trench with contrabands?

Lew Wallace.

Who would have led us, warriors plucky,
To bloody fields far in Kentucky?
But Wright said, No!—and that was lucky?

Lew Wallace.

Who sat his prancing steed astraddle,
Upon a silver-mounted saddle,
And saw the enemy skedaddle?

Lew Wallace.

And who, "wha hae wi' Wallace" fed,
On pork and beans and army bread,
Will e'er forget, when he is dead,

Lew Wallace?

Parson Brownlow

The Knoxville *Register* thus laments the release of the Parson from the prison of that city:

"In brief, Brownlow has preached at every church and school-house, made stump-speeches at every crossroad, and knows every man, woman, and child, and their fathers and grandfathers before them, in East Tennessee. As a Methodist circuit-preacher, a political stump-speaker, a temperance orator, and the editor of a newspaper, he has been equally successful in our division of the State. Let him but once reach the confines of Kentucky, with his knowledge of the geography and the population of East Tennessee, and our section will soon feel the effect of his hard blows. From among his own old partisan and religious sectarian parasites he will find men who will obey him with the fanatical alacrity of those who followed Peter the Hermit in the first Crusade. We repeat again, let us not underrate Brownlow."

The gallant Colonel Charles Anderson, of the 93d Ohio, in a speech in Columbus, said:

"The South laugh at the little shams of the hour with which they agitate us; but their purpose is deep and dark. They mean to carry out their system of 'oligarchy' at whatever cost. Looking upon slavery as I now do, having seen it from every side, and knowing that the South intend the destruction of this Union—were I to stand before the congregated world, I would declare it—I will hew slavery from crest to hip, from hip to heel, and cut my way through white, black, and yellow—nerve, muscles, bone—tribes and races, to the Gulf of Mexico, to save the Union."

CHAPTER XIX

An Episode of the War

During the early part of the rebellion, when the rebels were in force on Munson's Hill, McClellan laid a plan to surround and capture them. This plan was only known to McClellan, General Scott, and Colonel Scott, a relation of the General, by marriage. As the troops started out at night, for their assault, a signal rocket went up from Washington. On their arrival at Munson's Hill, the bird had flown. McClellan, being informed of this, immediately called on General Scott, finding there Colonel Scott. He immediately said to the General: "The enemy have been warned of our movements by a rocket; they must have been so warned by one of us. Which is the traitor?" No answer was given. McClellan then called on the President, and mentioned the above facts, stating his conviction that Colonel Scott was the delinquent, and insisted upon his immediate imprisonment, or his banishment, or his own resignation. Then followed General Scott's resignation, then his journey to Paris, and the self-banishment of Colonel Scott.

A Laughable Incident

Considerable merriment and not a few immodest expressions were elicited at Washington, one day, by the action of the patrol, who perambulate the Avenue on horseback, a terror to all fast riders. On this occasion they made an onslaught upon the darkeys, who, for some time past, had luxuriated in the uniform of United States volunteers. How the articles of wearing apparel were obtained by the contrabands alluded to we have not inquired. The patrol rode up to each unfortunate "Sambo" that made his appearance, and proceeded to divest him of each of the articles enumerated, save where the bare necessity of the case would not admit of such a procedure. Caps, vests, and coats rapidly disappeared from "Sambo's" body, and were deposited in the street at the feet of the horses.

"Take off your breeches," we heard escape the lips of one of the patrol. The darkey grinned, then rolled his eyes, gazed at some ladies passing, and then, with an astonished countenance, looked up into the face of the patrol. "Massa," he said, "I aint got nuffin else on when I take dese off." This was something of a puzzle to the guard on horseback, and so, not wishing to shock the modesty of the street, "Sambo" was allowed to depart with his linen and trowsers.

Old Mrs. Wiggles on Picket Duty

"As for sleeping on a picket," said Mrs. Wiggles to the three-months volunteer who had dropped in to see her, "I don't see how they can do it without hurting them. Sleeping on a post would be a good deal more sensible, unless there's a nail in it, which might be prejudicious for the uniform. Every one to his taste, and such things as where a man shall sleep is at his own auction; but nobody can help thinking that either a picket or a post is a very uncomfortable place to sleep on. At any rate, there isn't much room for more than one in a bed."

General Manson

Brigadier-General Manson was in camp at Glenn's Fork, Pulaski County, eighteen miles from the scene of the Mill Spring battle, and, with his brigade, made a forced march that distance, over horrible midwinter roads, arriving just in time to engage honorably in the fight. The gallant 10th Indiana lost seventy-five men. Its colonel, commanding the brigade as above, is an officer of great bravery and ability. His conduct at the battle of Rich Mountain, in Western Virginia, as colonel of that regiment, and his experience in the war with Mexico, constitute a happy preface to his late brilliant achievement. This same 10th Indiana is fully up to the feat of rapid marches. At one time, being detailed to go to Greensburg from Campbellsville, to repel an anticipated attack of Secesh, the march was made by the Hoosier boys in three hours, a distance of twelve miles, eight of which was over a dirt-road that had had the advantage of a hard rain the night previous.

God Bless the Soldier

A young and beautiful lady of Louisville (Minnie Myrtle) says; "God bless the soldier!" O, could we but look into the almost bursting heart of the rough-clad, tired soldier, as he plods his way, weary and worn, casting a glance, at intervals, to see one kind smile, to hear one kind and gentle voice to remind him of home, and the "loved ones" left far behind to the mercies of a cold and heartless world—could we but look into that fond heart and see the aching void, we would clasp that hand tenderly, and draw him gently to our homes, a welcome guest. O, did you but think, for a moment, of the sacrifice made by the ones you term "striplings," you would smother the thought before it rises to your pure lips, and your cheeks would burn with the sisterly blush, and your lips would breathe a prayer instead for the wanderer.

Come with me to yon snow-covered cabin. 'Tis a rude hut; but pause ere you enter, and behold the scene: An aged mother, bowed in deep and earnest prayer; and, as she prays for her jewels, a smile, not of sadness, but a settled calmness, gives place to one of extreme agony; her boys—she has but two, the pride of her declining years—both she gave, as did "Abraham of old," a living sacrifice upon the "altar of her country." Come with me to yonder habitation, not of wealth, but comfort. Hark! What shriek was that which rent the air? A widowed mother kneels beside the fatherless babe, and asks God in mercy to let the bitter cup pass from her. Another sacrifice to the dark and bloody ground! Pause, then, sisters, and give that thought not utterance. Your lips should breathe a prayer for the friendless soldier. If you have a brother, then love the soldier for your brother's sake; and if you have none, the honest-hearted soldier will be a brother and protector. But, O, for the love of God, speak kindly to the soldier.

A Negro's Pedigree of Abraham Lincoln

A full-blooded African, who was taken prisoner on the steamer Lewis, on which he is now employed as a cook, in the service of the United States, was encountered one evening by the surgeon of one of the naval ships, who asked him his name. "Nathaniel," replied the negro. "Any other name?" said the doctor; to which Sambo replied: "Why, de last name is always de massa's name—Massa Johnson." "What do the people say this war is about?" asked the doctor. Nat replied: "Why, sir, dey say that some man, called Linkum, is going to kill all de women an' de children, an' drive de massa away; and all colored folks will be sold to Cuba." Nathaniel then proceeded to give some new and highly interesting particulars respecting the genealogy of the family of the Chief Magistrate of the United States. "Dey say his wife was a black woman, and dat his fadder and mudder come from Ireland," said he, speaking with emphasis. The doctor indignantly refuted the aspersions cast upon the family of the President, and disabused the mind of the negro of the false impressions which he had received from the Secessionists of the place.

One morning I accosted a contraband named Dick, who was employed in the fort. "Have you any other name?" said I. "Dey calls me Dick, de Major," was his answer. In reply to interrogatories, he gave an account of his life. "I was born in Virginny," said he, holding on the rim of a slouchy felt hat, and raising it at every inquiry. "Massa sold me, fore I was old 'nuff to know my mudder, to a preacher man in Florida. Bimeby massa die, and missus, she had a musical turn o' mind, and swapped me off for a fiddler; but de people all got de laf on de ole 'oman, for in two or free months the old fiddler died, and she lost us both," and the darkey laughed vehemently.

A Middle Tennessee Preacher

A Secesh preacher, who was elected to a captaincy in the Home-Guards at Chattanooga, hearing they were likely to be called out, sent in the following note:

"dear curnel i beg to resind my commishen. Being a disciple of Krist i can not take up the sord."

A Laconic Speech

An amusing sword presentation took place one day in camp. The 78th Pennsylvania presented a sword to their colonel, William Sirwell. Captain Gillespie spoke as follows:

"Here *we* are, and here *it* is. This is a bully sword, and comes from bully boys; take it, and use it in a bully manner."

Colonel Sirwell replied:

"Captain, that was a bully speech. Let's all take a bully drink."

CHAPTER XX

CAMP NEAR GALLATIN, TENN.,
November 20, 1862.

A trip from the tunnel to Gallatin, and back, is a good day's sport, for it behooves all to be on the alert, to avoid being captured by citizen guerrillas. A number of this brigade have already been "gobbled up," while out hunting luxuries at farm-houses. This became so frequent that the General in command issued an order prohibiting the boys from leaving camp without special permission.

Folks at home have frequently heard of the strong Union sentiment pervading Tennessee, but, "cuss me" if I haven't hunted in vain for the article during the past two weeks, and, with no exception whatever, save among the laboring class, have I found an out-and-out Union man. They answer with a "double meaning," when questioned, and are *professed* Union men while the army is here, and strong Secessionists when the rebel army can protect them.

The fact is, all the true Union men have been driven by the merciless foe into the woods—at any rate from their homes. Acts of the most fiendish barbarity have been committed, and the aiders and abettors are within a few miles of this camp, unmolested, enjoying the comforts of a home, while the true patriot, driven from his family to the hills of his native State, is

"Unsheltered by night, and unrested by day;
The heath for his barracks—revenge for his pay."

An incident occurred in General Fry's division a few days since. Two of the 2d Minnesota Regiment, John A. Smith and Mr. Mervis, both of St. Paul, went out, by permission of their captain, in search of butter and eggs. They took two good horses with them, and although a week has passed, neither men nor horses have returned. The sequel proves that these men were captured by armed residents of this neighborhood, as yesterday a company were sent out for forage, and with them a number of servants were sent for eatables. Arriving at the house of 'Squire McMurray, a well-known Secessionist, who has two sons in the rebel army, the boys made inquiries of the servants in regard to their missing comrades, and found out they had been taken by a party of guerrillas from near this very house. The old scoundrel McMurray openly exulted over the fact, and thought it very comical to have the "Yankees" jerked up once in awhile. "It will teach them," said he, "to stay at home." The boys wanted to purchase some chickens and turkeys, but he refused to sell to "Yanks," swearing his turkeys were not fattened for "Down-easters." Mrs. McMurray hurriedly came out, and ordered all her black servants in the house, as she said she didn't want her niggers contaminated with "sich white trash."

About two hours after this conversation the brigade teams *drove up*, and soon *drove off* with ten loads of corn and oats, amounting to sixty dollars. 'Squire McMurray refused to receive a voucher offered by the Quarter-master, and said they were of no account to him—it was only a trick of the Abolition Government to rob the farmers; they had already sixty wagon-loads, and he guessed he could spare a few more. This man has a splendid farm, finely stocked with valuable imported Cashmere sheep, some of them worth from four to five hundred dollars apiece. This man is living in luxury, and upon ground that should be occupied by the poor and devoted families of those who, by his connivance, have been driven forth upon the world. Yet the great shield of the law—the law he has so basely violated, the Constitution he has, and yet does, openly defy—is made his safeguard. Is it at all astonishing our men weary of this favoritism, this premium upon traitors?

Let me tell your readers of what I was an eye-witness, a few evenings ago. You that have comfortable homes and warm firesides, with no war at your doors, can have but a faint idea of the horrors that are broadcast over this once happy country. A poor woman came to the commanding General of this brigade and begged for protection. She lived eight miles from this camp, and the rebels had threatened to burn her barn and house. Now, what do you think was this woman's offense? Her husband had joined the Union army at Nashville last August, and when, a few days afterward, he returned to arrange his family affairs, the "guerillas" found out his return, and five of the incarnate fiends walked into his house, and while he was seated at the table, partaking of his breakfast, these men shot him—there, in the presence of his wife and six children, these fiends, that our worthy President deliberately "commutes," murdered their only protector; and now, not satisfied with their former atrocity, they return to drive the poor widow and her children from the desolate little homestead!

O! if there is one hell deeper than another, please, God, send these wretches, who would persecute a poor woman thus, to it!

The General, upon hearing the story of her troubles, sent out two companies of the 2d Minnesota Regiment to guard and bring into camp her children, and what few chattels were left. Company A, under Captain Barnes, and Company G, under Captain Keifer, were assigned to perform this act of deserved charity.

It was ten o'clock at night, cold and windy, the rain penetrating to the very bones, and dark as Egypt, when the two companies returned with Mrs. Crane and her six children. One rickety wagon, a mangy old horse, a cow, some bedding, and a few cooking utensils, were the trophies of the trip. These things told a tale of poverty, but they were all the poor widow of the murdered soldier possessed.

The children were all barefooted, and most scantily attired; the little ones shivered with the cold, and the older ones wrapped their tattered garments closer as the wind played rudely with them. A little four-year-old boy eyed the soldiers with a side glance, and clung to his mother, as she held her infant to her breast.

If I were to decide what to do in such a case, I would quickly turn out Mr. 'Squire McMurray, and let Mrs. Crane and her little ones possess the well-stocked farm. To-day the General is endeavoring to get transportation to Indiana for this family, at the expense of the Government.

An old negro resident near this camp, in conversation, a few days since, said to me:

"Look-a-heah! all you white folks, when any debbeltry is done, allers lay it to Massa John Morgan."

"Well," said I, "don't he do a large share of it?"

"Yes, he does do a heap; but, Lor bress you, massa, gib de *debble* his due; he don't do de half what de white folks say. You see dat tunnel, don't you?" said he, rolling the white of his eyes to the obliteration of all sight of the pupil.

"Yes, I see it," I replied.

"Well, sah! Massa Morgan had no more to do wid dat tunnel dan you do yourself. Morgan *warnt* no way nigh dis place when dat was done; de folks what lib all round here was de *Morganses* what do dat work; why, dey done toted rails for *free* days, and packed 'em in dat tunnel, and we darkeys had to help 'em, and den dey set 'em on fire, and sich a cracklin' as you nebber heard, and in less dan a week ebbery body all over de country was a-tellin' about how as *John Morgan burnt de tunnel*."

Impudence of the Rebels

"Here, sir, I've got an order for you," said an acknowledged well-known rebel citizen, as he entered the head-quarters of the General commanding the Third Brigade of the First Division of the Ohio. From the pompous manner of the Tennesseean, the General didn't know, for a moment, but that he was about being ordered under arrest by the citizen. The General merely replied in his usual style:

"The hell you have, sir! Who is it from?"

"From General Fry, sir."

"Ah! let me see it."

The order was produced. It requested the General not to allow too much of any one man's stock of corn to be taken. The General read the *request*, and instantly inquired of the Tennesseean: "Are you a Union man?" and as instantly received the reply of "No, sir, I am not."

"Then, G— —d d— —n you, sir, how dare you have the impudence to come within my lines?"

The Tennesseean, seeing he had a man of the pure grit to deal with, shook slightly in his boots, and did not put on so much "style," and was about to explain something, when the General interrupted him with a quick order to leave forthwith, or he would have a dozen bayonets in his rear "d— —n quick."

"But, General, how shall I get out of camp? Won't you *please* give me a pass?"

"Me give a pass to a rebel! No, sir. How did you get within my lines?"

"Why, sir, I just walked straight in."

"Well, sir, you can just walk straight out, and if ever I see you inside my lines again, I'll have you sent where you belong; and, after this, when you have any 'order' for me, if it is from General Halleck, 'or any other man,' don't you dare to bring it, but *send* it in to me, or you will rue the day."

A Pathetic Appeal

I found the following "pathetic" appeal from the women of New Orleans. It was laid carefully by, with a lock of hair, bearing the inscription, "To Mary Looker, from her cousin Jane. Please send this appeal to all our male friends around Gallatin."

"AN APPEAL FROM THE WOMEN OF NEW ORLEANS.

"To every Soldier:

"We turn to you in mute agony! Behold our wrongs, fathers! husbands! brothers! sons! We know these bitter, burning wrongs will be fully avenged. Never did Southern women appeal in vain for protection from insult! But, for the sakes of our sisters throughout the South, with tears we implore you not to surrender your cities, 'in consideration of the defenseless women and children.' Do not leave your women to the merciless foe! Would it not have been better for New Orleans to have been laid in ruins, and we buried beneath the mass, than subjected to these untold sufferings? Is life so priceless a boon that, for the preservation of it, no sacrifice is too great? Ah, no! ah, no! Rather let us die with you! O, our fathers! rather, like Virginius, plunge your own swords into our breasts, saying, 'This is all we can give our daughters.'

"THE DAUGHTERS OF THE SOUTH.

"New Orleans, *May 14, 1862.*"

CHAPTER XXI

CAMP AT TRIUNE, TENNESSEE,
April 26, 1863.

Last Thursday was a "gay day" for a portion of the Third Division. General Schofield, thinking it requisite to lay in a good supply of provender, ordered out one hundred and fifty wagons, to go on an errand of mercy to our benighted "brethren of the South," and *borrow* of them some corn, oats, and fodder, for Federal horses. Well, as it is a recognized breach of etiquette to send such a train without escort, therefore, the General sent a retinue, consisting of the 35th Ohio, under Colonel Long; 9th Ohio, Colonel Josephs; 17th Ohio, Colonel Durbin Ward; 31st Ohio, Colonel Phelps; also, the 87th Indiana, Colonel Shyrock; and the 2d Minnesota, under Colonel George; together with two pieces belonging to the 4th Regular Battery, under Lieutenants Rodney and Stevenson. We went forward with the determination of obtaining food—"peacefully, if we could; forcibly, if we must;" but we had to use the rebel women's motto, lately made public in Richmond, "Food or Blood." Our new commander accompanied the expedition. We started, after partaking of an early breakfast, and crossed Harpeth River about nine o'clock. I had forgotten to mention that the 1st East Tennessee Cavalry were along: the rebels haven't forgotten it, however, as they were ordered to the front, and, as I am fond of seeing them "go in," I was appointed chief aid and bottle-holder to the command under Majors Burkhardt and Tracy, and had a splendid opportunity of seeing the "Secession elephant." After passing through the town of College Grove, we commenced feeling our way carefully, as we wished to make our visit a sort of "surprise party" to the "brethren in arms;" as a matter of course, this was only the "by-play," for while the Tennessee boys were unloading their muskets, the teamsters were loading corn and oats from Secesh cribs. They are excellent *cribbage*-players by this time.

As our cavalry advanced, the rebel cavalry fell back, declining to hold any communication. Major Tracy and "ye correspondent" went off the main road, in pursuit of knowledge, and came upon half a dozen negroes working in a field. The Major introduced "ye innocent lamb" as General Morgan, and demanded of the darkeys if any d——d Yankees had been about there lately. The darkeys replied very evasively; would not say a word that would injure the cause of the Union forces; denied all knowledge of them or their whereabouts. There were some two or three hundred fat sheep on the farm, and a good lot of cattle. I suggested the propriety of driving them within our lines, but was astonished when the Major told me it was "against orders" to do so. All the males of the family who owned the negroes and *other cattle* were in the rebel army—the master and two sons. While talking there, we heard firing, and so started for the fun, and soon came upon some of the "gentry," yclept "butternuts." The Major had about twelve men in the lead; a few others, with the colors, remaining a quarter of a mile to the rear—the *regiment* a mile in rear of the advance. When we arrived at what is known as Tippets's farm, the rebels, who were sheltered by Wilson's house, poured a volley down the road, and without inquiring the cause of such unkind treatment, on their part, this "individual" *retired* some twenty yards. I have before heard the sound of the Enfield-rifle ball, and have heard many persons say, 'tis "quite musical;" but *"I can't see it."* The boys advanced in the most daring manner on the open road, while the *valiant* and *"noble chivalry"* of Alabama kept continually retreating. In order to obtain a better view of the fight, and watch the maneuvers of the combatants, I went upon the side-hill of an open field to the left of the road, and while quietly looking on, three rebs came out from behind Wilson's house, and, without as much as saying, "By your leave," they blazed away at me. Isn't it a shame that these fellows should act so? Why, they *"busted* the Constitution all to the devil," in firing at *me.* The Major kindly rode up and told me, in his usual bland and benign style, that I was a d— —n fool; that "them fellers was a-shootin' at me." I merely replied that I guessed he was mistaken, as I saw the bullets *plowing* the field some twenty yards in front of me. While this conversation was going on between the Major and myself, the rebels reloaded their guns and gave us another trial of their skill, and settled the dispute at once, as I had asseverated; their bullets would not reach that distance. The Major was right, for a little while the nastiest shriek I ever heard came from that volley. The Major's horse didn't like it much, and *cavorted* like the "fiery, untamed steed" ridden by the fair "Adah Isaacs." Then we changed our base: we went toward the chaps, and, when they would get ready to fire, put spurs to our horses and ran from them. This so delighted the "rebs," that we gratified them with two or three trials, and every time we ran, they shouted and said *bad words.* After placing five men in ambush, we retired, as if leaving the field, and as the traitors were advancing directly into the trap of three hours' hard setting, the Wilson family came to the door and told them to go back, as the "Yankees" were in the orchard there by Tippets's house. The men were then within two hundred yards of the ambush, and, upon being so informed, hastily wheeled their horses and left on a double-quick. This act on the part of a citizen rebel so exasperated the men that Wilson was given one hour to get out of the house with his furniture, as all houses used for military purposes, signal stations, etc., would meet with destruction.

While the house was burning, the women boasted they had warned them, and would do it again. One virago-looking Secesh asseverated, in a voice of unearthly screechiness, that they had lots of "*Southern friends, and millions of money.*"

The citizens along the road will learn a lesson by this occurrence. It will teach them not to make signal stations of their houses.

Blowing Horns Unconstitutional

Another source of annoyance to our men was the frequent blasts upon dinner-horns. These "quiet, peaceful" citizens, as our men advanced, gave the enemy information by this *blasted* method. Upon being questioned as to the "cause why" they did so much blowing, they replied, "They were calling in the boys from the field, for fear they would get shot;" and Mrs. Tippets said, "'T was near dinner-time." One of the men said he would like something to eat, and went in the house, but no sign of dinner preparation could be seen. Major Tracy took the horn from Mrs. Tippets, at which the lady (?) protested most violently; said there "was no reason in that man," and asked me, "if it wasn't agin the Constitution for that feller to take that horn."

I told her, in a *pacific manner*, that that was nothing; Tracy took from ten to fifteen horns a day. She didn't see the joke, and I became disgusted with her want of penetration, and left.

Mr. Wilson and a man who was in his employ were brought into camp as prisoners. Mr. Wilson protested he didn't tell the States-rights men any thing, and held that he "couldn't hender the women talkin'."

About four o'clock we commenced a retrograde movement for the "old camp," and soon caught up with the big train, filled with all the delicacies of the season, for the brute portion of our division.

The Miss Fanny Battles who is now so sweetly sojourning in the Seminary at Columbus, Ohio, under the guardianship of "Uncle Samuel," was a resident of this county. Our troops were encamped upon the Battles farm for a month. Miss Battles was very industrious in circulating about the country. When she was taken, she had her *drawers* stuffed with letters, and was trying to steal through our picket-lines. The *Secretary* of State, or those connected with the *bureaus*, will, we hope, see that there are no more such *drawers* allowed within the lines.

The Difference

At the house of a Mr. Bolerjack are the wounded men belonging to the 1st Tennessee Cavalry. I called there yesterday, and, in conversation with Mr. B., he expressed surprise at what he termed the difference between our wounded and the rebel wounded. He said that he had a house full of Secesh at one time, but that they kept moaning and groaning all night and day, and kept his family busy, while our men have never muttered, but, on the contrary, are always cheerful, and only anxious to get back in their saddles.

CHAPTER XXII

Reward for a Master—Turning the Tables

The darkeys of Secession masters fairly flocked into camp on many occasions. When near Lebanon, Ky., a bright darkey, very witty, kept the camp alive with his humor. During the day some Kentuckians had posted up in camp an advertisement: "One Hundred Dollars Reward. Ran away from the subscriber, my man Bob," etc. Jim Duncan, the darkey I have referred to, soon after issued the following, and posted it beside the other:

Fifty Cents Reward.—Ran away from dis chile, an' leff him all alone to take care of his-seff, after I done worked twenty-six years for him faithfully, my massa, "Bill Duncan." Massa Bill is supposed to have gone off wid de Secesh *for to hunt for his rights*; and I 'spect he done got lost. Any pusson 'turnin' him to dis chile, so dat he can take keer ob me, (as he allers said niggers couldn't take keer demselves,) will be much oblige to dis chile.

N. B.—Pussons huntin' for him will please look in all de "lass ditches," as I offen heern him tellin' about dyin' dar.

'Specfull' submitted, JIM.

The poster created a great deal of merriment in camp, while the residents thought Jim a very sassy nigger.

Dan Boss and His Adventure

All railroad men know Dan Boss, of the Pittsburg, Fort Wayne, and Chicago Railroad. Dan was in Louisville, on Government business, during the raid, with a lot of cars. Dan thought he would ride out a few miles on the Bardstown pike one fine afternoon, with a friend, and for this purpose hired a fine horse and buggy. Dan went out gaily, and in fine spirits, jokingly observing he was about to reconnoiter. Only ten miles from the city Dan was captured. The rebels demanded a surrender of all his personal effects, which consisted of a rare lot of old passes over all the railroads in the United States, several "bottles," etc. Dan told them he was all right on the goose, and they told him to turn round and go back; upon which Dan was delighted, thinking he had deceived them, when he was accosted by several more of the gang, who wanted to try the speed of Dan's horse. Dan begged for the horse; said it wasn't his, to which the rebs replied, "Well! as it is not *'yourn,'* why, we'll take care of it," and then drove off, leaving Dan and his friend to foot it home.

Major Pic Russell

Says that, on the march to Louisville from Huntsville, Ala., he met hundreds of stragglers from Bragg's army. One tall specimen of Secesh, going back to his Southern home, the Major halted.

"Hallo!" said the Major, "where are you going?"

The fellow looked at the Major very intently, and replied, "Home, sir."

"Where do you live?" inquired Russell.

"Lewis County, Alabama!"

"Why," said the Major, "you don't think you will ever be able to walk all that distance, do you?"

"Well, I do," was his response. "I tell you, Major, I wouldn't take *five hundred dollars for my chance.*"

The distance to his home was over seven hundred miles, through Kentucky, Tennessee, and Northern Alabama.

The Major told me it was a common sight to see them trudging along, singing merrily, no doubt thinking of *"Home, sweet home."*

A Visit to the Outposts with Gen. Jeff C. Davis

General Davis I found an active, intelligent gentleman, with an eye denoting great determination, and very pleasing in his conversational powers; always on the alert, leaving nothing to subordinates that he could do himself. The General's division commanded the Shelbyville pike. I spent two nights with Colonel Heg, who had a brigade occupying the most dangerous position. The 25th Illinois and 8th Kansas were in his brigade.

Colonel Heg's regiment is mostly composed of Norwegians, or Scandinavians. They are generally from, and are known as the 15th Wisconsin; are a splendid body of well-disciplined men, and all speak our language fluently. I heard an amusing anecdote of one of their captains, who, a short time since, took a lot of rebel prisoners. As this Norwegian captain had them drawn up in line, he said to them, in broken English, and in accent very like the German: "Say, you fellers, you putternuts, I vant you all to schwear a leetle. It do you goot to schwear mit de Constitution.

I schwear him tree year ago; now you schwear him. Now, recollect, you schwear him goot; no d——n nonsense. You schwear him, and keep him down, and not *puke him up again*!"

The 24th Illinois are close at hand, also the 8th Kansas. These boys are in view of the rebels every day.

There is in the 24th Illinois Regiment a very clever officer who has an intolerably red nose. He says he can't "help it;" he strives to temper it, but it is no go. A friend inquired of him, how much it cost to color it out here; his reply was, "$2.50 a canteen."

The "rebs" played quite a trick upon the chaplain of the 24th Illinois. After they received his papers, they refused to send any in return. This would have been termed a nasty *Yankee trick*, had any of our boys committed such a breach of faith with them. But such is Southern *honor*.

Rebel Witticisms

The following is copied from the Chattanooga *Rebel*:

If it is true that General Marmaduke hung the regiment of armed negroes at Helena, he certainly made a center shot at old Abe's emancipation-insurrection scheme; for he "knocked the *black* out" every time he hung a darkey.

We do not know for certain that the price of negroes is going up; but there must have been a slight *advance* upon a regiment of them at Helena, the other day, if the wires were correct.

Grant's permitting his dead soldiers to decay and create a stench around Vicksburg presents the worst feature of the Yankee *die-nasty* we have yet had to chronicle.

Richmond papers announce that Hooker has again, "changed his base." He took it out of the saddle awhile ago, to go and tell old Abe "how the thing was did."

The soil of the South is becoming so fertilized with. Yankee bodies, that we will be able to raise nothing but wooden nutmegs after the war.

The "typos" of the *Rebel* suggest the necessity of the immediate return of Vallandigham, and our finishing up the Yankee raid on Vicksburg. Both exciting subjects cause too heavy a "run" on the capital "V" box.

The Yankee officers who lead armed negroes against the Southern people will have "a *high* old time," for our boys will certainly hang them "as high as Haman."

The Chicago *Tribune* says: "There are already twenty thousand colored troops in the Federal army." Does he mean the *blue-bellied* ones, or the black ones?

"Breakers ahead" for Yankee merchantmen! The Alabama and Florida! If they are not breakers to the ships, they will soon break all the ship-owners.

The Yankee corpses lying around Vicksburg are becoming fetid as fast as the living ones are becoming *de*-feated.

Hight Igo, ye Eccentric Quarter-master

Everybody in the Third Division of Crittenden's corps knows the Quarter-master of the 35th Indiana, Hight Igo; in fact, his fame is not confined to General Van Cleve's division. No, sir! not by any means! His eccentricities are the theme of conversation from Triune to Stone River, from "Kripple Kreek" to Nashville.

His first introduction to the favorable notice of high military authority occurred at Louisville. Shortly after the gallant 35th came into service, he stopped General Wood one day in the streets of Louisville, to inquire upon the subject of "yarn socks." The General informed him he never transacted business on the street, and suggested the propriety of calling at head-quarters. A short time after this the General met Igo on the street, and having heard something queer about Igo's forage account, requested information in regard thereto. Igo coolly remarked: "General, I never transact business on the street. You will please call at my quarters, when I shall be happy to afford you an insight into my affairs."

The next day a couple of the General's staff-officers called upon the incorrigible Igo, to investigate matters, and they investigated "in a horn." Igo remarked that, if they had waited until next morning to make their report, things would have worked; but they foolishly went into the presence of the General immediately upon their arrival; and when they reported "Quar-hic-termaster Igo's busi-ness all-hic-sound," the General "couldn't see it," and dispatched another officer, who could resist the blandishments of whisky-punch long enough to conduct the investigation.

The result of this move was a rather tart request—from the Quarter-master-General's Department—for Lieutenant Igo to send all the papers belonging to his department to Washington, for adjustment; a request which our friend complied with by heading up vouchers, receipts, requisitions, etc., in an ammunition-keg, with a letter stating that, inasmuch as the Department had a great many more clerks at its command than he had, and were probably better acquainted with the "biz" of making out quarterly reports or returns, they might be able to understand how things stood between him and the Government; confessing, at the same time, that he "couldn't make head or tail out of the blasted figures." In due course of mail Igo received a communication from the Department, informing him that if he did not immediately send in his report for the quarter ending on the 31st of October, he would find himself in Washington, under arrest. To this Igo answered thus:

Sir—Yours of — date received. Contents noted. I have long been desirous of visiting the city of "magnificent distances," but have not hitherto been able to realize sufficient funds at any one time to gratify that desire; I therefore gratefully avail myself of your obliging offer to defray the expenses of my journey, and most respectfully suggest the propriety of your "going on with your rat-killing." I am, sir, your obedient servant,

MARTIN IGO,
Lieutenant and A. A. Q. M., 35th Ind. Vols.

This closed Igo's official correspondence with the Department at Washington. He had the "*good luck*" to be captured by Morgan last fall, and, of course, Morgan destroyed all his papers. That struck a balance for him for the quarter ending last October. He had another stroke of good fortune at Stone River, on the 1st of January, in having a wagon captured. Of course, all his papers were in that identical wagon. He was very indignant that a battle did not take place about the last of March, as that would have saved him a heap of trouble. Do not think, however, that our Quarter-master has done any thing that will not bear investigation, for a more honest or conscientious man is not to be found in the Quarter-master's Department; but Igo has a holy horror of vouchers and invoices, and receipts all in triplicate; and small blame to him for it.

Fling out to the Breeze, Boys!

Dedicated to the Second Brigade, Second Division,
M'cook's Corps.
by W. A. Ogden.

Fling out to the breeze, boys,
That old starry flag—
Let it float as in days famed in story;
For millions of stout hearts
And bayonets wait,
To clear its old pathway to glory.

When the first wail of war
That was heard on our shore

Re-echoed with fierce promulgation,
Columbia's brave sons
Then rallied and fought,
In defense of our glorious nation.

From East, West, North, and South,
Their numbers did pour,
Alike seemed their courage and daring;
While boldly they stood,
As the fierce battle raged,
Each nobly the proud contest sharing.

Those patriots have passed—
They now sleep 'neath the sod;
But *their* flag shall be *our* flag forever!
We'll boldly march forward,
And strike to the earth
The fiends who it from us would sever.

Hark! hark! from the South
Comes a sound, deep and shrill—
'Tis the sound of the cannon's deep rattle!
Up! forward! brave boys,
And beat back with a will
The foe from the red field of battle.

We'll rally and rally,
And rally again,
To our standard now pennoned and flying;
And we swear, 'neath its bright folds
Of crimson and gold,
To *own* it, though living or dying.

Then fling to the breeze, boys,
That dear, blood-bought flag—
It must float as in days famed in story;
For millions of *stout hearts*
And *bayonets* wait,
To clear its old pathway to glory.

CHAPTER XXIII

CAMP NEAR GALLATIN, TENN.,
December 14, 1862.

After a careful investigation of the facts relative to the late fight at Hartsville, having visited the battle-field, and having conversed with numerous officers and privates who were wounded in that engagement, I am satisfied that gross injustice has been done the noble raw recruits of the 106th and 108th Ohio Regiments. I am not biased in the least on account of their being Cincinnati men, although I confess to a city pride; and I feel the greatest satisfaction in telling you that those regiments acted in the most heroic manner. That a few acted cowardly and shirked their duty, there is no doubt; but that the entire regiments should bear the blame is very hard.

I notice the Louisville *Journal* is particularly severe on the men and officers; and, also, that W. D. B. "pitches in," and terms them "Scott's Cowardly Brigade."

W. D. B. goes into *minutiæ* in regard to Scott, who, he says, commanded. He is entirely mistaken. Scott, finding the place a dangerous one, requested, a week previously, to be allowed to rejoin his regiment, and his request was granted. The Scott who had command, and was relieved, belonged to Turchin's old regiment, and was their Lieutenant-Colonel. Scott told Colonel Moore of the dangers of the post, and Colonel Moore, feeling his weakness, protested against being left there. The fault lies beyond these new regiments.

Why were three regiments of raw recruits placed in such a dangerous position, with but two guns and a handful of cavalry? As soon as the fight began, a courier was sent to Castilian Springs, a distance of only five miles, for reinforcements. The brigade was sent, but arrived too late. Instead of marching by column, on a double-quick, these men were deployed as skirmishers. The 106th and 108th Ohio and 104th Illinois held the ground for full two hours, until completely surrounded and driven to the brink of the river, where another large force of rebels awaited them. Yet these undisciplined men are called cowards—these men, who bravely held the ground, against odds of three to one, against the disciplined rebels belonging to the 2d and 9th Kentucky, and under the immediate command of Morgan! Yet these men are to bear the disgrace and receive the anathemas of the press, in order to shield some imbecile officer!

I paid a visit to the hospital to-day, and I tell you it was a pitiable sight to see a large room crowded with the gallant wounded. They told me they didn't care for the wounds, but to be so maligned was more than they could bear. One noble fellow read the remarks of the Louisville *Journal*, and the big tears rolled down his manly cheek, as he made the remark to me, "Good God! *is that all the thanks we get for fighting as we did?*"

Newspapers may publish what they please, but here is a fact that speaks loud in praise of the daring Ohio boys, and proves that the 106th and 108th fought well: it is, that Company G, of the 106th, lost every commissioned officer, two sergeants, one corporal, and twelve privates.

Colonel Moore, Lieutenant-Colonel Hapeman, and Major Wiedman refused to be paroled.

Lieutenant Gessert, of the 106th, tells me he was present, a week since, when a colored boy came to Lieutenant Szabo, of the 106th, who was on picket. The boy stated that he overheard Morgan tell his master he was laying a plan to "capture them d— —d Cincinnati Dutch within three days." The boy was sent to head-quarters, where he repeated his story, but no notice was taken of it.

To-day, Dr. Dyer, surgeon of the 104th Illinois, who went over the field directly after the fight, and assisted in dressing the wounds of our men, handed me a green seal ring belonging to Adjutant Gholson. The rebels had stripped the body of boots, coat and hat, and, fearing this ring would be taken, the Doctor placed it in his pocket.

The Doctor says a rebel captain took a fancy to his (the Doctor's) hat, and insisted upon buying it—swore he would shoot him if he didn't sell it; and told him he went in for raising the black flag on the d— —d Yankees.

The Doctor quietly went on with his work, attending to the wounded, while the rebel captain was robbing the dead.

I telegraphed you in regard to Adjutant Gholson's death. He died heroically leading his command. His praise is upon every tongue. I will send his body home on to-day's train.

ALF.

The lines following are a touching tribute to the memory of one of the noblest young men sacrificed in the war. Captain Gholson was a brave, earnest, talented, honorable man, in whose death his many friends feel a sorrowing pride:

To the Memory of Captain W. Y. Gholson

'Neath Western skies I'm dreaming,
This drear December morn,
Of joys forever vanished,
Of friendships rudely torn;

Of the friend so lately taken
From the heartless world away;
Of the well-beloved warrior
Now sleeping 'neath the clay.

The links of youthful friendship,
Unsullied kept through years,
Grim Death hath rudely shattered —
Ay, dimmed by Memory's tears.

Thou wilt be missed sincerely
By the well-remembered band,
Who've proved, through endless changes,
United heart and hand.

Thy mother's pain and anguish
Through life will never cease;
The grief she's now enduring
No earthly power can ease.

A father mourns the idol
Which God hath taken home,
Hath borne to sunnier regions,
Where guardian spirits roam.

And for the grieving sister,
Whose joyous days are o'er,
There cometh gleams of sunshine
From yonder golden shore.

From the throne of God eternal,
Where the angel roameth free,
He speaketh words of music
To parents dear, and thee.

To friends and weeping kindred
He speaketh words of cheer:
"Be ye prepared to meet me,
Prepared to meet me here."

LIZZIE A. F.

Colonel Toland vs. Contraband Whisky

"Volunteer" told me a good story of one of the gallant 34th Ohio and Colonel Toland.

During their stay at Barboursville, the Colonel noticed, one day, an extraordinary number of intoxicated soldiers in camp. Where they obtained their whisky was a mystery to the command. The orders were very strict in regard to its prohibition. After considerable effort, the Colonel succeeded in finding out the guilty party. The culprit had a little log hut on the banks of the Guyandotte River, and was dealing it out with a profuseness entirely unwarranted. The Colonel sent his orderly for Corporal Minshall, of Company G. On his arrival, the Colonel said:

"Corporal, you will take ten men, sir, and go to the whisky-cabin on the banks of the Guyandotte, seize all the whisky you find, and pour it out."

"All right," said the Corporal; "your order will be obeyed forthwith."

The Corporal got his men together, and ordered them to string all the canteens they could find around their necks. On arriving at the cabin, they seized upon and "poured out" the whisky. After a thorough loading-up, the Corporal returned and reported at head-quarters.

"You poured it out, did you?" inquired the Colonel.

"Yes, sir," categorically replied the Corporal.

The Colonel noticed a canteen about the Corporal's neck, and thought he smelled something, and, looking him steadily in the face, repeated:

"You poured it out, sir, did you?"

"Yes, sir," emphatically replied the Corporal.

"And where did you pour it, sir?"

"In our canteens, Colonel," he replied.

For a moment his eyes flashed with anger; but, on second thought, the joke struck him as being too good, and the pleasant smile so characteristic of the Colonel wreathed his face in a moment.

"Well, Corporal," continued he, "I suppose that is some of the 'poured-out' in your canteen, eh?"

"Yes, sir," he replied, with the utmost *sang froid*, and, at the same time, gracefully disengaging the strap from his neck, said, "Won't you try some, Colonel?"

"I don't care if I do," said the Colonel; whereupon he imbibed, saying, as he lowered the vessel, "Not a bad article—not a bad article; but, Corporal, next time I send you to pour out whisky I will tell you *where* to pour it."

CHAPTER XXIV

War and Romance

During the late movement against Vicksburg the national transports were fired upon by a rebel battery at Skipwith Landing, not many miles from the mouth of the Yazoo. No sooner was the outrage reported at headquarters than the Admiral sent an expedition to remove the battery and destroy the place. The work of destruction was effectually done; not a structure which could shelter a rebel head was left standing in the region for several miles around.

Among other habitations destroyed was that of a Mrs. Harris, a widow lady, young, comely, and possessed of external attractions in the shape of a hundred and fifty "negroes," which she had contrived to save from the present operation of "the decree," by sending them up the Yazoo River. But Mrs. Harris was a rebel—intense, red-hot in her advocacy of Southern rights and her denunciation of Northern wrongs. Although she had not taken up arms against the Government, she was none the less subject to the indiscriminating swoop of the Proclamation; her niggers, according to that document, were free, and if the Confederacy failed, she could only get pay for them by establishing her loyalty in a court of justice. Her loyalty to the Yankee nation?—not she! She was spunky as a widow of thirty can be. She would see Old Abe, and every other Yankee, in the happy land of Canaan before she would acknowledge allegiance to the Washington Government. Nevertheless, being all she possessed of this world's valuables, she would like to save those niggers.

"Nothing easier," suggested Captain Edward W. Sutherland, of the United States steam-ram Queen of the West, who, attracted by her snapping black eyes, engaged in a friendly conversation with the lady after burning her house down. "Nothing easier in the world, madam."

"How so, Captain? You don't imagine I will take that odious oath, do you? I assure you I would not do it for every nigger in the South."

"But you need not take that oath, madam—at least not *the* oath."

"I do not understand you, Captain," said the widow, thoughtfully.

"I said you need not take the oath of allegiance; you can establish your loyalty without it—at least," with a respectful bow, "I can establish it for you."

"Indeed! How would you do it, Captain?"

"Simply enough. I am in the Government service; I command one of the boats of the Western navy—technically denominated a ram, madam—down here in the river. Of course, my loyalty is unimpeached, and, madam, I assure you it is unimpeachable. Now, if I could only say to the Government, those niggers are mine"——

The Captain waited a moment, to see what effect his speech was producing.

"Well!" said the widow, impatiently tapping with her well-shaped foot one of the smoking timbers of her late domicile.

"In short, my dear madam, you can save the niggers, save your conscientious scruples, and save me from a future life of misery, by becoming my wife!"

The Captain looked about wildly, as if he expected a sudden attack from guerrillas. The widow tapped the smoldering timber more violently for a few minutes, and then, turning her bright eyes full upon the Captain, said:

"I'll do it!"

The next arrival at Cairo from Vicksburg brought the intelligence that Captain Sutherland, of the ram Queen of the West, was married, a few days since, on board the gunboat Tylor, to Mrs. Harris, of Skipwith Landing. Several officers of the army and navy were present to witness the ceremony, which was performed by a Methodist clergyman, and Admiral Porter gave away the blushing bride. She is represented to be a woman of indomitable pluck, and, for the present, shares the life of her husband, on the ram Queen of the West.

Colonel Fred Jones

I was with him on his last trip from Cincinnati to Louisville, and from thence to the army. Little did I think it was the last meeting. Noble Fred! He has left a name that will never be erased from honor's scroll. A writer in the Cincinnati *Commercial*, who knew him from boyhood up, says:

"He is a native of this city, and favorably known as one of our most brilliant young men.

"Colonel Jones was a graduate of Woodward High School, of this city, receiving his diploma, with the highest honor of his class, in 1853. He then entered the law-office of Rufus King, Esq. as a student, and evinced, in the pursuit of a legal education, a remarkable zeal and talent. Two years ago he was elected Prosecuting-Attorney of the Police Court, which office he held at the breaking out of the war, in 1861. It was but a few days after the first call for troops, when he threw his business into the hands of a brother lawyer, and became a soldier. He was first an adjutant to General Bates, but, in June, 1861, he received a lieutenant-colonel's commission in the 31st Ohio, with which he went into active service. He was afterward transferred, with the same rank, to the 24th Ohio, of which regiment he became colonel in May last.

"He distinguished himself at the Battle of Shiloh, to which, indeed, he owed his promotion. He enjoyed the highest reputation with his superiors as an officer.

"Colonel Jones was about twenty-seven years of age, of fine appearance, with a peculiarly happy manner and disposition. He was a very fine *extempore* orator, and possessed great military ardor from childhood. The writer, a fellow-student, remembers him as captain of a company of school-boys, at Woodward, which, drilling for pastime, became very proficient in tactics.

"We can pay no more eloquent tribute to his memory than the mute impression his history will impart. He is dead! Our city has offered no heavier sacrifice in any of her sons, and parted with no purer of the jewels which have been so rudely torn from her."

Hanging in the Army

HEAD-QUARTERS 3D DIVISION, 14TH ARMY CORPS, MURFREESBORO, *June 6, 1863.*

William A. Selkirk, who resided in an adjoining county, murdered, in a most brutal manner, a man by the name of Adam Weaver. Selkirk was a member of a roving band of guerrillas. He entered, with others, the house of Weaver, who was known to have money, and demanded its surrender. Weaver, not complying, was seized, his ears cut off, his tongue torn out, and he was then stabbed. These facts being proved to the court, Selkirk was condemned to death.

At twelve o'clock, yesterday, the crowd commenced congregating at the Court-house, eyeing with curiosity a large, uncovered ambulance, in which was built a platform. The trap was a leaf, acting as a sort of tailboard to the wagon. This trap, or leaf, was supported by a strip of wood that ran into a notch, similar to the old figure-four trap. Attached to the ambulance were six splendid horses. At one o'clock two regiments of infantry, under Colonel

Stoughton, arrived upon the ground and formed in line. The ambulance and military then moved along to the jail; the rough wooden coffin was placed in the vehicle, and the prisoner then, for the first time, made his appearance. He had a pale and care-worn look, and a decidedly Southern air. His step was firm, and he got into the wagon with but little assistance. He was accompanied by Father Cony, chaplain of the 35th Indiana. The procession then moved off toward the gallows, erected a short distance from the town, upon the Woodbury pike. The eager crowd thronged the avenues leading to the place of execution—rushing, crushing, cursing and swearing, laughing and yelling. Samuel Lover, the Irish poet, describes, in his poem of "Shamus O'Brien," a hanging, thus:

> "And fasther and fasther the crowd gathered there,
> Boys, horses, and gingerbread, *just like a fair*;
> And whisky was sellin', and 'cosamuck' too,
> And old men and young women enjoying the view;
> And thousands were gathered there, if there was one,
> Waiting till such time as the hanging would come."

The morbid appetite depicted upon that sea of upturned faces was terrible to think of.

By the kindness of Colonel Stoughton, I was given a very prominent place in the procession.

General Order No. 123, from head-quarters, was read. The prisoner then knelt, and was baptized by the clergyman before mentioned. After the baptism was over, Rev. Mr. Patterson, of the 11th Michigan, made a most fervent and eloquent prayer, the prisoner on his knees, with eyes uplifted to heaven, and seemingly praying with all the fervor of his soul. After Mr. Patterson had finished praying, the prisoner was told he had five minutes to live, and to make any remarks he wished. Selkirk arose, with steady limbs, and said:

"Gentlemen and friends: I am not guilty of the murder of Adam Weaver; I did not kill him. I hope you will all live to one day find out who was the guilty man. I believe my Jesus is waiting to receive my poor soul. I am not guilty of Weaver's murder. I was there, but did not kill him."

He then knelt down and joined in prayer. After prayer was over, he stood up, and stepped on the scaffold again, to have the fatal rope placed around his neck. While the rope was being adjusted, he prayed audibly, and his last words on earth were:

"Sweet Jesus, take me to thyself. O, Lord, forgive me for all my sins;" and again, as the person who escorted him was tightening the rope, he said,

"For God's sake don't choke me before I am hung." Then, when the black cap was drawn over his eyes, he seemed to know that in a few seconds he would be consigned to "that bourne from whence no traveler returns," and said, "Lord, have mercy on my soul."

The words were scarcely uttered, when that which was, a few moments before, a stout, healthy man, was nothing but an inanimate form. As the "black cap" was about being put on him, Sarah Ann Weaver, the youngest daughter of the murdered man, Adam Weaver, made her appearance inside the square, and quite close to the scaffold. She asked Captain Goodwin and Major Wiles the privilege of adjusting the rope around his neck, but they would not grant it. She is a young woman of about seventeen years, rather prepossessing and intelligent looking. She stood there unmoved, while the body hung dangling between heaven and earth. She seemed to realize that the murderer of her father had now paid the penalty with his life. I asked her what she thought of the affair, and she curtly remarked: "He will never murder another man, I think." After the body had remained about fifteen minutes swinging in the air, and surgeon Dorr pronounced life extinct, it was cut down and put in a coffin. The assemblage departed, some laughing, some crying, and some thinking of the fate of the deceased.

General A. J. Smith vs. Rusty Guns

Last winter General Smith's head-quarters were on board the steamer Des Arc; he was in command of a division of Grant's army. One day, on a trip from Arkansas Post to Young's Point, there were on this boat three companies of a nameless regiment. Now it happened that these men had rather neglected to clean their guns, which the sharp eye of the old veteran soon discovered. It was in the morning of our third day out, the wind was blowing terribly, and the weather unusually cold, rendering it very unpleasant to remain long on the hurricane-roof, that the General came rushing into the cabin, where nearly all the officers were comfortably seated around a warm stove.

"Captain," exclaimed the General, in no very mild tone, addressing himself to the commander of one of the aforesaid companies, "have you had an inspection of arms this morning?"

"No, General," timidly replied the Captain, "I have not."

"Have you held an inspection of your company at any time since the battle of Arkansas Post, sir?" sharply asked the General.

"No, sir; the weather has been so unpleasant, and I thought I would let my men rest awhile," hesitatingly replied the Captain, already nervous, through fear, that something disagreeable was about to turn up.

"You thought you'd let them rest awhile? Indeed! The d——l you did! Who pays you, sir, for permitting your men to lay and rot in idleness, while such important duties remain unattended to? What kind of condition are your arms in, now, to defend this boat, or even the lives of your own men, in case we should be attacked by the enemy this moment? What the d——l are you in the service for, if you thus neglect your most important duty?" fairly yelled the old General. And then, starting menacingly toward the quaking captain, said he, imperatively:

"Mount, sir, on that roof, this moment, and call your men instantly into line, that I may examine their arms."

"And you," resumed he, turning to the lieutenants, who commanded the other companies, "are fully as delinquent as the captain. Sirs! I must see your men in line within ten minutes."

It is scarcely necessary to state that the officers in question made the best of their time in drumming up their men, whom they found scattered in all parts of the boat. Finally, however, the companies referred to were duly paraded on the "hurricane," and an abridged form of inspection was gone through with. The General, finding their arms in bad condition, very naturally inflicted some severe talk, threatening condign punishment in case such neglect should be repeated.

But during the time in which one of these companies was falling in, which operation was not executed with that degree of promptness, on the part of the rank and file, satisfactory to the lieutenant commanding, that officer called out, in a most imploring strain, "Fall in, gentlemen! Fall in, lively, gentlemen!" That application of the word "gentlemen" fell upon the ear of General Smith, who, turning quickly around, hastily inquired:

"Are you the lieutenant in command of that company, sir?" addressing the individual who had given the command in such a polite manner.

"Yes, sir," replied the trembling subaltern.

"Then, who the d——l are you calling gentlemen?" cried the General. "I am an old soldier," continued he, approaching and looking more earnestly at the lieutenant, "but I must confess, sir, that I never before heard of the rank of gentleman in the army. Soldiers, sir, are ALL supposed to be gentlemen, of course; but, hereafter, sir, when you address soldiers, remember to say soldiers, or men; let us have no more of this 'bowing and scraping' where it is your duty to command."

Then, turning upon his heel, his eyes snapping with impatience, the old gentleman gave vent to the following words:

"*Gentlemen! gentlemen, forsooth!* And *rusty guns! Umph!* The d——l! I like that! Rusty guns! and gentlemen!"

CHAPTER XXV

A Trip into the Enemy's Country

TRIUNE, TENNESSEE,
March 8, 1863.

After a four-days' trip, without tents, we are once more in camp. Last Tuesday afternoon General Steadman ordered Colonel Bishop, of the 2d Minnesota, to take his regiment, a section of the 4th Regular Battery, under Lieutenant Stevenson, and six hundred of Johnson's 1st East Tennessee Cavalry, and proceed forthwith to Harpeth River. Anticipating a fight, I went with the detachment. As we passed through Nolinsville and Triune the few butternut inhabitants gazed with apparent envy at our well-clad soldiers. About nine o'clock at night we reached the river. Here the infantry bivouacked for the night; the artillery planted their pieces in eligible positions, while the cavalry crossed the river and commenced to search for rebel gentry who were supposed to be on short leave of absence at their homes. Quite a number of *citizen* soldiers were thus picked up. Major Tracy, of the cavalry, then proceeded, with a dozen men, to the residence of General Starnes, and surrounded it, hoping to find the General at home. But the bird had flown the day previous. The Major, however, being a *searching* man, and full of inquiry, looked under the beds, and in the closets, and asked who was up-stairs. "No one," was the reply, "but my brother, and he has never been in the army." Major Tracy took a candle, went up, saw the young man, and asked where the man had gone who had been in bed with him. The young man protested no one had been there, and Mrs. Starnes pledged her word, on the *"honor of a Southern lady,"* that there was no one else in the house. But Tracy turned down the sheets, and, being a discerning man, discovered the imprint of another person in the bed, and, from the distance they had slept apart, he felt sure it was not a woman. So telling Mrs. S. he hadn't much faith in the honor of a Southern woman, under such circumstances, he thought he would take a peep through a dormer-window that projected from the roof; there, sure enough, sat Major Starnes, a son of the rebel general, in his shirt-tail, breeches and boots in hand, afraid to stir. It was a bitter cold night, and the poor fellow shook like an aspen leaf.

He presented at once a pitiable yet ludicrous aspect. After collecting some twenty or thirty horses, they returned to their head-quarters, this side of the river. At night, not relishing the thought of sleeping on a rail, I had the good fortune of sharing a bed with Lieutenant Stevenson, who commanded the battery.

As we anticipated, an early "*reveille of musketry*" awoke the party, and mounting my sorrel Rosenante, I proceeded to investigate "why we do these things," or to learn what the *quarrel is all about*. Crossing the river, I caught up with Major Tracy just as he was returning from his expedition to General Starnes's house. It was about eight o'clock as we came in sight of College Grove, a little village about a mile beyond Harpeth River. Here we turned toward Triune, and had left College Grove half a mile to the rear, when we heard the rebels firing upon a few stragglers of the Tennessee Cavalry. Major Tracy promptly countermarched his battalion, which was in the rear, and double-quicked back to the school-house at the town, and within a hundred yards of the rebel cavalry, who were drawn up in a line, in the front and rear of some houses, on the right of the road. The Major, seeing they outnumbered him two to one, halted, and sent word back to Major Burkhardt to reinforce. He then formed a line of battle across the road, awaiting the other battalion. Just as it arrived, Major Tracy thought he saw signs of wavering in the rebel line, and immediately ordered Squadron E to "Forward, by platoons! Double-quick! Charge!" and galloping to the front, along with Lieutenant Thurman, away they go. The rebels waver, break, and now comes the chase. The Major gains upon their rear, and brings rebel No. 1 to the dust, by the aid of a Smith & Wesson revolver. The Major, now wild with excitement, threw his cap in the air, and, hallooing for the boys to follow, continued the chase. The race was fully a three-mile heat, in which we captured fifty-nine rebels. Thirteen were *wounded by the saber*, four very severely. There were not more than fifteen or twenty of our men close on their rear at one time, and as the rebels turned out on the road-side to surrender, the Tennessee boys never stopped to make sure of them, but yelled to them to drop their guns and dismount, and if they stirred before they returned, they would murder them. After going as far as the few thought it safe, they returned to camp, bringing the prisoners, horses, and various implements of warfare, "sich" as fine English shotguns and the like.

This was certainly one of the most gallant affairs of the season, and may be considered among the most successful charges of the war; for, while not a man of ours was injured, fifty-nine rebels were taken, and I saw more saber cuts that day than any time since I have been with the army.

At noon, General Steadman arrived with the 35th and 9th Ohio, together with another section of battery, under Lieutenant Smith, commanding

Company I, 4th Regular Artillery, and the whole brigade moved at once across the river, and marched out in search of the enemy. We soon came upon their picket-fires, the pickets having skedaddled. We rested for the night at Riggs's Cross-roads, and continued the march in the morning. By nine o'clock we met the rebels, drawn up in line of battle, about a mile north of Chapel Hill. The Tennessee Cavalry were in the advance; General Steadman and staff occupied the crest of a hill, in full view of the rebels, and where we all could see the movements of the butternuts; the 9th Ohio arriving, was immediately deployed to the right, the 2d Minnesota and 35th Ohio and 87th Indiana to the left, the battery taking the center. The rebels, consisting of two thousand five hundred of Van Dorn's forces, ran helter skelter through Chapel Hill, and turned to the left—the Tennessee Cavalry again proving their valor by sabering half a dozen of the 7th Alabamians. The rebels, as they retreated across Spring Creek, formed a line, and gave us a brisk little brush; but our men steadily advanced, driving them back, and, crossing the creek, were in their late camp. We skirmished and drove them some three miles beyond the river, and found we were within one mile of Duck River, eleven miles within and beyond their line. Not knowing what forces might come to their aid, the General did not further pursue them; but, on returning, we destroyed their camp, setting fire to all the houses and large sheds they had been using for shelter. A church, among the rest, was destroyed, as it had been used by rebel officers for head-quarters. On the return, a great many colored men, women, and children begged to be allowed to come with us.

To-day, (the 8th,) Sabbath devotions were disturbed by General Steadman ordering the 35th Ohio and a section of battery, under Lieutenant Rodney, of the 4th Artillery, to feel the rebels at Harpeth; so again I thought I might catch an item, and went to the front. The impudent scamps had crossed, and were within four miles of our camp. The Tennessee Cavalry drove them back across the river. The rebels occupied a hill on the opposite side, adjoining the residence of Doctor Webb. After several little brushes by cavalry, our artillery opened upon the line formed by two thousand six hundred rebels, under Patterson and Roddy, of Van Dorn's division, who were supported by two regiments of infantry. They stood but two rounds from the Napoleons, before moving off in disorder. Our line advanced, when, much to our astonishment, the rebels opened up a battery from in front of Doctor Webb's house, which was sharply replied to by Lieutenant Rodney, who sent his compliments to the "gay and festive cusses," inclosed in a twelve-pounder, and directed to Doctor Webb's house; it was safely *delivered*, as we saw it *enter the house*. Again their four-pounder belched forth, and one of their shots fell directly in front of the 35th Ohio ambulance, but luckily it did not burst. After holding our position four hours, and driving the rebels back to their dens, we returned to camp.

Colonel Moody and the 74th Ohio

In the fight at Murfreesboro, General Rosecrans said the 74th Ohio behaved nobly. After General McCook's right had been turned, the whole rebel force came against General Negley's division, to which this regiment belongs. After the 37th Indiana had retired, it being terribly cut up, the 74th was ordered to take its place amid such a shower of shot and shell as has scarcely fallen during the war.

This regiment did not leave its position until an order came from Colonel Miller, commanding the brigade; then, slowly and stubbornly, it came from that well-fought field, leaving many of its members, "who never shall fight again," dead upon it. On the Friday following that bloody Wednesday, they were "in at the death," in the triumphant charge of our left. Its commander, Colonel Moody, is "the fighting Parson" of the Cumberland Army. Calmly and steadily he led his men into the seven-times heated furnace of battle, and,

"As the battle din,
Came rolling in,

his voice of cheer and encouragement was heard above its roar. Just before they came into the whizzing storm, he said: "Say your prayers, my boys, and give them your bullets as fast as you can." A conspicuous mark, he was struck by balls in three places, and his horse shot from under him; but he took no notice of the hits. Once, during the thickest of the fight, he rode along the line, and was cheered by his men even in the roar of battle.

Side by side with Colonel Moody rode, during both battles, the gallant Major Bell, the new field-officer of this regiment. Ohio's 74th is justly proud that she has the experience of a gray-headed Colonel united with the "dash" of a young Major. This regiment has won for itself a place among the "crack" regiments of our army; and General Rosecrans told it to-day that he would have to call it "the fighting regiment."

Colonel Moody on the Battle-field

The Ohio *Statesman*, speaking of Colonel Moody at the late battle at Murfreesboro, has the following:

"Colonel Moody has been so long accustomed to 'charge home' upon the rebellious 'hosts of sin,' from the pulpit, that he finds himself in no uncongenial position in charging bayonet upon the rebellious hosts of Davis and the Devil upon the battle-field. And, as in the former position he ever acquitted himself right valiantly, so, in this latter position, he is equally heroic and unconquerable.

"His escape from death in the late fight was so wonderful as to seem clearly Providential. His friends and members of his church in Cincinnati had presented him with a pair of handsome revolvers. One of these he wore in the breast of his coat during the fight. A partially-spent Minié-ball had struck him on the breast, pierced his coat, and, striking the butt of his pistol, splintered it to pieces directly over his heart, *but went no further*. The stroke was so violent as to hurl him from his horse by the concussion, and he lay, for a moment, insensible. Consciousness soon returned, and, mounting his horse, he raged on through the battle like an enraged lion. He won the most hearty congratulations from General Rosecrans himself. So much for having one's life saved by a *bosom* friend."

CHAPTER XXVI

A Wedding in the Army,

And, as it is from the pen of the worthy Chaplain, J. H. Lozier, it is perfectly reliable.

About as pleasant and romantic a wedding as anybody ever saw, lately took place in this department. Immediately after the battle, a soldier of the 15th Indiana took sick, from exposure in the fight, and was taken to Hospital No. 5. Among the attendants there was a pretty little "Yankee girl," whose charms occasioned an affliction of the heart which baffled the skill of all the doctors, and they were compelled to call for the services of the chaplain.

There are obstructions in "the course of true love," even in Tennessee, and one of these was the difficulty of procuring "the papers," as there was no clerk's office in the county, or, at least, no clerk to attend to the office. Again were the resources of the General commanding brought into requisition, and again did he prove himself "equal to the emergency." The following document, authorized by General Rosecrans, dictated by General Garfield, and promulgated by Major Wiles, shows how men get licenses to marry in those counties in this department where martial law alone exists:

State of Tennessee,
Rutherford County. *Greeting:*

To any person empowered by law to perform marriage in Tennessee:

You are hereby authorized to join together in marriage Joseph A. Hamilton and Francillia L. Bean, and this shall be your authority for so doing.

Witness my hand and official seal of the Provost-Marshal-General, Department of the Cumberland.

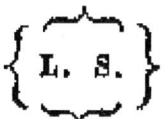

State of Tennessee,
Rutherford County.

WILLIAM M. WILES,
Major 44th Indiana, and Provost-Marshal-General,
Department of the Cumberland.

Be it remembered that, on this 12th day of May, A. D. 1863, personally appeared before me, Major William M. Wiles, Provost-Marshal-General, Department of the Cumberland, one W. T. Mendenhall, Assistant Surgeon of Hospital No. 5, of lawful age, who, being duly sworn, on oath says that he is acquainted with Joseph A. Hamilton and Francillia L. Bean; that said parties are of legal age to marry, without the consent of their parents or guardians, and that he knows of no lawful reason why said parties should not marry.

[Signed]   W.   T.   MENDENHALL.
Subscribed and sworn to this 12th day of May, A. D. 1863.

WILLIAM M. WILES,
Major and Provost-Marshal-General, Department of
the Cumberland.

Now, therefore, I, William M. Wiles, Major of 44th Indiana Volunteers, and Provost-Marshal-General, Department of the Cumberland, in consideration of the fact that this county has been placed under military law, and civil courts and laws, with their officers, are not in existence, do empower John Hogarth Lozier, a regularly ordained minister of the Methodist Episcopal Church, and Chaplain of the 37th Regiment of Indiana Volunteers, to join in *Holy Matrimony* the above-named parties, and this shall be his full and proper authority for so doing.

Given this 12th day of May, A. D., 1863. Witness my hand and seal, the day and year above mentioned,

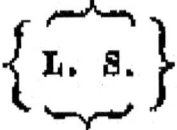

W. M. WILES,
Major and Provost-Marshal-General, Department of
the Cumberland.

Accordingly the happy pair, together with a large concourse of officers and soldiers, and a delightful sprinkling of pretty Northern belles, met on the battle-field, in a grove on the banks of Stone River, on the precise spot where the bridegroom, with his regiment, the noble 15th Indiana, fought on the memorable 31st of December. A large, flat rock stood up prominently, and upon this the bride and groom, with their attendants, and the chaplain, took their position, while an eager throng gathered around to witness the interesting ceremony. After announcing the "license," as above given, the chaplain asked the usual questions as to "objections." There was a moment's silence, in which, if any man had dared to object, he would have done so at the peril of an immediate "plunging bath" in Stone River, for the boys were determined to see the ceremony completed. The chaplain then proceeded, in solemn and impressive tones, to perform the ceremony, at the conclusion of which they dropped upon their knees, and a solemn invocation being uttered, they arose, and having pronounced them husband and wife, he introduced them to the audience. Then followed a rare scene of unrestrained social enjoyment. The mingling of shoulder-straps with plain "high-privates," and of "stars" with "stripes," was truly refreshing. We observed three Major-Generals, McCook, Crittenden, and Johnson, besides any amount of "lesser lights," among the crowd.

I see, by a late Chattanooga *Rebel*, that the editor of that "delectable sheet" is in grief because he has been told that Miss Fannie Jorden, who resides near our camp, is about to marry Captain Kirk, of General Steadman's staff. The *Rebel* says: "We are sorry to hear that the niece of the gallant Colonel Rayne has so far forgotten herself as to engage to marry one of the 'Lincoln horde.'"

We have had the pleasure of meeting Miss Fannie upon several occasions. She is a very nice young lady, and is not aware of any such engagement. Captain Kirk is pretty good-looking; but, we rather guess he is not on the right side of Jorden this time. If the young lady marries, 'tis more likely she will emigrate to Minnesota than Ohio. We sincerely hope our neighbor of the *Rebel* will not have cause to "come to grief." He had better mind his own business, and let the soldiers here attend to the "Union" unmolested.

A strange family feud, quite "Corsican" in its character, came to light some time ago, while we were at Cunningham's Ford.

There were two families, Bently by name, residing there. These brothers had not spoken to each other for forty years. They nor their families have had any intercourse whatever; never recognizing each other, though they had resided side by side, farms adjoining. One could not go to church, or meeting of any kind, or to town, without passing his brother. While we were there, the elder brother died, and he was buried by his children. The other family knew nothing of it, until told by our soldiers. The cause of the estrangement was, that, in dividing the land left them, more than forty years ago, one claimed the line was drawn some ten feet too far south, thus losing to the other about six acres of ground, the value, at that time, being about twenty-five cents per acre. This feud is now an inheritance, we suppose, to be handed down forever. Can't you send out a missionary?

Those who can afford it are now enjoying in camp all the luxuries of the season. I received an invitation to dine out yesterday. The following bill of fare was partaken of in a beautiful arbor:

BILL OF FARE.

Mock Turtle Soup.

Turkey.	*Roast Beef.*
Ham and Eggs.	*Roast Mutton, with Currant Jelly.*
Radishes.	*Lettuce.Onions and Potatoes.*
Custard.	*Lemon Pies.Pound Cake. Jellies.*

The whole concluding with elegant "Mint Juleps," with straws in them.

In the 1st Brigade, under Colonel Connell, each company has a large brick cooking-range erected, and their system is really worthy of emulation. This entire division is supplied with fine fresh bread every day. The division baker has three Cincinnati bake-ovens, from which he turns out from three to five hundred loaves a day, besides pies innumerable. It is under the foremanship of Mr. John Wakely, a well-known Cincinnati baker. This arrangement is a great saving to the Government in the way of transportation, etc.

I heard a first-rate story, which, although it did not occur in this division, is too good to lose. A private soldier, named Cupp, who is a German, belonging to the 1st Missouri Cavalry, and now one of the body-guard of General Granger, was out to the front a few days ago, and seeing a "stray rebel," "made for him." The chase commenced—away went Mr. Reb and Cupp. Having the fleetest horse, Cupp gained upon him rapidly, crying, "Halt! halt! halt!" every leap his horse would make. But the rebel, bent on getting away, heeded not the call. At length the Dutchman reached his rear, and, swinging his saber heavily over his head, charged the rebel, and brought him to a *"dead stand."*

"Ah ha!" said the now excited Cupp, "how you vass all de viles? D——n you, anoder time I hollers halt I speck you stop a leetle, unt not try to fool mit me so long, you d——d rebel."

Dishonest Female Reb

A rebel sympathizer and his wife, a cross-eyed specimen of the *genus homo*, came within our lines and delivered themselves up, to be where they could get something to eat. Captain Parshall, of the 35th Ohio, being Provost-Marshal of Triune, and supposing them honest refugees, endeavored to secure comfortable quarters for the woman at the house of Dr. Williams. Dr. Williams is a stanch Union man, and willing to do all in his power for suffering humanity. The Doctor told the Captain that the lady was welcome, but that his wife was away from home.

Captain Parshall had kindly provided quarters for the husband who, as he was about going, gazed cautiously around, and eyed the Doctor from head to foot, then looked at the woman with an "affectionate" stare, and, with a long-drawn sigh, exclaimed:

"Well, Doctor, I guess I'll risk her with you."

In about an hour the Captain was startled with the sudden appearance of Doctor Williams, much excited, who begged that he would have that woman taken away, right off, as she was a thief.

The Captain went over immediately, and interrogated the woman, but she stoutly denied the charge. The Captain, however, noticed a very heavy bust where a bust shouldn't be with so hatchet-faced a woman, and asked her what she had in her bosom.

She replied, that was common with her "every grass;" but the Captain "couldn't see it," and indelicately placed his masculine fingers within the sacred precincts, and drew forth two children's dresses, one from each side; finding she was fairly caught, she begged for mercy; said she didn't know what "possessed her," and declared that was all she had. The Captain told her he would have to hang her if she didn't deliver up every thing. She became frightened, and then commenced the peeling of petticoats, shawls, chemises, pillow-slips, etc., much to the amusement and contempt of all honest people.

Suffice it to say, the woman, with her husband, was sent back to Dixie, to feed upon corn-bread and water, as the Union people of this neighborhood didn't wish to be contaminated by such trash.

The Doctor's wife has since returned. She told me the story, and declares she won't leave the Doctor to keep house any more, as she won't trust him alone.

To the Thirteenth Ohio

by Martha M. Thomas.

Our Fathers House is threatened, boys!
The Union, grand and free,
Has warmed an adder in its heart
That saps its great roof-tree.
We've sworn to hold it pure, boys—
A first love's holy shrine;
A home for all the homeless, boys,
For "auld lang syne."

Its foemen are our brothers, boys;
But still we must not falter;
Though dear to us those who offend,
They must die by lead or halter.
Our Father's House is ours in trust,
From Washington's own line;
The Union knows no Pleiad lost
For "auld lang syne."

The rafters of the old house, boys,
Must never know pollution;
Its cement was our father's blood,
Its roof the Constitution;
And though, like prodigals astray,
Its sons eat husks with swine,
And feel the rod, we'll kill the calf,
For "auld lang syne."

Then let the bugle sound, my boys
And forward to the strife;
We'll thrash our rebel brothers well,
E'en though it cost our life.
And when we've whipped them into grace
And made each dim star shine,
We'll open wide our Father's door,
For "auld lang syne."

CHAPTER XXVII

The Oath

BY THOMAS BUCHANAN READ.

HAMLET—Swear on my sword.
GHOST (below)—*Swear!*—[*Shakspeare.*

Ye freemen, how long will ye stifle
The vengeance that justice inspires?
With treason how long will you trifle,
And shame the proud name of your sires?
Out, out with the sword and the rifle,
In defense of your homes and your fires.
The flag of the old Revolution
Swear firmly to serve and uphold,
That no treasonous breath of pollution
Shall tarnish one star on its fold.
Swear!
And hark, the deep voices replying
From graves where your fathers are lying,
"Swear, O, swear!"

In this moment who hesitates, barters
The rights which his forefathers won,
He forfeits all claim to the charters
Transmitted from sire to son.
Kneel, kneel at the graves of our martyrs,
And swear on your sword and your gun:
Lay up your great oath on an altar
As huge and as strong as Stonehenge,
And then with sword, fire, and halter,
Sweep down to the field of revenge.
Swear!
And hark, the deep voices replying

From graves where your fathers are lying,
"Swear, O, swear!"

By the tombs of your sires and brothers,
The host which the traitors have slain;
By the tears of your sisters and mothers,
In secret concealing their pain
The grief which the heroine smothers,
Consuming the heart and the brain
By the sigh of the penniless widow,
By the sob of her orphans' despair,
Where they sit in their sorrowful shadow,
Kneel, kneel, every freeman, and swear;
Swear!
And hark, the deep voices replying
From graves where your fathers are lying,
"Swear, O, swear!"

On mounds which are wet with the weeping
Where a nation has bowed to the sod,
Where the noblest of martyrs are sleeping,
Let the winds bear your vengeance abroad,
And your firm oaths be held in the keeping
Of your patriot hearts and your God.
Over Ellsworth, for whom the first tear rose,
While to Baker and Lyon you look;
By Winthrop, a star among heroes,
By the blood of our murdered McCook,
Swear!
And hark, the deep voices replying
From graves where your fathers are lying,
"Swear, O, swear!"

A Conservative Darkey's Opinion of Yankees

There was a large Union meeting in Nashville, and an old house-servant of one of the most aristocratic rebel families, who hates "Lincolnites" and "poor white trash" as heartily as Jeff Davis does, was walking slowly along the square as the grand procession was forming. Soldiers were moving about in great numbers, the cavalry galloping to and fro, regiments were forming to the sound of lively music, citizens and visitors thronged the sidewalks, children ran about with banners, and thousands of flags fluttered like fragments of rainbows, from the various buildings. The conservative contraband paced slowly along, rolling his distended eyes in all directions, apparently overwhelmed by the exhibition and bustle around him. Approaching our friend, he exclaimed:

"My God! what are we Southern folks coming to? Massa said, a year ago, dat de Yankees done gone away forever. Now dey is swarmin' about thicker dan locusses. Dey runs dere boats on our ribber; dey is pressin' all our niggers; dey lib in our houses; dey drivin' our wagons, and ringin' our bells; dey 'fisticatin' our property; dey eatin' up our meat and corn; dey done killed up mose all of our men; and, 'fore God, I spec dey are gwine to marry all our widders!"

And, heaving a deep groan from the bottom of his continental waistcoat, he shook his head in sadness, and passed slowly onward, to the joyful chimes of the church-bells and the soul-stirring strains of "Yankee Doodle."

Visit to the Graves of Ohio and Indiana Boys

Traversing the field of battle, near Murfreesboro, a few days after the rebel defeat, I could but contrast, in my mind, the terrible quiet with the terrific din and roar of battle of which it was the late scene.

The *debris* of battle is strewn for miles and miles. Thousands upon thousands of cannon-balls and shell lie upon the field. The woods present the appearance of having been visited by a tornado, and here and there a pool of blood marks the place where some devoted hero has rendered up his life.

The heavy cedar wood is nearly three miles from Murfreesboro, to the right of the pike, going south. The rocks bear evidence of the struggle, for thousands of bullet and shell traces may be seen. The smaller branches of trees are cut as if a severe hail-storm had visited the spot. Let us dismount and read the names of those soldiers who fell here. They have been given a soldier's funeral. Ah! the names here denote this as a part of the gallant Rousseau's division; for on rough pieces of board we read: W. McCartin, Hamilton, Ohio, Company F, 3d Ohio; F. Burley, Hamilton; John Motram, Company I, Cardington, Ohio; H. K. Bennett, Company A, 3d Ohio; M. Neer, Company D, 3d Ohio. And close beside, a brother Indiana soldier sleeps—Joseph Guest, 42d Indiana.

Just across the pike, on the left going south, is the grave of A. Hardy, 6th Ohio; and opposite this is the spot where Lieutenant Foster, of the noble 6th, yielded up his life, and was buried. Close by is a log house, perforated with shot and shell. Here some of our wounded sought shelter during the storm of iron hail, but were mercilessly driven out by the shot poured into their intended refuge. To the left of this house are numerous graves. Among them, Francis Kiggins, Company K, H. Borrien, Company H, W. Keller, Company H, all of the 24th Ohio; Alf Goodman, 58th Indiana; Noah Miller, 58th Indiana; E. D. Tuttles, Company B, C. McElvain, Company A, Levi Colwright, James Wright, C. A. McDowell, Company K; J. B. Naylor, H. Lockmeyer, A. B. Endicott, Company A; J. Cunningham, E. Skito, J. Reavis, H. Cure, Company D, all of the 58th Indiana.

Near this the 26th Ohio lost John Tagg, John Karn, F. Singer, and Charles Bartholomew; Mark E. Rakes, of the 88th Indiana, and George Kumler and William Ogg, of the 93d Ohio, are buried here, together with John Van Waggoner and Lieutenant Black, of the 58th Indiana. And still further to the left, along the Chattanooga Railroad, are the remains of Elias M. Scott, 82d Indiana; near this, but across the road, on the skirt of a wood, are Sergeants Potter and Puttenry, of the 24th Ohio, Henry Allen, of the 65th Ohio, and Frank Nitty, of the 58th Indiana. Continuing our course to the left, just crossing a dirt-road leading toward Murfreesboro, upon a little knoll, are the ruins of a once handsome mansion. Behind an upright Southern timber-fence, just back of the still-standing negro-quarters, there is a beautiful cluster of prairie-roses in full leaf. The waving branches, as they bend to the right, cover the graves of three Cincinnati boys, two of whom I knew intimately. Go ask their comrades, and they will bear willing evidence to the chivalrous bearing of the two noble youths, Ally Rockenfield and little Dave Medary. Beside them is the grave of W. S. Shaw, whom I did not know personally. I am told he died while bravely doing his whole duty. The branches of the same friendly rose-bush, bending to the left, cover the graves of Captain Weller, Lieutenant Harmon, and Major Terry; all of the 24th Ohio, forming a beautiful emblem of the unity of those two splendid regiments, the 6th and 24th. Continuing still further to the left, we cross Stone River, where our forces did such good fighting under Crittenden. Just after crossing this stream, upon the first knoll, beneath a large oak, are the remains of Sergeant Jacob McGillen, of Hamilton. He belonged to the 69th Ohio. An incident in regard to this noble youth was told me by a gentleman who knew him well. When that noble man, William Beckett, of Hamilton, was doing all in his power to assist in raising the 69th Regiment, a number of the "*Southern Rights*" sympathizers tried to dissuade McGillen from joining—bidding him to hold off until substitutes were called for, and then, if he would go, they would buy him. He, however, spurned their base offers, and enlisted; and, when crossing the river amid the leaden hail, he received a bullet in his arm; he hastily tied up the wound, and, though weakened from loss of blood, rejoined his command, and the second ball piercing his breast, he fell. Nearly opposite his resting place lies Captain Chandler, of the 19th Illinois.

I have been told, by those high in command, that more *individual prowess* was manifested upon this battle-field than any during the war. There were more hand-to-hand encounters, more desperate fighting—men selling their lives as dearly as possible. As to their General, there is but one acclamation: General Rosecrans has endeared himself to the whole army; they love him as a child should love its father; and all are satisfied that, had it not been for the surprise upon the right, and Johnson's defeat, the battle would have ended with the total annihilation of the Southern army.

Nashville Convalescents—A Death in the Hospital

On my way back to Nashville I called at the different hospitals, and saw quite a number of the wounded. The surgeons were doing all they could toward sending them home. Doctor Ames and Doctor Stevens, of the 6th Ohio, in fact, all the surgeons seemed assiduous in their attentions to the wounded. As a matter of course, many thought they were neglected; but there were so many to be attended to.

I met Major Frank Cahill. He told me he had six thousand convalescents under his charge at Nashville.

General Mitchell was kept very busy, although but few passes were given to any going South; but Lieutenant Osgood, his chief business man, was up night and day, ready, at all times, to expedite those going in search of the wounded Union soldiers. Lieutenant Osgood certainly did more business in one day than many men, who are called fast, could do in a week. To know that he did his duty, I will state that Secessionists hated him, and Union men spoke in high terms of him.

A young lad, who had been sick for a long time, died; his name was William Stokes, and his home was near Dayton, Ohio. The boy had been honorably discharged, but there were no blanks, and *red tape* forbids a surgeon, no matter how high his position, to grant the final discharge without the blank forms. For five weeks this poor home-sick boy, only eighteen years of age, worried along, continually speaking of his mother and home; but the inexorable law kept him there to die.

Henry Lovie Captured

At Bowling Green I met Henry Lovie, the artist; he had been grossly abused by a party of a dozen butternuts, at a little town called "Cromwell," (what's in a name?) They accused him of being a nigger-thief—a d——d

Abolitionist, and were sworn to hang him. His servant, however, happened to have his free papers, and Lovie, exhibiting to them passes from McClellan, Rosecrans, and other "high old names," they were disposed to cave a little. "Our traveling artist" for Frank Leslie took a horse for self and one for servant, riding twenty-eight miles, fearing the butternuts might receive reinforcements, and reached Bowling Green by early dawn, through mud, slush, snow, and rain. Lovie wants to enlist a company to go and take "Cromwell," and requested me to see Tom Jones & Co. in regard to the matter.

CHAPTER XXVIII

CAMP NEAR TRIUNE, TENNESSEE,
April 24, 1862.

I arrived in camp day before yesterday, and immediately reported for duty.

Last night General Schofield took command of this division, General Steadman having been assigned to the Second Brigade. General Schofield comes to us with the highest recommendations for gallant daring, and his appearance among the boys was the signal for a neat ovation. He was serenaded by a crowd of singers, and, upon the conclusion of a patriotic song, he came to the front of his head-quarters and made a telling speech, which was enthusiastically received by his command. General Steadman being called for responded, regretting to part with his old command, but rejoicing that he had been superseded by a gentleman and a soldier so worthy of the position that had been assigned him. General Steadman assured the General that he had as fine a set of soldiers as were to be found in the Army of the Cumberland; men who had been tried and never found wanting; men whom he assured General Schofield would go wherever ordered, and against any foe. After the adjournment of the public demonstration, the two generals, with their staffs, were handsomely entertained by Captain Roper, where song, sentiment, and recitation were the order of the evening—Colonel George, Colonel Vandeveer, Colonel Long, and other notables being among the guests.

While thus enjoying ourselves, the General received a telegraphic dispatch from head-quarters, announcing the capture of McMinnville by our forces.

The command of the Third Division, we feel confident, is in vigilant hands. Brigadier-General Schofield has heretofore proved his efficiency in Missouri. His staff consists of Major J. A. Campbell, A. A. S.; W. M. Wherry, Aid-de-camp; A. H. Engle, Aid-de-camp and Judge Advocate; Captain Kirk, Quarter-master; Captain Roper, Commissary; Captain Budd, Inspector of Division, and Doctor Gordon, Medical Director.

The East Tennessee Cavalry still continue to prove their gallantry. I spent a pleasant afternoon with them yesterday, and paid a visit to their hospital. I saw six of the noble fellows who were wounded in a late fight. About ten days ago, Colonel Brownlow, a regular "chip of the old block," took a part of the regiment out some twelve miles from camp, toward Duck River, and, coming upon a large party of secesh, gave them a "taste of his quality." A short time after, the Colonel, with nine of his men, became detached from the main body, and found themselves completely surrounded by the rebels, and were within thirty yards of the foe, who ordered the Colonel to surrender. A moment's parley with his men, and the Colonel, with the boys, rode toward the rebels, and, with a few adjectives, quite *unparliamentary* to ears polite, much to their surprise, dashed through their line. This audacity saved them; for, before they had time to recover from their surprise, Brownlow and his men were beyond their reach. I was told, by one of the prisoners, that, at one time, twenty rebels were firing at that "little cuss in the blue jacket," as they called the Colonel, during the day's performance. Several splendid charges were made by these Tennesseeans.

James Mysinger, of Company I, from Green County, after being mortally wounded—the noble fellow—fired three shots. The Colonel dismounted to assist the dying soldier, who, with tears in his eyes, said:

"Colonel, I've only one regret—that I am not spared to kill more of those wretched traitors. Tell me, Colonel," continued he, "have I not always obeyed orders?"

"Yes, Mysinger, you are a noble fellow, and have always done your duty," said the Colonel, patting him on the cheek, and brushing the cold sweat from his brow.

"Now, Colonel," said he, "I am ready to die."

Oliver Miller, Company C, received a severe wound in the arm. He is only seventeen years of age. John Harris received three balls. Robert Adair was wounded in the head. William Riddle was completely *riddled*, receiving one ball and four buck-shot. David Berry had his thigh broken, jumping from his horse. Berry's father was murdered by rebels at Cumberland Gap. His head was placed upon a block and cut off, by order of Colonel Brazzleton, of the 1st East Tennessee rebel cavalry. Nearly all these men have not only their country's wrongs to avenge, but the wrongs heaped upon their fathers, mothers, and sisters. I spent an hour in conversation with these wounded men, and all were laughing and talking in the best of spirits. Such men are invincible.

A brother of Colonel Brownlow, who is now on a visit to this camp, informs me that he had it from the most reliable source, that the rebels in and around Knoxville were actually suffering for food. An order was issued by the rebel commander at Knoxville, a few days since, to seize all the hams, sides, and bacon belonging to private parties, leaving only fifty pounds for each family. A Mrs. Tillery, of Knox County, residing twelve miles from Knoxville, when her house was visited for the purpose of being pillaged, in the fulfillment of this order, expostulated with the lieutenant in command. She told him that fifty pounds would not keep her family two weeks, and she had no way of obtaining more. Notwithstanding her entreaties, the rebel lieutenant ordered fifty pounds to be weighed and given to her. He had scarcely given the order when Mrs. Tillery drew a pistol and shot the lieutenant through the heart. The rebel detail left the meat, and took off the corpse of their commander. The spirit of discontent is manifesting itself in various ways among even the most ultra rebels. They are getting tired of seeing their country devastated by the two armies, and are anxious for a settlement; and it only awaits the *daring of a few* to inaugurate a "rebellion within a rebellion," which, if once started, will spread like wild-fire.

Picket Duty and its Dangers

Of all the duties of a soldier, outpost duty is the most trying and dangerous. Courage, caution, patience, sleepless vigilance, and iron nerve are essential to its due performance. Upon the picket-guards of an army rests an immense responsibility. They are the eyes and ears of the encamped or embattled host. Hence, if they are negligent or faithless, the thousands dependent upon their zeal and watchfulness for safety, might almost as well be blind and deaf. The bravest army, under such circumstances, is liable, like a strong man in his sleep, to be pounced upon and discomfited by an inferior foe. For this reason the laws of war declare that the punishment of a soldier found sleeping on his post shall be death.

But although the peril and responsibility involved in picket duty are so great, the heroes who are selected for it rarely receive honorable mention in our military bulletins. Their collisions with the enemy are "skirmishes." The proportion of killed and wounded in these collisions may be double or triple what it was at Magenta or Solferino, but still they are mere "affairs of outposts." "Our pickets were driven in," or "The enemy's pickets were put to flight," and that is the end of it. Presently comes the news of a brilliant

Union victory; and nobody pauses to consider that if our pickets had been asleep, or faithless, or cowardly, a Union *defeat* might, nay *must*, have been the consequence.

We forget what these men endure—their risks, their privations, their fatigues, their anxieties, *their battles with themselves*, when sleep—more insidious than even the lurking enemy in the bush—tugs at their heavy eyelids, and their overwearied senses are barely held to their allegiance by the strongest mental effort. The soldier who rushes to the charge at the command of his officer is animated by the shouts of his comrades, inspirited by the sounds of martial music, and full of the ardor and confidence which the consciousness of being intelligently led and loyally supported engenders. He sees his adversaries; he fights in an open field; his fate is to be decided by the ordinary chances of honorable war. Not so the picket-guard. He is surrounded by unseen dangers. The gleam of his bayonet may, at any moment, draw upon him the fire of some prowling assassin. If he hears a rustling among the leaves, and inquires, "Who goes there?" the answer may be a ball in his heart.

A Gallant Deed and a Chivalrous Return

In the recent movement of Stoneman's Cavalry, the advance was led by Lieutenant Paine, of the 1st Maine Cavalry. Being separated, by a considerable distance, from the main body, he encountered, unexpectedly, a superior force of rebel cavalry, and his whole party were taken prisoners. They were hurried off as rapidly as possible to get them out of the way of our advancing force, and, in crossing a rapid and deep stream, Lieutenant Henry, commanding the rebel force, was swept off his horse. As none of his men seemed to think or care any thing about saving him, his prisoner, Lieutenant Paine, leaped off his horse, seized the drowning man by the collar, swam ashore with him, and saved his life, thus literally capturing the captor. Paine was sent to Richmond with the rest of the prisoners, and the facts being made known to General Fitz-Hugh Lee, he wrote a statement of them to General Winder, Provost-Marshal of Richmond, who ordered the instant release of Lieutenant Paine, without even parole, promise, or condition, and, we presume, with the compliments of the Confederacy. He arrived in Washington on Saturday last. This act of generosity, as well as justice, must command our highest admiration. There is some hope for men who can behave in such a manner.

But the strangest part of the story is yet to come. Lieutenant Paine, on arriving in Washington, learned that the officer whose life he had thus gallantly saved had since been taken prisoner by our forces, and had just been confined in the Old Capitol prison. The last we heard of Paine he was on his way to General Martindale's head-quarters to obtain a pass to visit his imprisoned benefactor. Such are the vicissitudes of war. We could not help thinking, when we heard this story, of the profound observation of Mrs. Gamp: "Sich is life, vich likevays is the hend of hall things hearthly." We leave it to casuists to determine whether, when these two gallant soldiers meet on the battle-field, they should fight like enemies or embrace like Christians. For our part, we do not believe their swords will be any the less sharp, nor their zeal any the less determined, for this hap-hazard exchange of soldierly courtesy.

CHAPTER XXIX

An Incident at Holly Springs, Miss.—The Raid of Van Dorn

The amount of public and private property captured and destroyed by the enemy is estimated at something over six millions of dollars. He had considerable skirmishing with our troops, whose effective force Colonel R. C. Murphy, commandant of the post, says was less than three hundred. The Confederates lost ten or twelve in killed and wounded, and we six or seven wounded, none fatally. Colonel Murphy says he received information from Grant too late to make the necessary arrangements for the defense of the place. Though there were less than three hundred effective Union soldiers in town, all the civilians, tradesmen, speculators, and promiscuous hangers-on to the army were captured, swelling the number who gave their parole to about fifteen hundred. The raid, as you may imagine, delighted the residents of Holly Springs, who turned out *en masse* to welcome their brief-lingering "deliverers," and were very active in pointing out the places where Northerners were boarding. Not a few of the precious citizens fired at our troops from the windows, and acted as contemptibly and dastardly as possible. The women, who had been rarely visible before, made their appearance, radiant, and supplied the rebel Yahoos with all manner of refreshments. "Good Union men," who had sold their cotton to the Yankees, shook the Treasury-notes in the faces of the Union prisoners, saying they had been paid for their property, and had the pleasure of burning it before the "d——d Abolition scoundrels' eyes."

Cincinnati Cotton-Dealers in Trouble

A number of cotton-buyers were robbed of whatever money they had on their persons, and some of them are said to have lost from five to ten thousand dollars apiece, which is, probably, an exaggerated statement. W. W. Cones, of Cincinnati, saved a large sum by an ingenious trick. He had twenty-eight thousand dollars on his person when the enemy entered the place, and immediately throwing off his citizen's garb, he attired himself in the cast-off gauntlets of a private soldier, entered the Magnolia House, employed as a hospital, and, throwing himself upon a bed, assumed to be exceedingly and helplessly sick, while the foe remained. As soon as the rebels had departed, he became suddenly and vigorously healthy, and walked into the street to denounce the traitors. He declared his eleven hours' sickness caused him less pain, and saved him more money than any illness he ever before endured. D. W. Fairchild, also of the Queen City, in addition to losing fifty bales of cotton, was robbed of his pocket-book, containing forty-five dollars, in the following manner: When captured, he was taken before General Jackson, popularly known as "Billy Jackson," considered a high representative of chivalry and soldiership in this benighted quarter of the globe. Jackson inquired of Fairchild, in a rough way, if he had any money with him? To which the party addressed answered, he had a trifling sum, barely sufficient to pay his expenses to the North. "Hand it over, you d——d nigger thief," roared the high-toned general, who, as soon as the porte-monnaie was produced, seized it, thrust it into his pocket, and rode off with a self-satisfied chuckle. What a noble specimen of chivalry is this Jackson! He has many kindred spirits in the South, where vulgar ruffians are apotheosized, who would, at an earlier time, have been sent to the pillory. "Sixteen-string Jack," and all that delectable fraternity, whose lives bloom so fragrantly in the pages of the saffron-hued literature of the day, would have spat in the faces of such fellows as Jackson, had they dared to claim the acquaintance of persons so much their superiors.

When the rebels were playing the part of incendiaries in town, they set fire to the building containing a great quantity of our ammunition, shells, etc. The consequence was a tremendous explosion, which broke half the windows, and many of the frames, in town, rattled down ceilings, unsettled foundations, and spread general dismay. Women and children screamed, and rushed like maniacs into the streets, and fell fainting with terror there. For several hours the shells continued to burst, and, I have heard, two or three children were killed with fragments of the projectiles. Two days after, I saw families suffering from hysterics on account of excessive fright, and several seemed to have become quite crazed therefrom.

Troubles of a Reporter

One morning, hearing that John Morgan was at Elizabethtown, Ky., I determined to go as near as possible, and find out the condition of things, and see the fight that was in expectancy. Proceeding as far as I could by rail, I hired a carriage and horses, hoping to reach Munfordville in time for a big item.

I had proceeded some five miles when a party of eight men, whom I at once determined were guerrillas, rode hastily to the carriage, and demanded my credentials. I exhibited a free pass over the Ohio and Mississippi

Railroad, four Provost-Marshal's passes, a permission to leave the State of Ohio, also one to leave Kentucky, and a ten-cent Nashville bill. I was afraid to show them my letter from General Starbuck, of the *Daily Times*.

After looking at them awhile, they were passed round to the balance of the fiendish-looking rascals, and I was kept in terrible suspense ten minutes longer.

I tried to get off several of my well-authenticated bad jokes, but I choked in the utterance, and my smile was no doubt a sardonic grin. I wiped the perspiration from my brow so frequently that one of the most intellectual of the "brutes" relieved the monotony of the occasion by observing that it was a very hot day, to which I acquiesced, feeling quite glad to have a guerrilla speak to a prisoner.

The countryman who had driven me thus far was speechless. He thought of his carriage and horses, and visions of their being immediately possessed by Morgan or Forrest had rendered him powerless. After a few questions as to where we left the train, and as to the number of passengers on board, the citizen cavalry, or Union guards, as they proved to be, told us we might proceed, that we were all right, but to be very careful, as Forrest was reported near that region; they hardly thought it safe to attempt to get to Green River.

This brewed fresh trouble to me, the owner of the horses and carriage refusing positively to proceed on the journey. In vain I expostulated, telling him I would pay for his horses out of the *sinking fund* of the *Times* office, in case of their loss. It was no go, and I was compelled to retreat. I felt very much like building some fortifications in the woods, and making a stand, but, remembering the saying, "Discretion is the better part of valor," retreated, and fell back upon the National Hotel, in Louisville, with all the luxuries prepared by Charley Metcalf, Major Harrow, and Colonel Myers.

CHAPTER XXX

A Reporter's Idea of Mules

Junius Browne, describing a mule and his antics, says: "Now, be it known, I never had any faith in, though possessed of abundant commiseration for, a mule. I always sympathized with Sterne in his sentimental reverie over a dead ass, but for a living one, I could never elevate my feeling of pity either into love or admiration. The mule in question, however, seemed to be possessed of gentle and kindly qualifications. He appeared to have reached that degree of culture that disarms viciousness and softens stubbornness into tractability. I believed the sober-looking animal devoid of tricks peculiar to his kind, such as attempting to run up dead walls in cities, and climb trees in the country, mistaking himself for a perpetual motion, and trying to kick Time through the front window of Eternity. I was deceived in the docile-looking brute. He secured me as his rider by false pretenses. He won my confidence, and betrayed it shamefully. That he was a good mule, in some respects, I'll willingly testify; but in others, he was deeply depraved. He exhibited a disposition undreamed of by me, unknown before in the brothers and sisters of his numerous family. In brief, he was a sectarian mule; a bigot that held narrow views on the subject of religion; believed Hebrew the vernacular of the devil, and regarded the Passover with malevolent eyes. Confound such a creature, there was no hope for him! Who could expect to free him from his prejudices? He hated Moses for his fate, and Rebekkah for her forms of worship. He was insane on Judaism. He was a monomaniacal Gentile. Who could make out a mental diagnosis, or anticipate the conduct of a mule afflicted with religious lunacy? Well for your correspondent had he discovered beforehand the bias of the brute, or suspected he was a quadruped zealot! Much might have been saved to him, and more to a number of unoffending gentlemen from church, as the sequel of my 'o'er true tale' will prove.

"The train got off about eight o'clock, on a cloudy, rainy, muddy, suicidal morning, and the material that composed it was worthy of illustration by Cruikshank. The procession was singularly varied, and supremely bizarre. There were the army-wagons, with sick and wounded soldiers, lumbering heavily along; the paroled prisoners wading through the mire; cotton-buyers, on foot and on horseback; members of the twelve tribes of Israel, with all possible modes of conveyance—in broken buggies, in dilapidated coaches, on bare-boned Rosinantes, on superannuated oxen, with fragmentary reins, rope reins, and no reins; spurring, swearing, hallooing, and gesticulating toward Memphis, in mortal terror lest the rebels would capture them again, and some of their hard-earned gains. Pauvre Juils! They would have excited the pity of a pawnbroker, if he had not known them, so frightened and anxious and disconsolate they looked. They could not have appeared more miserable if they had just learned that a brass watch they had sold for silver had turned out gold. The mule trotted along briskly and quietly enough until he beheld the grotesque vision of the heterogeneously-mounted Israelites. Then he displayed most extraordinary conduct. He pawed, he hawed, he kicked, all the while glancing at the sons of Jerusalem, and braying louder and more discordant every moment. I could not understand the mule's idiosyncrasies. Possibly, I thought, the doctrine of the metempsychosis may be true, and this brute, in the early stages of its development, once have been in love. He has a fit on him now, I fancied—he is once more possessed of a petticoat. Why not? If love converts men into asses, why should not asses, in their maddest moments, act like men in love? The mule's ire was culminating. I dug my spurs into his side. Vain effort! He was bent on mischief, and malignant against the persecuted race. If he had been in the House of Commons, (and many of his brethren are there,) I know he never would have voted for the admission of Jews into the English Parliament. Before I could anticipate his movement, he rushed at several pedestrian Hebrews and kicked the wind out of their stomachs and three pairs of green spectacles from their noses. While endeavoring to recover their glasses, the mule knocked their hats off with his hoofs, and impaired the perfect semicircle of their proboscis, thus imitating the rebels—by destroying their bridges totally. The infuriated brute then ran for an old buggy, and, by supreme perseverance, kicked it over, and its two Hebrew occupants, into the road, where they fell, head-foremost, into the mire, growling profanely, like tigers that have learned German imperfectly, and were trying to swear, in choice Teutonic, about the peculiar qualities of Limburger cheese. In their sudden subversion, the Israelites dropped three fine watches out of their pockets, and the mule, with an unprecedented voracity, and determined on having a good time, ate the chronometers without any apparent detriment to digestion. The owners of the watches were frenzied. They glanced at my beast, and were about to devour him, hoping thereby to get the timepieces back. They did not violate the third commandment. They could not. They were too mad. They merely hissed rage, like a boiling tea-kettle, and grew purple in the face, and spun round in the road, from the excess of their wrath. Your correspondent was alarmed. He feared the mule would devour the Hebrews themselves, and he knew, if that were done, the animal would explode, and said animal had not been paid for. No time was given for reflection. Off ran the mule again, and made a pedal attack on a small Hebrew with a huge nasal organ, seated on top of a decayed coach, drawn by a horse, a cow, and three negroes. The quadruped made a herculean effort to kick the diminutive Shylock from his seat, but all in vain. The altitude was too great, and, in the midst of his exertions, he kicked himself off his feet, and fell over into a gulley, in which he alighted and stood on his head, as if he had been trained in a circus. The position was admirable, and so worthy of imitation that I stood on my head also, in two feet of mire, and beckoned with my boots for some passing pedestrians to come and pull me out, as they would a radish from a kitchen-garden. The mule resumed his normal position speedily, and went off in his well-sustained character of a Jew-hunter. I was less fortunate. Three teamsters drew my boots from my feet, and tears from my eyes, before they could extricate me. And when I was removed from *terra firma*, I resembled a hickory stump dragged out by the roots, or a large catfish that had left his native element, and, seized with a fit of science, had endeavored to convert himself into a screw of the Artesian well. Placed feet downward on the ground again, I could not thank my deliverers or swear at the mule. I was dumb with astonishment and the mud, having swallowed eighteen ounces avoirdupois weight of the sacred soil of Mississippi while endeavoring to express my admiration of the performance of the mule. When I had removed the mire from my optics, in which cotton-seed would have grown freely, I beheld the mule in the dim distance. I could not see the brute plainly, but I could determine his course by the frequent falling of a human figure along the road. I knew the figures were those of his enemies, the much-abused Hebrews—that he was still wreaking his vengeance on the representatives of Israel—that he was fulfilling the unfortunate destiny of a misguided and merciless mule. Strange animal! Had the honest tradesman ever sold his grandfather a bogus watch? or inveigled his innocent sire into the mysterious precincts of a mock-auction? Alas! history does not record, and intuition will not reveal.

"My narrative is over. I did not go to Memphis. I returned, limping, to town, mentally ejaculating, like many adventurous gentlemen who, before me, have recklessly attempted to ride the peculiar beast, 'D——n a mule, any how!'"

Letters from Kentucky

Early in September, 1862, I was sent by General Starbuck & Co., proprietors of the Cincinnati *Daily Times*, to reconnoiter in Kentucky. My first stop was a very pleasant one—at the Galt House, Louisville. From that place I wrote incident after incident concerning the most inhuman barbarity that had been enacted by citizen guerrillas and butternut soldiers. Louisville was in a foment of excitement, and if the rebels had only possessed the dash, there was scarce a day but they could have made a foray upon the "Galt," and captured from forty to fifty nice-looking officers, from brigadier-generals down to lieutenants.

It was supposed the Government could spare them; else why were they in the North, when they should have been in the South?

While there, I met Lieutenant Thomas S. Pennington, of Columbus, Ohio, a gentleman of intelligence, who told me HE SAW CITIZENS OF RICHMOND (Kentucky) who had pretended to be FRIENDLY WITH OUR MEN, SHOOT THEM DOWN AS THEY WERE RETREATING THROUGH THEIR STREETS. G. W. Baker, the regimental blacksmith of the 71st Indiana, who resides in Terre Haute, was in the city in charge of a number of horses left in Richmond. As our boys, worn-out and unarmed, retreated through the place, Mr. Baker says the men fired from their windows and doors. J. C. Haton, of Point Commerce, Indiana, also corroborates this fiendish piece of work upon the very men who had for days stood guard over their private property. All agree that more of our men were killed by these incarnate fiends in citizens' clothing than by the secesh in uniforms. Many of the pretended friendly citizens went out (says Lieutenant Pennington) to aid us, and then treacherously picked off our officers. Colonel Topkins, of the 71st Indiana, died nobly, leading his men, who, although undisciplined, stood bravely by their gallant colonel while there was a shadow of hope. Twice was his horse shot beneath him; and mounting the third horse, he received two bullets. A number of his boys hastily gathered around him. His last words were: "Boys, did I do my duty?" With tears coursing their manly cheeks, they replied: "You did, Colonel." "Then," said he, "I die happy." Major Concklin, of the 71st, whom I reported wounded, died shortly afterward. Coming from Shelbyville, I passed more than one hundred wagons, all heavily loaded with the wreck of the late battles, many of the wounded being brought to this city.

Chaplain Gaddis and the 2d Ohio

Charley Bunker, in writing from the 2d Ohio, says: "This is the Sabbath, which, under present circumstances, can only be known by the neat appearance of the boys, in their shiny boots and clean, boiled shirts, as they make their early morning entrée for company inspection of arms and accouterments, after which, all is dullness and vacuity. There is a sensible void, apparent to all, requiring something to remove the depressing dullness now surrounding them; and that something is to be found only in the presence of an accommodating and pleasing chaplain. Being to-day in the camp of the 2d Ohio Regiment, I observed this lack of a clerical adviser, in the absence of Brother M. P. Gaddis, the pleasing and affable chaplain of this gallant band of patriots. Brother Gaddis, being naturally of a pleasing and accommodating disposition, has won the confidence and favor of his entire command, and is an ever-welcome guest wherever he may chance to offer his presence. But one instance can be recorded wherein the parson has met with refusal of friendship and favor—and this can be credited to nothing but the present distracted condition of our unfortunate country. But, even in this instance, the kind and accommodating nature of the chaplain was fully manifested; forgetting all party or political prejudices, he viewed all the circumstances with a happy mind and Christian heart. The following are the circumstances of the above-mentioned case: On the first advance of the national army from Louisville toward the land of Dixie, a portion of our forces marched along the turnpike, passing in their route the time-noted tavern-stand, distant some twenty miles north of Bowling Green, and known to all travelers as "Ball's Tavern." On the evening of the arrival of the forces under the immediate command of General Mitchel, at this place, one of the buildings attached to the premises accidently caught fire."

Chaplain Gaddis Turns Fireman

The 2d Ohio Regiment being encamped near the premises, and observing the flames bursting from the roof of the building, Brother Gaddis, with a number of others, instantly made their way to the building to save the entire property from destruction. Entering the building, they made their way to the top of the house, where the fire was then raging, and commenced tearing away the wood-work near the devouring element. No water being convenient, they were obliged to resort to the snow as a substitute, which, at that time, covered the ground, to subdue the flames. Having partially succeeded in checking the raging of the fire, a small aperture was made in the roof of the building, and Dave Thomas, the sutler of the 2d Ohio, being the smallest one of the party, was thrust through the hole in the roof, and made a desperate onslaught upon the fire, while Brother Gaddis continued to hand up the snow in hats and caps to the daring firemen on the roof, until the fire was entirely extinguished. The following day Brother Gaddis, knowing the former reputation of the tavern, and, as is natural with all clerical exponents, preferring *fried chicken to hog meat*, and warm rolls to hard crackers, wended his way to the tavern, with a craving appetite, and the full expectation of a kind welcome and an agreeable entertainment.

Before proceeding further, I must here state that, attached to these premises, is a noted subterranean recess, which has ever been the attraction of all travelers who have chanced to pass over this frequented thoroughfare, and is known as the "Diamond Cave."

Gaddis and the Secesh Grass-Widow

Entering the dwelling, Brother Gaddis sought the landlady, Mrs. Proctor, or the late widow Bell, but now the wife of a Proctor, who, by-the-by, is at present to be found in the ranks of the rebel army, the madam's entire sympathies leading in the same direction. Addressing the landlady in his usual winning manner, Brother Gaddis requested the privilege of remaining as a guest of the house, and enjoying the luxuries of her well-stored larder and the comforts of her well-furnished rooms. What was the surprise of the chaplain to find in the landlady a real she-devil in politics, and utterly inexorable to all appeals to her charity and hospitality. In her remarks, she observed that "He was on the wrong side of the fence; that she had entertained, the day before the arrival of the Union troops, a company of three hundred gentlemen, (referring to that number of rebel cavalry,) and that they had treated her like a lady, and paid her for what they had received"—(in *Confederate scrip*). In reply, Brother Gaddis, not wishing to be deprived of her coveted entertainment, inquired "What was the difference which side of the fence he was on, so that he conducted himself with propriety, and paid her for her trouble?" asking if his money was not as good as that of those of whom she spoke. She answered, "No!" and positively refused to entertain any of the "hated Yankees" in her house.

"Turchin's Got Your Mule"

A planter came to camp one day,
His niggers for to find;
His mules had also gone astray,
And stock of every kind.
The planter tried to get them back,
And thus was made a fool,
For every one he met in camp
Cried, "Mister, here's your mule."
Chorus.—Go back, go back, go back, old scamp,
And don't be made a fool;
Your niggers they are all in camp,
And Turchin's got your mule.

His corn and horses all were gone
Within a day or two.

Again he went to Colonel Long,
To see what he could do.
"I can not change what I have done,
And won't be made a fool,"
Was all the answer he could get,
The owner of the mule.
Chorus.—Go back, go back, go back, old scamp,
And don't be made a fool;
Your niggers they are all in camp,
And Turchin's got your mule.

And thus from place to place we go,
The song is e'er the same;
'Tis not as once it used to be,
For Morgan's lost his name.
He went up North, and there he stays,
With stricken face, the fool;
In Cincinnati now he cries,
"My kingdom for a mule."
Chorus.—Go back, go back, etc.

CHAPTER XXXI

A Visit to the 1st East Tennessee Cavalry

The cavalry had been kept very busy during the months of March and April; the picket-duty was arduous and severe, but the East Tennessee soldiers stood up to the rack manfully. I had been with them on nearly all their expeditions; shared their toils and dangers, until I felt I was a part and parcel of their "institution." Colonel Johnson, at this time, was in Nashville, raising a brigade; the command of the regiment, therefore, devolved upon Colonel Brownlow.

The Colonel had frequently invited me over to the camp, but other engagements had as frequently deterred me from accepting the invitation.

I was seated, one beautiful afternoon, in the tent of Doctor Charles Wright, of the 35th Ohio, conversing with Colonel Brownlow, when Major Tracy, of the Tennessee regiment, with two or three others, agreed that "now was the appointed time." A horse was proffered me by John Leiter, Esq., and I proceeded forthwith to the head-quarters of the renowned East Tennesseeans. Arriving there, the Major requested that I would entertain the boys, who, as well as they knew me personally, did not know me *facially*— did not know the "power of facial expression."

Major Tracy ordered the assembly-call sounded, which was done, and, in a short time, five or six hundred men were congregated in front of head-quarters, and as those in the rear could not have a good view of the speaker, the Major ordered the front rank to kneel, or squat. The boys had been told that Alf was going to give them some "fun;" that Alf was to amuse them for awhile.

During the congregating of the crowd, I was in the tent—the audience in waiting. Major T. went to the front and announced that the Rev. Ebenezer Slabsides, from Middle Tennessee, would address the congregation. A table was placed, and I had taken a "*posish*," with spectacles mounted on my nose, when, just as I had commenced the discourse, by saying: "My Beloved Brethering," I heard a strange voice say:

"We didn't come to hear no sermon—we come to hear Alf. Put that fellow out!"

Another voice said: "That's a burlesque on our parson."

Still I went on, thinking all would be quiet. Presently a big, tall E. T. C. fellow shouted "Move him, move him!" and shouts of "Alf! where's Alf?" resounded all over. Here I tried to divest myself of my spectacles, but they stuck, and before I could identify myself to the crowd as to who I was, I received a *knock-down* argument.

I changed my base of operations, and retreated to the Major's tent. Here two stalwart fellows laid violent hands upon me, and each one getting hold, tried to pull me *through the tent-pole*. Seeing a fine opportunity for a strategical maneuver, I succeeded in planting a heavy blow on the proboscis of one of my tormentors, which bedizzened his vision. Again I changed my base, and got to another tent. By this time the camp was wild; a few, who knew me, were taking my part; blows fell thick and fast, but I succeeded in guarding my head. I had no relish for cavalry on the brain just then. During the melée they robbed me of a watch and about fifteen dollars in money. *"But they can't do it again! Hallelujah!"*

The news of my *defeat* spread like wild-fire over the camp before tatoo; the entire division were talking of it, and serious consequences were feared; the cavalry soldiers did not dare show themselves near the 2d Minnesota for several days, I being quite a favorite with those boys, and that being my home for the time. The most exaggerated stories were told of the affair.

In a few days all was quiet on the Harpeth, and again I was with the boys, who all made the most ample apologies, and expressed sorrow for what had occurred.

Colonel Brownlow called upon me the next day, in condolence, renewing the invitation, but the remembrance of my former reception deterred me from making the journey. Some weeks after the occurrence, I was commissioned by the proprietors of the Cincinnati *Commercial* to proceed to Murfreesboro as their "Special," and telegraphed to General Garfield for the requisite permission. Judge of my surprise upon receiving the following dispatch from General Garfield:

HEAD-QUARTERS ARMY OF THE CUMBERLAND, Murfreesboro, *May 10, 1863.*

Alf Burnett — *Sir:* The commanding General has heard of the occurrence at Triune, and refuses you permission to come to Murfreesboro.

J. A. GARFIELD,
Brigadier-General and Chief of Staff.

I immediately dispatched a batch of letters from prominent Generals; also sent forward several fine introductory letters that I held, addressed to General Rosecrans and General Garfield. A regular diplomatic correspondence was opened, and, after hearing the evidence, I received a telegram to this effect:

Alf Burnett—Report forthwith at these Head-quarters.

J. A. GARFIELD.

By order of Major-General Rosecrans.

I arrived at Murfreesboro the following day, but did not "*report*," for I felt somewhat chagrined at the General's crediting the stories that he had heard. The succeeding day, however, I met General Alex McCook, and his brother, the gallant Colonel Dan McCook, who told me that the General wanted to see me immediately; that the greatest anxiety was felt at head-quarters for my appearance; that I had been the subject of conversation for an hour past. I immediately dismounted and walked into the house, presenting my card to an orderly, and, in a moment, General Garfield came to the door with a cordial welcome and a hearty laugh, took me by the hand and introduced the "Preacher from Hepsidam" to Major-General Rosecrans. When this was done, another outburst of laughter was the result.

Major-General Turchin, Major-General Thomas, and the staffs of those heroes were present. General Garfield and "Old Rosey" formed the party whom I was apprised were a court-martial now duly convened to try the "Preacher from Hepsidam." General R. asking me if I was ready for trial, I told him I was, if he had a pair of spectacles in the "court" room. So he called the court to order, sent for a few of his staff, who were absent, and requested General Garfield to get me a pair of spectacles from an adjoining room. General Rosecrans took advantage of General Garfield's absence to tell me that General Garfield had once been a "Hard-shell" Baptist preacher, and requested me, if I could, by any possibility, "bring him in," to do so. The sermon was given, and, afterward, the "Debate between Slabsides and Garrotte," together with other pieces. At the conclusion of the "trial," the court unanimously resolved that I should not only be honorably acquitted of all charges, but that I was henceforth to be allowed the freedom of the Army of the Cumberland. "And," said the General, "in explanation of my dispatch to you, refusing you permission to come here, some one told me you were giving a mock-religious sermon which so disgusted the religious sensibilities of the E. T. C. that they mobbed you; and I thought if you could do any thing to shock their feelings, you must be a devil with '*four horns;*' but, with such a face as you make, no wonder they were deceived."

Old Stonnicker Drummed Out of Camp

The illustration of this scene will be recognized by thousands of our soldier-boys who were occupiers of Virginia soil, upon the banks of the Elkwater, for some months during the summer and fall of 1861. Old Stonnicker's was a name familiar as a household word, and many were the pranks played upon the poor old man. Ignorant, beyond description, he yet had twice been a "justice" of the peace, and, as he said, "sot on the bench."

OLD STONNICKER DRUMMED OUT OF CAMP.

The scene illustrated is where Stonnicker was arrested by a "special order" from the 6th Ohio, and tried by an impromptu court-martial, for selling liquor to soldiers. The mock-trial took place amid the most grotesque queries and absurd improvised telegraph dispatches—the hand-writing of the telegraphic dispatches being sworn to as that of the individuals from whom they were just received, the oath being, "As they solemnly *hoped for the success of the Southern Confederacy.*" The poor wretch had actually been detected in selling, contrary to express orders, liquor to soldiers. He employed counsel, but, notwithstanding all they could do, he was sentenced, by Major Christopher, to die. He received his sentence with moanings and anguish; he was too frightened to notice the smiles or laughter of the crowd. He got on his knees and begged for mercy, and, after an hour of suspense, the Court relented, and commuted the sentence to being drummed out of camp. It is at this juncture the artist has seized the occasion to illustrate the scene.

Stonnicker is a by-word to all the boys of Elkwater notoriety to this day, and was, at one time, "*a password*" at Louisville.

Poor Stonnicker is dead. In trying, last fall, to ford that mad torrent, Elkwater, during a storm, he was swept from his horse and drowned.

Andy Hall, Ned Shoemaker, Doctor Ames, and other notables of the "times that tried men's *soles*," were the recipients of the hospitality of another of the family of Stonnickers, who lived up a "ravine" about a mile nearer Huttonsville. Doctor Ames had musk upon his handkerchief, which the young lady, (?) Miss Delilah Stonnicker, noticing, as she waited upon the Doctor at the supper-table, exclaimed: "'Lor', Doctor, how your *hankercher* stinks!"

"Does it?" said the Doctor, coloring up to his very eyes, roars of laughter proceeding from all present.

"Yaas; it stinks just like a skunk."

"Why, Miss Delilah, do you have skunks out here?" inquired the Doctor.

"Yaas, lots on 'em up the gut out thar."

Now and Then

Written by Enos B. Reed,

and Recited by Mr. Alf Burnett, at the Benefit of the Ladies' Soldiers' Aid Society of Cincinnati, Saturday Evening, January 31st, 1863.

In other days, as it has oft been told
By those who sleep beneath the grave's dank mold,
In this, our loved, but now distracted land,
Men dwelt together as a household band;
Brothers they were, but not alone in name,
Sons of Columbia and Columbia's fame—
They loved the land, the fairest 'neath the sun,
Home of the brave—the land of Washington!

Peaceful the rivers as they flowed along
The plenteous fields, where swelled the harvest song;
Peaceful the mountains, as they reared on high
Their snow-capped peaks unto the azure sky—
Peaceful the valleys, where contentment smiled,
Blessing alike the parent and the child—
Peaceful the hearts which owned a country blest,
And owned their God, who gave them peace and rest!

The happy matron and the joyous maid
Alike were blest—the unknown traveler stayed
His weary limbs beneath their roof-tree's shade,
While home from toil the husbandman returned,

His honest hands the honest pittance earned,
Willing to share his humble meal with one
Whether from Winter's snows or Southern sun.

No North—no South, in those the better days—
Our starry flag o'er all—its genial rays
Glistened amid New England's dreary snows,
Or shone as proudly where the south wind blows:
One flag, one nation, and one God we claimed,
And traitors' lips had never yet defamed
The land for which our fathers fought and bled—
Hallowed by graves of honored patriot-dead!

Fruitful the earth, and fair the skies above;
The days were blissful, and the nights were love;
We were at peace—our land and freedom gained—
Our fair escutcheon with no blot e'er stained—
But all did honor to the fair young State
Who made herself both glorious and great;
Our Eagle—emblem of the happy free—
Was free to soar o'er foreign land or sea!

But darkness came, and settled like a pall
Funereal, on our hearts; o'er one and all
It cast its blighting, withering wing,
A horrid, shapeless, and revolting thing—
While dove-eyed Peace bowed down its gentle head
And wept for those, though living, worse than dead;
And blood, like rivers, flowed from hill to plain
'Till land and sea knew not their ghastly slain.

The Northern snows incarnadined with gore—
The Southern vales with blood, like wine, ran o'er—
The battle raging in the morning sun,
At night, the warfare scarcely yet begun—
The sire, in arms to meet his foeman-son,
Brother, to seek his brother in the strife,
Rushed madly on—demanding life for life!
And children, orphans made—and worse than widowed,
wife!

And this the land which erst our fathers blest,
Favored of Heaven—the pilgrim's hope of rest—
Now cursed by traitors, who with impious hands
Have dared to sunder our once-hallowed bands—
Have dared to poison with their ven'mous breath
All that was fair—and raise the flag of death;
Have dared to blight the country of their birth,
Striving her name to banish from the earth!

God of our fathers! where your lightnings now,
To blind their vision, and their hearts to bow?
Traitors to all that manhood holds most dear,
Without remorse, with neither hope nor fear,
They trail our starry banner in the dust,
And flaunt their own base emblem in the gust;
Like the arch-fiend, who from a Heaven once fell,
They'd pull us down to their own fearful hell!

A boon! O God! a boon from thee we crave—
Shine on this gloomy darkness of the grave;
Stretch forth thine arm, and let the waves be still,
And Union triumph, as it must and will.
God of our Fathers! guide our arms aright,
Be near and with us in the deadly fight;
Columbia's banner may we still uphold,
And keep each star bright in its azure fold.

We mourn for those who sleep beneath the wave,
Or on the land have found a soldier's grave;
Each heart will be an altar to their fame,
And ever sacred kept each glorious name.
We'll honor those who nobly fought and bled,
And fighting fell, where freedom's banner led;
Each soldier-son, we'll welcome to our arms,
When strife has ceased its din and dread alarms!

Our soldiers, home returning from the wars,
Our dames shall nourish—honored scars
Shall mark them heroes, and they live to tell

How once they battled—battled brave and well—
For home and country—mountain, plain, and dell—
And how the nation like a phenix rose
From out its ashes, spite of fiendish foes;
Then once again Columbia shall be blest—
Home of the free, and land for the oppressed!

CHAPTER XXXII

An Incident of the 5th O. V. I

There is no regiment in the service that has won more enviable renown than the glorious old 5th; and, although I have met them but twice in my peregrinations, I can not let them go unnoticed in this volume. Many of the boys I knew intimately—none better than young Jacobs, who was killed near Fredericksburg, Virginia. A writer in the Cincinnati *Commercial*, soon after his death, penned the following merited tribute to his memory:

Noble deeds have been recorded, during the past two years, of the faithful in our armies, who have struggled amid carnage and blood to consecrate anew our altar of liberty—deeds which have stirred the slumbering fires of patriotism in ten thousand hearts, and revived the nation's hope. I can well conceive that it would be asking too much to record every merited deed of our brave officers and men; but, while too many have strayed from the ranks when their strong arms have been most needed, will you allow a passing tribute to the memory of one who was always at his post of duty?

Henry G. Jacobs, a private in Company C, 5th Regiment O. V. I., who was killed in battle near Fredericksburg, Virginia, was the second son of E. Jacobs, Esq., of Walnut Hills. He enlisted in May, 1861, and had, consequently, been in the service two years. Since his regiment left Camp Dennison, he had never been absent from it a day until he fought his last battle. I need not speak of his deeds of personal bravery, for he belonged to a regiment of heroes. For unflinching courage on the field of battle, the 5th Ohio has few parallels and no superior. In that respect, the history of one is the history of all. In the battle of Winchester, Henry escaped with two ball-holes in his coat. In the battle of Port Republic, only one (a young man from Cincinnati) besides himself, of all his company who were in the action, escaped capture. They reached the mountains after being fired at several times, and, two days after, they arrived at their camp. At the battle of Cedar Mountain the stock of his gun was shattered in his hands by a rebel shot. He was in the battles of Antietam and South Mountain, and in over twenty considerable skirmishes.

Last autumn, his sister wrote, urging him to ask for a furlough and visit home, if but for a few days. His answer was: "Our country needs every man at his post, and my place is here with my regiment till this rebellion is put down." No young man could be more devotedly attached to his home, yet he wrote, last winter: "I have never asked for a furlough since I have been in the service; but, if you think father's life is in danger from the surgical operation which is to be performed upon his arm, I will try to get home; for you do not know how deeply I share with you all in this affliction."

His talents and education fitted him for what his friends considered a higher position than the one he occupied. Accordingly, application was made to the Governor to commission him as a lieutenant in one of the new regiments. In signing the application, Professor D. H. Allen, of Lane Seminary, prefaced his signature as follows: "I know no young man in the ranks who, in my opinion, is better qualified for an officer in the army than Henry C. Jacobs." In this opinion W. S. Scarborough, Esq., Colonel A. E. Jones, and many others who were personally acquainted with him, heartily concurred. Such encouragement was received from the Governor as led his sister to write, congratulating him upon the prospect of his appointment. His answer was: "I had rather be a private in the 5th Ohio than captain in any new regiment. In fact, I do not want a commission. When I enlisted, it was not for pay; I never expected to receive one dollar. I have fought in many battles, and served my country to the best of my ability; and I wish to remain in the position I now occupy till the war is over."

It is not only to offer a tribute to the memory of Henry that I would intrude upon your readers, but, by presenting an example, encourage faithfulness and patriotic devotion to the cause of liberty. If any man, officer or private, has been more faithful, his be the higher monument in a grateful nation's heart when treason is no more. He shouldered his musket, and it was at his country's service every hour till it was laid down beside his bleeding, mangled body, on the banks of the Rappahannock. If my country ever forgets such heroes as these, her very name should perish forever. Young men whose hearts are not stirred within them to rush into the breach, avenge the fallen brave, and save their country, are making for themselves no enviable future. Who that calls himself a man will sit with folded arms and careless mien, under the shade of the tree of liberty, while the wild boar is whetting his tusks against its bark, and the gaunt stag rudely tears its branches? It was planted in tears and watered with blood; and if you do not protect it now, your names will perish.

Henry had made two firm resolves: one was to keep out of the hospital, and the other was to keep out of the hands of the rebels. He would not be taken a prisoner, and, if die he must, he preferred the battle-field to the hospital. He has realized his wish, and though the bitterness of our anguish at his loss may only wear out with our lives, our country, in his death, has lost more than his kindred. We are making history for all time to come. Eternity will tell its own story of unending joy for those who have freely shed their blood to lay a firm foundation for the happiness of millions yet unborn.

> "Give me the death of those
> Who for their country die;
> And O! be mine like their repose,
> When cold and low they lie!

> "Their loveliest Mother Earth
> Entwines the fallen brave;
> In her sweet lap who gave them birth
> They find their tranquil grave."

How to Avoid the Draft

During the troubles of raising men, a rough-looking customer, determined upon evasion, called upon the Military Commission, when the following colloquy ensued, the individual in question remarking:

"Mr. Commissioner, I'm over forty-five."

"How old *are* you?"

"I don't know how old I am; but I'm over *forty-five*."

"In what year did you make your appearance on this mundane sphere?"

"I don't know what you mean; but I'm over forty-five."

"When were you born?"

"I don't know; but I'm over forty-five."

"How am I to know you are over age?"

"I don't know and I don't care; but I'm over forty-five."

"When were you forty-five?"

"I don't know; but I know I'm over forty-five."

"You must give me some proof that you are over age."

"I've been in the country thirty-six years, and I'm over forty-five."

"That does not prove that you are too old to be drafted."

"I don't care; I know I'm over forty-five."

"I shall not erase your name until you prove your age."

"I tell you I've been in this country thirty-six years, and I went sparking before I came here, and I'm over forty-five."

"Will you swear it?"

"Yes, I'm over forty-five. D——d if I aint over forty-five."

"Well, I will exempt you."

"I don't care whether you do or not, for *I've got a wooden leg.*"

New Use of Blood-hounds

One fine summer's Sunday afternoon, as a steamboat was stopping at a landing on the Mississippi to take in wood, the passengers were surprised to see two or three young, athletic negroes perched upon a tree like monkeys, and about as many blood-hounds underneath, barking and yelping, and jumping up in vain endeavors to seize the frightened negroes. The overseer was standing by, encouraging the dogs, and several bystanders were looking on, enjoying the sport. It was only the owner of some blood-hounds training his dogs, and keeping them in practice, so as to be able to hunt down the runaways, who often secrete themselves in the woods. It was thought fine sport, and useful, too, in its way, ten years ago.

But now the same hounds are being made use of, all through Alabama and Mississippi, and, we have no doubt, in other of the Southern States, to hunt down white men hiding in the woods to escape the fierce conscription act, which is now seizing about every man under sixty years of age able to carry a gun. Nor is this the worst. It is found that those camped out are supplied with food brought them by their children, who go out apparently to play in the woods, and then slip off and carry provisions to their fathers. To meet this exigency, blood-hounds are now employed to follow these little children on their pious errands, and the other day a beautiful little girl was thus chased and overtaken in the woods, and there torn in pieces, alone and unaided, by the trained blood-hounds of Jefferson Davis! Nor is this a solitary case. It appears that many white men, women, and children have thus been sacrificed, in order to carry out the conscription act in all its terrors.

In a large number of cases, those who are thus hunted down are such as have in some way exhibited Union proclivities; for, although such have ceased to offer any opposition to the rebels, they do not like taking up arms against the flag of the Union, to which many of them have, in former days, sworn allegiance. These persons, and all suspected, are especially marked out as objects of the conscription and the blood-hound, be their ages and fighting qualities what they may. And these are the men hunted down with dogs, and their wives and their children, if they attempt to follow them. There are, however, many men not Unionists, and willing to contribute of their property to any amount to support the rebels, but now being drawn into the conscription, or, having tasted the desperate neglects of the rebel service, have deserted, and will not again take up arms. Their wives are ladies, most delicate and tender, and their children brought up with a refinement and delicacy of the most perfect character, until this war began. And these are the women that now have to wander alone in the woods, in search of their husbands and brothers and sons; and these are the little girls, who, going to carry food to their relatives, are liable at any moment to be overtaken by swift hounds, let loose and set upon their track by the agents of Jefferson Davis.

It may be doubted if war itself, ever but once in the history of mankind, proved so disastrous to a people, by the hands of those engaged in carrying it on. Perhaps, in the final destruction of Jerusalem, there may have been scenes of greater and more fiendish cruelty by the factions of John and Simon destroying each other, while both were at war with the Romans. And what must be the state of the South, when a delicate woman, who would hardly set her feet on the ground for delicacy, and used to have servants to attend upon her every wish and want, is reduced to straits like these, and children are torn to pieces by the dogs of humble hunters after white flesh for Jefferson Davis's shambles!

Keep the Soldiers' Letters

Mother, father, brother, sister, wife, sweetheart, keep that bundle sacredly! Each word will be historic, each line invaluable. When peace has restored the ravages of war, and our nation's grandeur has made this struggle the most memorable of those great conflicts by which ideas are rooted into society, these pen-pictures of the humblest events, the merest routine details of the life led in winning national unity and freedom, will be priceless. Not for the historian's sake alone, do I say, keep those letters, but for your sakes who receive them, and ours who write them. The next skirmish may stop our pulses forever, and our letters, full of love for you, will be our only legacy besides that of having died in a noble cause. And should we survive the war, with health and limb uninjured, or bowed with sickness or crippled with wounds, those letters will be dear mementoes to us of dangers past, of trials borne, of privations suffered, of comrades beloved. Keep our letters, then, and write to us all the home news and "gossip." Bid us Godspeed. Speak kindly, loving, courageous words to us. If you can't be Spartans—and we don't want you to be—be "lovers, countrymen, and friends." So shall our feet fall lighter, and our sabers heavier!

Proposition to Hang the Dutch Soldiers

The following specimen of "chivalric" literature is copied from the Knoxville *Register*, of June 12, 1862:

Of late, in all battles and in all recent incursions made by Federal cavalry, we have found the great mass of Northern soldiers to consist of Dutchmen. The plundering thieves captured by Forrest, who stole half the jewelry and watches in a dozen counties of Alabama, were immaculate Dutchmen. The national odor of Dutchmen, as distinctive of the race as that which, constantly ascending to heaven, has distended the nostrils of the negro, is as unmistakable as that peculiar to a polecat, an old pipe, or a lager-beer saloon. Crimes, thefts, and insults to the women of the South invariably mark the course of these stinking bodies of *sour-krout*. Rosecrans himself is an unmixed Dutchman, an accursed race which has overrun the vast districts of the country of the North-west.... It happens that we entertain a greater degree of respect for an Ethiopian in the ranks of the Northern armies, than for an odoriferous Dutchman, who can have no possible interest in this revolution.

Why not hang every Dutchman captured? We will, hereafter, hang, shoot, or imprison for life all white men taken in the command of negroes, and enslave the negroes themselves. This is not too harsh. No human being will assert the contrary. Why, then, should we not hang a Dutchman, who deserves infinitely less of our sympathy than Sambo? The live masses of beer, krout, tobacco, and rotten cheese, which, on two legs and four (on foot and mounted), go prowling through the South, should be used to manure the sandy plains and barren hill-sides of Alabama, Tennessee, and Georgia.... Whenever a Dutch regiment adorns the limbs of a Southern forest, daring cavalry raids into the South shall cease.... President Davis need not be specially consulted; and if an accident of this sort should occur to a plundering band, like that captured by Forrest, we are not inclined to believe our President would be greatly dissatisfied.

"My young colored friend," said a benevolent chaplain to a contraband, "can you read?"

"Yes, sah," was the reply.

"Glad to hear it. Shall I give you a paper?"

"Sartin, massa, if you please."

"What paper would you choose?" asked the chaplain.

"If you chews, I'll take a paper of terbacker."

The Stolen Stars

[At a dinner party, at which were present Major-General Lewis Wallace, Thomas Buchanan Read, and James E. Murdoch, a conversation sprung up respecting ballads for the soldiers. The General maintained that hardly one had been written suited for the camp. It was agreed that each of them should write one. The following is that by General Wallace:]

When good old Father Washington
Was just about to die,
He called our Uncle Samuel
Unto his bedside nigh;
"This flag I give you, Sammy, dear,"
Said Washington, said he;
"Where e'er it floats, on land or wave,
My children shall be free."

And fine old Uncle Samuel
He took the flag from him,
And spread it on a long pine pole,
And prayed, and sung a hymn.
A pious man was Uncle Sam,
Back fifty years and more;
The flag should fly till Judgment-day,
So, by the Lord, he swore.

And well he kept that solemn oath;
He kept it well, and more:
The thirteen stars first on the flag
Soon grew to thirty-four;
And every star bespoke a State,
Each State an empire won.
No brighter were the stars of night
Than those of Washington.

Beneath that flag two brothers dwelt;
To both 't was very dear;
The name of one was Puritan,

The other Cavalier.
"Go, build ye towns," said Uncle Sam,
Unto those brothers dear;
"Build anywhere, for in the world
You've none but God to fear."

"I'll to the South," said Cavalier,
"I'll to the South," said he;
"I'll to the North," said Puritan,
"The North's the land for me."
Each took a flag, each left a tear
To good old Uncle Sam;
He kissed the boys, he kissed the flags,
And, doleful, sung a psalm.

And in a go-cart Puritan
His worldly goods did lay;
With wife and gun and dog and ax,
He, singing, went his way.
Of buckskin was his Sunday suit,
His wife wore linsey-jeans;
And fat they grew, like porpoises,
On hoe-cake, pork, and beans.

But Cavalier a Cockney was;
He talked French and Latin;
Every day he wore broadcloth,
While his wife wore satin.
He went off in a painted ship—
In glory he did go;
A thousand niggers up aloft,
A thousand down below.

The towns were built, as I've heard said;
Their likes were never seen;
They filled the North, they filled the South,
They filled the land between.
"The Lord be praised!" said Puritan;
"Bully!" said Cavalier;
"There's room and town-lots in the West,
If there isn't any here."

Out to the West they journeyed then,
And in a quarrel got;
One said 't was his, he knew it was,
The other said 't was not.
One drew a knife, a pistol t' other,
And dreadfully they swore;
From Northern lake to Southern gulf
Wild rang the wordy roar.

All the time good old Uncle Sam
Sat by his fireside near,
Smokin' of his kinnikinnick,
And drinkin' lager-beer.
He laughed and quaffed, and quaffed and laughed,
Nor thought it worth his while,
Until the storm in fury burst
On Sumter's sea-girt isle.

O'er the waves to the smoking fort,
When came the dewy dawn,
To see the flag he looked—and lo!
Eleven stars were gone!
"My pretty, pretty stars," he cried,
And down did roll a tear.
"I've got your stars, old Fogy Sam,
Ha, ha!" laughed Cavalier.

"I've got your stars in my watch-fob;
Come take them if you dare!"
And Uncle Sam he turned away,
Too full of wrath to swear.
"Let thunder all the drums!" he cried,
While swelled his soul, like Mars;
"A million Northern boys I'll get
To bring me home my stars."<7p>

And on his mare, stout Betsey Jane,
To Northside town he flew;
The dogs they barked, the bells did ring,
And countless bugles blew.
"My stolen stars!" cried Uncle Sam,

"My stolen stars!" cried he,
"A million soldiers I must have
To bring them back to me."

"Dry up your tears, good Uncle Sam;
Dry up!" said Puritan,
"We'll bring you home your stolen stars,
Or perish every man!"
And at the words a million rose,
All ready for the fray;
And columns formed, like rivers deep,
And Southward marched away.

And still old Uncle Samuel
Sits by his fireside near,
Smokin' of his kinnikinnick
And drinkin' lager-beer;
While there's a tremble in the earth,
A gleaming of the sky,
And the rivers stop to listen
As the million marches by.

DEBATE

BETWEEN
REV. EBENEZER SLABSIDES AND HONORABLE FELIX
GARROTTE,
DELIVERED BEFORE
GENERAL ROSECRANS AND THE
SOCIETY OF THE TOKI.

DEBATE BETWEEN SLABSIDES AND GARROTTE.

The subject of discussion was—"Who deserved the greatest praise: Mr. Columbus, for discovering America, or Mr. Washington, for defending it after it was discovered?" The two characters are personated by an instantaneous change of feature.

[The Honorable Felix Garrotte arose, and said:]

MR. PRESIDENT, AND GENTLEMEN OF THIS
LYCEUM:

I suppose the whole country is aware that I take sides with Mr. Kerlumbus, and I hope, Mr. President, that I may be allowed to go a leetle into detail in regard to the history of my hero. I find, Mr. President, after a deal of research, that Mr. Kerlumbus was born in the year 1492, at Rome, a small town situated on the banks of the Nile, a small creek that takes its rise in the Alps, and flows in a south-westerly direction, and empties into the Gulf of Mexico.

Mr. Kerlumbus's parents were poor; his father was a basket-maker, and, being in such low circumstances, was unable to give his only son that education which his talents and genius demanded. He therefore bound him out to a shepherd, who sot him to watchin' swine on the banks of the Nile; and it was thar, sir, by a cornstalk and rush-light fire, a readin' the history of Robinson Crusoe, that first inspired in his youthful breast the seeds of sympathy and ambition. Sympathy for what? Why, sir, to rescue that unfortunate hero, Mr. Crusoe, from his solitary and lone situation upon the island of Juan Fernandeze, and restore him to the bosom of his family in Germany. He accordingly made immediate application to Julius Cæsar for two canoes and a yawl, eight men, and provisions to last him a three-days' cruise; but, sir, he was indignantly refused. He was tuk up the next day and tried by a court-martial for treason, and sentenced to two months' banishment upon the island of Cuba—a small island situated in the Mediterranean Sea—which has lately been purchased by the Sons of Malta for Jeff Davis.

But, sir, he was not to be intimidated by this harsh and cruel treatment. No, sir-ee; on the contrary, he was inspired with renewed zeal and energy; and I can put into the mouth of my hero the immortal words which Milton spoke to the Duke of Wellington, at the siege of Yorktown:

"Once more into the breach, dear friends!"

Well, after the tarm of his banishment had expired, he returned to Rome, and he found that Cæsar had died again, and that Alexander the Great had succeeded him. Well, he made the same demand of Alexander that he made of Mr. Cæsar, but he met with a similar denial; but, finally, through the intermediation of Cleopatra, (that was Aleck's first wife,) he ultimately succeeded.

It is unnecessary for me to go into a detail of his outfit and voyage. Suffice it to say, that, after having been tossed about upon waves that ran mountain-high, all his crew was lost, except himself and a small boy, and they were thrown upon the state of insensibility.

Well, when he came-to, he rose up, in the majesty of his strength, and found he was upon an island; so he pulled out his red cotton bandana handkercher, tied it to a fish-pole, and rared the stake of Alexander, and took formal possession of the territory in his name, and he called it San Salvador; that was in honor of Cleopatra's eldest daughter.

Well now, you see, Cleopatra was so well pleased with the honor conferred upon her daughter, that she migrated to this country for to settle; hence you see the long line of distinguished antecedents that she left here previously, and they are known as *pat*riots, from Cleo*patra*.

Now, sir, having accomplished the great and paramount object of his life, he was ready for to die. The natives, therefore, for intrudin' upon their sile, tuk him prisoner, stripped him of his hunting-shirt and other clothing, tarred and feathered him, and rid him on a rail! Thus perished that truly great and good man, who lived and died for mankind. One more remark, Mr. President, and then I am done; and I lay it down as a particular pint in my argument. If it had not have been for Mr. Kerlumbus, Mr. Washington would never have been born; besides all this, Mr. Washington was a coward. With these remarks, I leave the floor to abler hands.

> [Here Mr. Slabsides arose, much excited at hearing Mr. Washington called a coward, and said:]

Mr. President: I, sir, for one, am sureptaciously surprised at the quiet manner in which you have listened to the base suspersions cast upon that glorious and good man. Mr. Washington a coward! Why, sir, lockjawed be the mouth that spoke it. Mr. Washington a coward! Mr. President, my blood's a-bilin' at the idea. Why, sir, look at him at the battle of Tippecanoe! Look at him at the battle of Sarah Gordon! Look at him at the battle of New Orleans! Did he display cowardice thar, sir, or at any of the similar battles that he fout? I ask you, sir, did he display cowardice at the battle of New Orleans?

> [Mr. Garrotte arose, and responded to the question. Said he:]

The gentleman will allow me to correct him, one moment. Mr. Washington, sir, never fit the battle of New Orleans. He couldn't have fout that battle, for he'd been dead more'n *two weeks* afore that ar battle was ever fout. He never fit the battle of New Orleans.

Mr. Slabsides.—Will the gentleman—will Mr. Garrotte please state who it was that fit the battle of New Orleans? The gentleman has seen fit to interrupt me; will he please to state who it was fit the battle of New Orleans?

Hon. Felix Garrotte.—If the gentleman will have patience to turn to Josephus, or read Benjamin Franklin's History of the Black-Hawk War, you will thar learn, sir, that it was General Douglas that fit the battle of New Orleans.

Mr. Slabsides.—I thank my very learned opponent, not only for his instructions, but more especially for his corrections, in which he has shown himself totally ignorant of history, men, and things. I contend, Mr. President, notwithstanding the gentleman's assertion to the contrary, that Mr. Washington not only fit the battle of New Orleans, but that he is *alive now*, sir! I have only to pint you, Mr. President, and gentlemen of this lyceum, to his quiet and retired home at *Sandoval*, on the banks of the Tombigbee River, whar he now resides, conscious of his private worth and of the glorious achievements heaped upon his grateful brow by his aged countrymen; and allow me to call your attention to the fact that General Douglas never fit the battle of New Orleans. He couldn't have fout that battle, cause he was dead. Yes, sir, and I can prove it, if you'll have the patience to turn and look over Horace Greeley's History of the Kansas Hymn-book War; for there you will find that General Douglas, at the head of an army of negroes, made a desperate charge on Mason and Dixon's line, and Horace said he never breathed afterward.

[Hereupon the speaker left in disgust at the ignorance of his opponent.]

A Sermon from the Harp of a Thousand Strings

preached before General Rosecrans and staff.

THE PREACHER FROM HEPSIDAM.

THE PREACHER FROM HEPSIDAM.

My Beluved Brethering:

I am a plain and unlarnt preacher, of whom you've no doubt heern on afore; and I now appear to expound the scripters, and pint out the narrow way which leads from a vain world to the streets of the Juroosalum; and my tex which I shall choose for the occasion is somewhar between the second Chronikills and the last chapter of Timothy Titus, and when found you will find it in these words: "And they shall gnaw a file, and flee unto the mountains of Hepsidam, whar the lion roareth and the whang-doodle mourneth for its first-born."

Now, my beluved brethering, as I have afore told you, I am an unedicated man, and know nothing about grammar talk and collidge highfaluting; but I'm a plain, unlarnt preacher of the Gospil, what's been foreordained, and called to expound the scripters to a dyin' world, and prepare a perverse generation for the day of wrath; "for they shall gnaw a file, and flee unto the mountains of Hepsidam, whar the lion roareth and the whang-doodle mourneth for its first-born."

My beluved brethering, the text says "they shall gnaw a file." It don't say they *may*, but they *shall*. And now, there's more'n one kind of file: there's the hand-saw file, rat-tail file, single file, double file, and profile; but the kind of file spoken of here isn't one of them kind neither, because it's a figger of speech, my brethering, and means goin' it alone, getting ukered; "for they shall gnaw a file, and flee unto the mountains of Hepsidam, whar the lion roareth and the whang-doodle mourneth for its first-born."

And now, there be some here with fine clothes on thar backs, brass rings on thar fingers, and lard on thar har, what goes it while they're young; and thar be brothers here what, as long as thar constitutions and forty-cent whisky last, goes it blind; and thar be sisters here what, when they get sixteen years old, cut thar tiller-ropes and goes it with a rush. But I say, my brethering, take care you don't find, when Gabriel blows his last trump, that you've all went it alone and got ukered; "for they shall gnaw a file, and flee unto the mountains of Hepsidam."

And, my brethering, there's more dam beside Hepsidam: thar's Rotterdam, Haddam, Amsterdam, mill-dam, and don't-care-a-dam; the last of which, my dear brethering, is the worst of all, and reminds me of a circumstance I once knew in the State of Illinoy. There was a man what built him a mill on the east fork of Auger Creek, and it was a good mill, and ground a site of grain; but the man what built it was a miserable sinner, and never give any thing to the church; and, my brethering, one night thar come a dreadful storm of wind and rain, and the fountains of the great deep was broken up, and the waters rushed down and swept that man's mill-dam into kingdom come, and, lo, and behold! in the morning, when he got up, he found he was not worth a dam. Now, my young brethering, when storms of temptation overtake ye, take care you don't fall from grace, and become like that mill—not worth a dam; "for they shall gnaw a file, and flee unto the mountains of Hepsidam, whar the lion roareth and the whang-doodle mourneth for its first-born."

"Whar the whang-doodle mourneth for its first-born." This part of the tex, my brethering, is another figger of speech, and isn't to be taken as it says. It doesn't mean the howlin' wilderness whar John the Hard-shell

Baptist was fed on locusts and wild asses; but it means, my brethering, the city of New Yorleans, whar corn is worth six bits a bushel one day, and nary red the next; whar gamblers, thieves, and pickpockets go skiting about the streets like weasels in a barnyard; whar they have cream-colored hosses, gilded carriages, marble saloons with brandy and sugar in 'em; whar honest men are scarcer than hens' teeth; and whar a strange woman once tuk in your beluved preacher, and bamboozled him out of two hundred and twenty-seven dollars; but she can't do it again, hallelujah! For "they shall gnaw a file, and flee unto the mountains of Hepsidam, whar the lion roareth and the whang-doodle mourneth for its first-born."

Brother Flint will please pass round the hat, and let every Hard-shell shell out.